Trekker

Trekker

Book II in the *Corps of Discovery* Series

James S. Peet

Trekker

Trekker

James S. Peet

2018

First Printing: 2018
Enumclaw WA 98022

ISBN: 978-0-9996093-2-3

Cover art by Jeanine Henning

To buy this (and future) books by James S. Peet in an e-book format, please go to **www.jamespeet.com**.

For my family

Trekker

CONTENTS

ACKNOWLEDGEMENTS

Special thanks to all that made this novel possible: Shannon Page, my editor; Jeanine Henning, the cover artist, the Beta Readers who provided some excellent feedback to make this novel better than the first draft – Domingo Chang, Pat Ingram, Dave Jeschke, and Dave Morris; Proof readers Becky Rush-Peet and Joseph Michael, and; Katie Peet (my youngest daughter, who is attending DigiPen Institute of Technology to earn a BFA in Digital Arts and Animation) for the cover concept art.

THE MEDITERRANEAN

Trekker

Mouth of the Rhône

Bill Clark wouldn't say he was a particularly skittish guy, but when your nascent fiancée fires a rifle off in your ear at two in the freakin' morning, it tends to make you a bit skittish. That's pretty much what happened to him, just minutes after crawling into his hammock. Granted, Meri Lewis wasn't shooting at him, nor even particularly close to him, or in his direction; and he wasn't even asleep yet, but any shot within twenty feet is too close when you're not expecting it.

Bill's first reaction was to roll out of his hammock, holding his personal defense weapon at the ready. Unfortunately, rolling out of a hammock involves gravity, and after slamming his face into the ground of Planet 42, courtesy of said gravity, he staggered to his feet. Scanning around the gravel bar in the light of a half-moon, Bill could see the love of his life aiming for another shot at whatever it was that had perturbed her in the first place.

As she shot again, the muzzle flash showed him the threat: a lion just outside the trip wire line. Bill brought his gun, a PDW-1, up to add his support and heard a crashing sound from the lion's position. More crashing echoed through the nearby forest. At that moment, Karen Wilson announced her engagement in the fracas by shining a small, powerful flashlight into the dark. The lion Meri had shot was down, possibly dead.

"Keep your eyes peeled," Karen warned, shining the light around with her left hand, rifle in her right. "Lions hunt in packs."

Then Ben Weaver made an appearance, also armed with the *Corps'* ER-1 rifle, a bolt action rifle with a low power scope mounted on it, identical to the ones Meri and Karen held.

After several tense minutes with no other sounds, not even the usual night sounds of bugs and birds, Karen said, "I think they're gone."

She ordered Bill, who was armed the lightest, to throw some more wood on the fire. Ben muttered, "That's it for sleep." Bill silently agreed.

Meri Lewis came into the fire's circle of light and Bill looked at her questioningly, concerned. She shakily smiled back at him and said she was okay, just scared. "No doubt," Bill said.

After circling the camp, Karen came back to Meri and asked how she was doing.

"Fine, but I can't wait to get off this beach."

"Yeah, well, another couple of days and we should be good to go." Karen glanced into the dark brush. "I'm thinkin' that bad boy you shot'll add to the larder."

After ordering Ben and Meri to keep watch, Karen and Bill dragged the lion's carcass back to the campfire, careful not to set off the tripwire. The huge carcass required both of them, particularly since neither of them was willing to set down their weapon.

As the fire roared to life, Bill shouldered his PDW. He and Karen cut up the dead animal while Ben and Meri continued to keep watch.

It had only been a couple of weeks since their sabotaged survey plane had crashed in the Eurasian mountains on this unexplored planet, a parallel Earth. They weren't quite used to the fauna they had to deal with. One thing was obvious, though: the animals, particularly the predators they had encountered so far, were not scared of humans.

Before setting out on the survey they had been told that it appeared the planet was a non-impact planet. This meant that the meteors that were suspected of slamming into the Laurentide Ice Sheet during the late Pleistocene, causing major flooding and climate change and leading to the extinction of most megafauna, never happened in this timeline.

So not only were the four crew members stranded 10,000 kilometers from any help, but they were also dealing with megafauna of the late Pleistocene. Not that all the animals were bad, but in just a couple of weeks they had been attacked by a pack of hyenas which were larger than their African cousins, and now a pride of lions. Fortunately, technology in the form of rifles and flashlights had triumphed over fangs and claws.

"Y'know," Bill said, "I was taught in survival school that fires kept the critters away. Sure doesn't seem that way to me."

"Well, I'm gonna disagree there, man o' mine," Meri said, her blue eyes laughing. "So far, other than that hyena, nothing's come into the camp. I spotted that lion out beyond the trip wire. I think it was trying to figure out how to get in but the fire kept it away."

Bill mulled that over, then reluctantly agreed with her. When it came to survival stuff and megafauna, she was far better versed than he. After all, he was only from Earth, while she was a native Hayeker who had earned a bachelor's degree in Exploration Science. If that wasn't enough, she was also the only child of the Commandant of the *Corps of Discovery*.

"Either way, we'll be out of here in a couple of days," Karen said. "Unfortunately, we can't carry as much food and water as I'd like, so we're almost at the limit of what we can carry. Simba over there might just top up the larder once we dry and jerk him. I want to sail fairly close to land until we pass through the Strait of Gibraltar. That way we can continue to get fresh game. Which reminds me, I want you two," she indicated Bill and Meri, "to gather up makings for bows and arrows tomorrow. I figure we'll be in that outrigger for about a month, so that should give us plenty of time to get them made."

Bill and Meri nodded acquiescence.

Sunrise came early, thanks to the time of year. Mid-June was still fairly cool at night, but the days on the southern coast of what was France on Earth were getting quite warm. As the sun came up, fish started jumping in the Rhône River, feeding on bugs on the water.

Karen suggested lion for breakfast. Knowing how much Bill and Meri enjoyed fishing, she added, "We'll be eating enough fish as we cross the Atlantic. No sense in burning out on it early."

Soon lion steaks were grilling over the campfire, pierced by sticks held by hungry Explorers. The rest of the lion would be turned into jerky, and some of that would be made into pemmican, depending on how much fat they could render from the carcass.

Yesterday, Karen had spied a number of oak trees several hundred meters from the river. She informed the crew that she and Ben would take a couple of baskets the crew had made and collect as many fallen acorns as they could find.

"When we get back we'll have a nut cracking party," she said, looking at Ben and Bill, both of whom raised their eyebrows and made mocking gestures of protecting their privates. The two women laughed, a much-needed break from the stress of the morning.

"I'll want you two to stay around camp and keep an eye on the meat," Karen said, after everyone has stopped laughing.

This, of course, set them all off again. Finally, wiping her eyes, she went on. "Take a moment to check the snares, and if you find any edible plants, collect them. We're gonna be pretty shy on veggies when we cross the ocean. And keep an eye out for whoever made that point," she said, referring to a stone artifact Ben and Meri had found on the opposite side of the lake from where they had crash landed. They had discovered a fire pit and the point, but no other signs of humans or other hominids.

Breakfast over, Karen and Ben each grabbed a basket and headed off into the forest east of the river. While they were gone, Bill and Meri did a quick walk around to each of the snares that had been set out yesterday. They found several rabbits and a couple of squirrels, all dead, all destined for the lunch stew pot. Smaller animals were consumed fresh, while the larger animals were being turned into long-term storage food.

They reset the snares, moving them to new locations nearby, but still along the game trails.

As they made their way back to camp, visible through the trees, they heard a rifle shot. Bill and Meri, their own rifles raised in the ready position as always, froze and looked in the direction of the shot, several hundred meters away. Another shot rang out.

"I hope they're shooting at something they found." Bill left unsaid the hope that they weren't shooting to protect themselves.

Meri said, "Me, too," in a low voice.

One of the most frustrating things about being stranded was the lack of two-way radios. While they each originally had one, the same electromagnetic bomb that destroyed their plane had also fried nearly all the electronics inside said plane. All that survived was one server, two field tablets, and a solar charger that were in a combination crash box/Faraday cage. Not being able to communicate, even over a couple of hundred meters, meant that something could be happening to one pair of Explorers and the others would know nothing about it. The only means of communication they had, other than yelling or shooting, were the small whistles each Explorer was issued.

After another minute passed with no further gunshots, Bill and Meri continued back to the campsite, stepping over the tripwire line and into the circle of hammocks.

Bill took the dead lagomorphs and rodents from Meri and began cleaning them: decapitating, removing feet, gutting, and then stripping off the skin. He had done a lot of hunting before joining the *Corps*, and killed and cleaned a fair amount of game, but it was still a task he didn't like. He liked animals, and didn't like seeing them suffer or die, despite how much he enjoyed eating them. As he cleaned the game, he thought about this, then told himself, *If I didn't kill them, I couldn't eat them. Then I'd be dead.* That brought back memories of his father, who would often say, "You don't work, you don't eat. You don't eat, you die."

His hands on the first squirrel, Bill thought of what he had read in an old western novel back in his Earth days. "A squirrel ain't nothing but a rat with a cute, fluffy tail." *All right, cute, fluffy-tailed rat, into the pot with you.*

Bill's father was a career military man in the U.S. Air Force. He had been a bit surprised when Bill announced, after graduating college, that he had joined the *Corps of Discovery* on Hayek as an aerial survey specialist. Hayek was the first multiverse planet discovered when Dr. Tim Bowman had invented the gate that allowed people to move between parallel Earths.

It was hard to believe that Bill's conversation with his dad had been only a year ago. In that one year, Bill had been through several months of training, had a propeller blade slice into a plane he was transitioning in and decapitate the instructor pilot, spent several more months on a survey in the Caribbean, and then spent the last two months on the Initial Survey of Planet 42, where they were currently stranded.

His job had been to use remote sensing platforms for mapping and, most importantly, to determine if any humans, civilizations, or proto-civilizations existed on the planets they were surveying. On the recent flight, Ben was the pilot and Meri the co-pilot. Karen had double duty. Not only was she the Survey Commander, but she was also an aerial survey specialist.

Bill had met Meri just before starting Explorer training, and the two had hit it off so well that they had moved in together after their first survey. When they moved into the small apartment Bill had said something to the effect of, "Geez, just like married people." Meri took that, in jest, to be a poorly worded marriage proposal. Ever since then she had called him her "sorta fiancée." Bill was secretly pleased with that and was planning on having the phrase changed, dropping the "sorta" part. Of course, that was before they crash landed in the Alps a couple of weeks ago.

It was still several hours before lunch, so Bill wrapped up the cleaned game in fresh leaves and set them in the shade. They would go in the stew pot an hour before lunch, with whatever edible plants they could find.

Soon, Ben and Karen hailed the camp, giving Bill and Meri fair warning that it was them and not some hungry pre-Holocene predator coming in for a snack.

As the nascent hunter-gatherers stepped over the trip wire, Meri asked if all was all right, and was told it was.

"We shot this monster-sized bull," Ben said by way of greeting, dropping his basket of acorns by the fire. "The thing's over two meters at the shoulder and must weigh at least a thousand kilos."

Karen nodded. "I think it's an auroch, or something similar. Either way, the damned thing's huge and should have plenty of fat on it." She set her basket of acorns next to Ben's.

Fat was pretty important for the stranded Explorers. Not many animals ate well enough to develop the marbled fat that domesticated grain animals had, which meant that all the protein the four crew members were getting was lean meat. Fat contained plenty of calories, so it was greatly desired. Fat was also used in the making of pemmican and soap. Pemmican, a long-term storage food, was made from ground up dried meat, clarified fat, and whatever nuts or berries could be found and added. The crew was hoping to carry as much as possible for their journey across the Mediterranean, and then across the Atlantic Ocean to North America, or Ti'icham as it was called on Hayek. Soap, of course, was useful for staying clean, something the *Corps of Discovery* considered one of the most important things Explorers could do when in the boonies, other than survey, that is.

"After lunch, Ben, you take Bill and clean the bull," Karen said. "Hang whatever you can't carry in a tree, so take some rope with you. It's probably gonna take several trips, and I'd like to get as much in before night. And definitely, before it attracts too many predators. We've already seen just how nasty some of them can be." With a grin, she said, "Meri and I'll just stay here and crack some nuts."

"Bad, Karen, just bad," Bill said, shaking his head in disbelief.

After lunch, the two men gathered their rifles, and some rope, and headed out beyond the trip wire. They walked with rifles ready, heads moving all around and up and down, looking for any potential threats. Both had been taught in survival school that threats could come from anywhere, including above, where some predators like to hang out and jump their victims.

In addition to their rifles, they carried backpacks full of survival equipment, a web belt, a survival vest, and their *Corps of Discovery* uniforms - also full of survival equipment. Bill estimated they each had well over two thousand dollars, or about two-fifths of a troy ounce's, worth of equipment on their bodies. The *Corps* standing rule was that any time an Explorer was on a survey planet, they carried their rifles and wore vests and belts. If they stepped away from the group, they took their packs. This was emphasized so much that every probationary Explorer, or "Probie" as they were called, was required to wear all survival equipment during training. It was now second nature to Bill.

As they walked through the forest, Bill could smell the rotting vegetation. It reminded him of the Cascade Mountains he used to hike in.

The two arrived at the dead auroch. Bill was amazed. *That thing's freakin' huge! It's larger than a bison.* Luckily, no other scavenger had arrived yet, but buzzards were starting to circle. As Bill kept watch, Ben commenced butchering the big bovine. It had already been gutted, so now the task was to quarter it, then hang the meat out of reach of scavengers. It didn't take Ben long, and soon they had over half the big bull in the air, strung between several large branches.

Bill cut a sapling down with a hatchet he kept on his belt, and the two strapped a large chunk of meat to it. Ben then used his canteen to wash the blood off his hands. No sense getting his rifle stock all sticky with blood.

When Ben's hands were clean and dry, Bill picked up one end of the pole and Ben the other. The two, rifles still at the ready, staggered back to camp with their heavy load.

The two women had already cracked open all the acorns and were leaching them in several small pots of boiling water to extract the tannin. Acorns were edible only after the tannin was removed, and boiling them in water was one way of doing that. The acorns would be used as flour, and also in stews.

"Drop it here," Karen said, indicating a spot near the fire. "We'll take care of it."

The men dropped their burden, untied it, then turned and headed back to the kill, rifles at the ready.

By the time night had fallen they had made several trips to haul in as much of the auroch carcass as possible. Karen called for a two-on, two-off watch for the night; that much meat would most likely attract predators and scavengers. The men were told to sleep first and were given four hours. They collapsed in their hammocks after a quick supper of stew.

They were awakened at two o'clock in the morning. *At least nobody's shooting this time*, Bill thought. Karen had made coffee, telling them to nurse it; she didn't want to use it all up in one night. Then the men stood watch with rifles at the ready and flashlights handy. The light from the campfire threw a circle around the camp, casting long shadows into the dark forest. Bill and Ben kept a watch for any reflections from eyes staring at the camp.

Over the course of the next four hours, nothing approached, nor were the trip wires activated. They could hear hyenas laughing at the auroch kill site, though, and Bill heard a wolf howl in the distance. *Great, just what we need,* he thought, *now it's either regular wolves or dire wolves. Hope they don't come 'round here.*

Bon Voyage

By the time daylight came, both men were feeling the effects of only eight hours of sleep over the last forty-eight hours. Of course, with the schedule they had maintained during the Initial Survey, this wasn't the worst they had felt. They had managed to keep busy during their watch tending both the fire and the meat-drying process, so that by the time the women climbed out of their hammocks the meat collected the day before had been turned into jerky. Of course, it helped that the women had already done most of the work the day and night before.

Bill made sure there was enough coffee made for everyone to have a cup. They all recognized their coffee habit was soon to come to a screeching halt, something none of them were looking forward to.

Meri said to Bill, "You must be exhausted."

"Why do you say that?" he asked.

"Your eyes look like blazing emeralds. They only do that when you're really tired. Usually they're a pretty nondescript hazel."

As she sipped her coffee Karen announced to the group, "I'd like to head out this morning. Best way to do that is to catch the outgoing tide." With a glance at the river, she added, "Looks like the tide's almost in right now, so that doesn't give us a whole lot of time to get ready. If need be, we can finish up the pemmican afloat."

Ben told her that all the meat gathered was now dried into jerky, suitable for either eating or grinding into powder for pemmican. "We've also clarified all the fat."

Using her best Captain's voice, Karen said, "Make it so, Weaver."

The three Earthlings got a chuckle out of that, but Meri just looked at them, confused.

"Old TV show," Bill explained.

"Ahh. Gotcha."

"Okay, Karen said. "The boat's ready to go, so all we need to do to launch is load her, and take her out. If anything's gonna happen, it's gonna happen once we're out there." Karen looked around at them expectantly, then sighed when nobody responded. "All right, finish your coffee and let's get things rolling. Ben and Meri, you finish up the food stuff and get it packed. Bill, you and I'll get the boat out on the water. If you're hungry, snack on some jerky. We've only got a couple of hours."

Bill finished his coffee, rinsed out the cup, and replaced it and the canteen on his belt. Grabbing a handful of jerky, he followed Karen to the outrigger canoe. The dried meat was palatable, but definitely not Oshiro's Teriyaki flavor. It was tough, slightly salty, with a smoky oak flavor. *Good thing I've got great teeth*, he thought. *No way I'd be able to handle this cardboard otherwise.* As one hand was occupied with his rifle, everything was done one-handed.

As they approached the dugout canoe, Bill admired their handiwork. *Not bad, considering all we used were axes, hatchets, and an adze.* The dugout was an outrigger canoe, modeled on the Polynesian style from Earth. It had main body with a single mast and an outrigger for stabilization. It had been made from a small-leaved lime tree, using what Karen called linden wood. Apparently, it was the same type of wood used by neolithic Europeans to make canoes back on Earth. The main canoe was almost twenty meters long and about a meter and a half wide, wide enough for a single person to sit and lie down in. The hull speed, or the maximum speed they'd be able to get to under sail, was almost 11 knots, or about 20 klicks an hour. The sail was made from one of the parachutes from the S-1 Monarch survey plane, left behind in Grand Lac de Laffrey, in the western Alps. A small wooden seat with a wooden bucket under it served as a toilet. Bill wasn't looking forward to using that.

It had taken a week to cut the tree, dig it out, and then struggle to get it to the campsite where they completed the work. Bill and everyone else hoped it would float. After all, they had quite an ocean voyage ahead of them. Nobody was excited about being cramped in the boat, which was why they had constructed a net across the span between the canoe and the outrigger. At least people would be able to safely leave the canoe for brief spells, if for nothing more than to stretch out on the net. They had also carved four rough paddles for near-shore use. They figured they would have time to finish carving them once underway.

The canoe sat on small logs that had been used to roll it from where they had cut it down. The plan was to continue to roll it until it was in the water. While Bill pushed the heavy canoe, Karen would take the log that it had just rolled off, walk to the front of the canoe, and set it down so the canoe would continue moving. As she did, she was constantly scanning for threats. They kept this up until the boat rested partially in the water and partially in the mud below the high tide mark. They had removed boots, shoes, and uniform pants for the last stretch to avoid getting mud all over everything, reasoning that it was far easier to clean skin than boots and clothing.

"Let's tie it up and start loading it," Karen said.

Bill tied the boat off to a large tree near the river bank. The two then washed the mud off their feet and ankles and put their clothing and boots back on.

By the time they made the short walk back to the campfire, they saw that all the food had been packed, and every container that could possibly hold food or water was doing so.

The two remaining tablets were put inside a waterproof bag that did double duty as a clothes washing machine. Inside were little knobbies that would agitate the clothing and do the cleaning. For now, though, they served to protect valuable items, such as the tablets, the small solar charger, the flashlights, and spare gunpowder. The rifles and PDWs would be wrapped in spare clothing and stashed in the backpacks once they were underway. The packs were somewhat waterproof, but not completely. The idea was to allow salt and moisture to do the least amount of damage possible.

Using some of the gear salvaged from the Monarch, they had placed several stanchions at various locations. To these were strapped the packs and survival belts. Survival vests would be worn at all times, and the life vests taken from the Monarch's inflatable would be worn by all at night. Karen had told the crew that she expected that if anyone fell overboard during the day they'd be immediately missed, but probably not so at night. "No sense taking any unnecessary risks."

During the week they had been food gathering, Karen had also told the crew to find makings for bows and arrows. "We'll have plenty of time to make them, and I want us ready to start using them the minute we get off that boat," she said. "Let's save the ammo for when we really need it."

Within a half-hour, everything was packed except the rifles, with all items either tied down, strapped to the boat, or set inside. The boat was ready to go before the high tide had fully come in. Following standard protocol, the fire was completely extinguished before they left.

Slipping out of boots, socks, and uniform pants, each Explorer entered the canoe, one at a time, passing their clothes and rifle over to the previous entrant. Each rifle was disassembled to reduce its length, wrapped in spare clothing and then secured in the owner's backpack. The final one to board was Ben, and he did so only after releasing the rope holding the canoe to the tree and then pushing the vessel further into the river.

As he hopped into the canoe, it started downriver on the outgoing tide.

Within minutes the outrigger approached the Mediterranean Sea. Each Explorer had found a place to sit and was easing the canoe along with their rough-hewn paddles. Other than survival school, the only ones with any prior sailing experience were Meri and Ben, Meri because her family owned a small cabin on the Nisqually River of Cascadia, with access to the Salish Sea, and Ben who grew up regatta racing in the Chesapeake Bay. Bill had been on a few boats, but not for more than a couple of hours, and the same for Karen.

The vessel started bobbing in the water as the small waves of the sea made their way up the mouth of the Rhône River. Bill hoped he wouldn't get seasick. Then he thought, *I hope nobody else gets seasick. That's all we need.*

Soon the boat was past the mouth of the river and fully into the Mediterranean. As it was now afternoon, the winds were blowing from the sea onshore. Bill remembered learning that the air above the land heated faster than that over the water, in his one physical geography class he took at the University of Washington.

Rather than head for the Strait of Gibraltar, Karen had decided on a mostly coastal route, explaining, "We're gonna be at sea for probably a month straight. Before we're forced to do so, though, I want to take advantage of the fresh water and food options available to us. So, the plan is to pull into rivers along the way and stay near shore for a full day. We'll load up on fresh water, bathe, and try to get fresh food, other than fish, at every opportunity."

Karen had had Bill plot out the possible rivers along the way, of which there were many. The first stop was to be one of a set of rivers on the south coast of France, approximately eleven hours sailing time away. Karen had explained that without navigation aids other than their chronographs and the sextant that came with the Monarch, they would have to plan for "close enough." They would aim for a spot near where they hoped to land and then sail down the coast looking for the mouth of the river.

Fortunately, the wind was with them. It was a moist wind, and Bill could feel the increased humidity, but it was nothing like what he had experienced during survival training on the Yucatan Peninsula. He spent the day thinking about their chances of survival. Others had managed to make it back to the Initial Point after similar mishaps, whereupon they were given the moniker of "Trekker." Bill couldn't remember hearing about any Trekkers that made it back from this far away, though. Most Trekkers only had to cross Ti'icham, with a few stranded several hundred kilometers from the nearest base.

Bill asked the group, "What's the longest distance you've ever heard anyone cross on a trek?"

The three thought about it. Then Meri, who grew up in the *Corps*, said, "There have only been a few who went down on an

Initial Survey. Janice Goodland is the most famous, and she went down on the east coast of Ti'icham." Janice Goodland was the head of the survival school for the *Corps of Discovery* and, despite being mauled by a Smilodon, managed to make the several-thousand-kilometer trek from the east coast to the Initial Point on the west coast. The Survival School was named after her.

"Wait a minute," Bill said. "I remember an outrigger canoe in the museum on base. Anyone recall the story on that?"

"That was a crew that went down on one of the islands in the Caribbean during a secondary survey," Meri said. "I don't remember if that was on the fourth or fifth planet, but it was fairly early on in the *Corps'* history. They only had to go a couple of hundred klicks."

That bit of information sobered the group up, and they got quiet for quite some time.

As the day wore on, the crew quickly learned what worked and what didn't. One of the things they discovered was that wood was a hard thing to sit on for hours, and it was worse if they didn't have a way to lean back and relax their back muscles.

"We'll probably have to use some of the cloth we have left, maybe a parachute or two, for our asses," Karen said, "but we're gonna have to go ashore and get some wood to make back supports. That doesn't have to be tonight, but let's make sure we've got them rigged up before we set sail again."

Bill and Meri had arranged it so that the two of them could sit together - well, as together as they could be sitting single file. Rather than face the bow, Meri had elected to face Bill who was riding in the stern.

The two quietly discussed whatever possible future existed considering their situation. They had already espoused their love for each other, and Bill told her that he had been waiting for them to get through their probationary year with the *Corps* before he was willing to ask her formally to marry him.

"I just wanted to be sure that I'd be around more than a year," he explained. "Now I'm not even sure if we'll be around more than a month."

Looking out over the wide sea, with gentle swells being pushed by the east wind, he had a thought.

"Listen, I don't know if this'll be legal in the eyes of the *Corps* and Hayek's laws, but how about we get married tonight? I bet Karen or Ben can perform the ceremony as captain of this vessel. That way, if anything happens, at least we'll have been married, even if for short while."

Meri smiled. "I gotta say, you're not the smoothest talker when it comes to marriage proposals. First the apartment, now this. No chivalry, no undying love, just an 'it should be okay' statement. Where's the romance? Where's that dashing guy who swept me off my feet?"

Bill was flabbergasted. He thought that everything he said was logical and made sense. Romance? She wanted romance on a trek in the middle of the ocean in a dugout canoe?

Fortunately, some deeper wisdom prevailed, and rather than voicing these thoughts, he got up and knelt in front of her. "Meriwether Lewis, will you do me the honor of becoming my wife?"

Meri squealed and wrapped her arms fiercely around Bill, almost knocking the two of them into the water.

All Bill could hear through the thrumming in his ears was the word 'yes' repeated over and over, between the kisses she was showering on him.

Karen, hearing the commotion behind her and turned around. "What's going on?"

Meri looked at her with a grin plastered across her face. "Bill just officially proposed".

"I'm gonna bet you said yes," Karen said dryly, getting a bobbing-head response in return.

"So, when's the big date, lover boy?" Ben called to Bill.

"How about tonight, when we make landfall?" Bill asked. "Can one of you perform the ceremony?"

"Heck, both of us can, him as pilot and me as Survey Commander," Karen said.

Landfall couldn't come soon enough.

It was dusk as they finally found one of the rivers they had been aiming at. The voyage had, with the exception of the proposal, been uneventful. Nobody had gotten sick, water hadn't come in over the gunwales, nothing went overboard, and nobody drowned. Life was good.

As they entered the river delta, Karen told the group that other than hammocks, survival belts, and rifles, everything else was to stay on board and that the canoe was to be beached and double tied. "I don't want us losing everything to the tide."

She then decided that rather than risk the canoe, Meri and Bill would stay aboard it overnight. "Call it a honeymoon," she said with a grin.

Just before landing, they extracted their rifles from the packs, reassembled them, and loaded them. Ben, being on the bow, jumped to shore as they partially beached the canoe. Taking the bow rope he ran to a nearby tree and secured it. The other three watched the surroundings, rifles at the ready.

Once the boat was secure, the rest disembarked. Survival belts were passed around and secured on all. Bill and Meri set out trip wires and then collected firewood while Karen and Ben set up their hammocks. Night was approaching, but fortunately, the late June day was a long one, so they still had some time before full dark.

Meri had managed to find several varieties of wildflowers, so she gathered them together and created a bouquet. Karen ordered Ben to serve as a witness and to use one of the tablets to record the event. He retrieved it from the canoe while the other three made their way to a point on the beach that looked out over the Mediterranean. To the east, the full moon was just rising.

Ben returned to the group with the tablet, turned it on, and began recording. Karen stood with the sea behind her, keeping an eye on both the betrothed and the forest behind them. Before Karen stood Bill and Meri, with Meri holding the wildflower bouquet. All three had their rifles slung over their shoulders.

"Meri, Bill," Karen said, "marriage is a solemn vow between two people, requiring each to devote themselves to the other. It's not always about love, but that helps." She smiled. "It's about family. The family you will become, and the family you will raise. It won't always be easy or fun, but it will always be something worth treasuring. Treasure that for as long as you can."

"I guess I better get on with the ceremony. Do you guys want the 'dearly beloved' part?"

Both shook their heads. Bill was so nervous, he was afraid his voice would have cracked if he tried to answer.

"Didn't think so," Karen said. She turned to Bill. "Bill, do you take this woman, Meriwether Lewis, to be your wife? To love, honor, and respect, for better or for worse, in sickness and in health, till death do you part?"

Bill looked at Meri and managed to get out, "I do," thinking very hard about the 'till death' part.

Karen then turned to Meri. "Meri, do you take this man, William Clark, to be your husband? To love, honor, and respect, for better or for worse, in sickness and in health, till death do you part?"

Meri quietly said, "I do."

"Then, by the power invested in me by the *Corps of Discovery* and the Canton of Yakama, I hereby pronounce you husband and wife."

The two stood there in front of Karen with huge grins.

"This is where you kiss the bride," Karen said pointedly to Bill.

Bill turned to Meri and gave her a rather chaste kiss, but she was having none of that. She grabbed him around the neck, pulled him in close, and gave him the kind of kiss that took his breath away. Karen clapped while Ben hooted with approval.

After the two separated, Karen said, "Ben and I'll stay in our hammocks and take the first two watches. You guys can have the last two. Try to get at least a little sleep." The last was said with a knowing grin.

The crew returned to the fire where a pot of jerky had been set to cook as a stew. Each dug their canteen cups from their belts and served themselves. After a quick meal, they cleaned their cups and sporks and put everything away.

Karen announced that since Ben had first watch, she was going to get some shuteye. Looking pointedly at the newlyweds she said with a grin, "Try to keep it down — some of us need some sleep."

"Yeah, I'm just gonna watch the forest. Why don't you two kids get some 'sleep'," Ben added.

Bill and Meri just shrugged their shoulders. Holding hands, they practically ran back to the canoe.

It's amazing just how loud the crashing of surf can be on an otherwise quiet night.

Bill had just shut his eyes from the third watch, hoping to finally get some sleep when he was rudely awakened by Meri. "Hey, sleepyhead. Wake up. We gotta go."

He came wide awake, rifle in hand. Looking around, he saw his wife standing over him, with a sky just lightening. "What time is it?" he muttered, looking at the chronograph strapped to his wrist, before remembering that his chrono was set to Alpha time. Alpha time was the time used for Hayek's capital of Milton, located in what was eastern Washington on Earth. On Hayek, it was in the Yakama Canton, just east of the Cascade Mountains. *Well, that does me no good,* he thought.

The sun was just rising above the ocean's horizon. Bill struggled out of the canoe and saw Ben and Karen already standing by the fire drinking coffee. As Bill joined them, Meri gave him a cup, but not before getting a morning kiss from him.

"Listen up, gang," Karen said. "As soon as possible, we'll be on our way. I'll try to get us into the next RON site before nightfall so we can do a little hunting."

RON was pilot-speak for Remain Over Night. "Bill identified our next stop as a bay called...?" Karen looked at Bill.

He pulled out his pocket notepad and flipped a few pages. "Bahia de Rosas. There's a couple of rivers that feed into it. It's about 130 klicks south of here, around the Cabo Creus Canyon, a cape that sticks out." He put his notepad back into its pocket. "That still leaves us over a thousand klicks from the Strait of Gibraltar."

"So, there you have it," Karen said. "Let's get this circus on the road."

After a quick breakfast of jerky, and once the hammocks were packed, three Explorers showered while Karen kept watch. The showers were nothing more than a shower head attached to a collapsible bottle, but it was enough to wash off the grime of the day before. One thing the *Corps of Discovery* took seriously was hygiene, hence the showers, toothbrushes, and laundry bag washers in all survival kits. As far as the *Corps* was concerned, cleanliness wasn't next to Godliness, it actually came first. Once the three were finished, dressed, and had rifles in hand, then Karen took her shower. After all the bottles were drained, they were filled with filtered water from the river. Nobody wanted to be out on the sea without enough water.

The four boarded the vessel and set sail within an hour after sunrise. It took a while to get out a safe distance from shore, tacking all the way, as the east wind was still upon them. Once far enough offshore to satisfy Karen's requirements, they headed south.

They rounded Cabo Creus Canyon on the Iberian Peninsula late in the afternoon and made their way into the bay. Landfall was on the beach near one of the two rivers. Once landed, the canoe was dragged ashore above the high tide mark, and camp was made again.

Bill and Meri offered to go hunting. Karen agreed, so they grabbed their rifles. Bill also brought a PDW in case they saw smaller game: anything deer-sized or less. The rifles used the 7.62 NATO round, which the *Corps* found to be ideal for most game. The PDW used a much smaller cartridge, the 5.7x28mm round, which was basically a hopped up .22 magnum round.

Other than the caliber size, there were many other things that differentiated the two firearms. The ER-1 was a bolt action rifle that had a detachable magazine in front of the trigger, a fixed stock that contained a spare five-round magazine and a cleaning kit, an integral bipod, a rifle scope, iron sights, and a 45-centimeter barrel. Bill still thought of it in standard measurement terms of 18 inches. This meant it had enough power to take out large game several hundred meters away.

The PDW, or more officially, the PDW-1, was more like a pistol with a collapsible stock. It was a semi-automatic weapon that fed from a magazine through the pistol grip, had a smaller scope with very little magnification, backup iron sights, and a short barrel, barely 30 centimeters, or 12 inches. Pistols were something the *Corps* didn't issue or recommend, due to a combination of a short range, underpowered ammunition for the job, and the overall excess weight it had in relation to its usefulness. A lot of time went into training Explorers how to use both rifles, so either one was considered sufficient for survival situations. The PDW was favored for hunting because its cartridge wasn't powerful enough for protection against most predators, and the crew wanted to save the larger cartridges for when absolutely needed.

Bill and Meri headed up the bank of the river, walking slowly, and listening. They would take two or three slow steps, toes down first, and then heels, rest, and listen. Bill was in front in case they spotted a deer or goat. They had been taught this technique in survival school — the one with the more powerful rifle came second to provide security for the one hunting up front.

They hadn't gone far when Bill spotted a clearing by the river. As they approached, they saw a small herd of goat-like animals, maybe gazelle. The horns on the lone male amazed Bill, seeming to curve in all directions, but winding up pointing back. They were also ridged. Bill looked the herd over and, using his chin, pointed to a female goat who looked neither pregnant nor nursing. Meri nodded, keeping her attention on the male, in case he decided to defend his flock.

As Bill was preparing to shoot, Meri did a slow scan around them, making sure nothing was sneaking up on them. She knew better than to have both of them pay attention to one area when threats existed all around.

Bill took careful aim and placed the scope's crosshairs right behind the ear of the goat he had chosen. Gently easing the trigger back with his index finger, he was surprised when the rifle actually fired, just as he should have been. Since the recoil of the PDW was practically nonexistent, Bill could watch the bullet strike the goat exactly where he aimed. The animal dropped like a rock. The rest of the flock, alarmed by the shot, jumped and moved a few feet, looking around. He debated on shooting a second goat but decided against it. *We've got enough dried meat, and this'll be enough for tonight and tomorrow.*

As he and Meri began walking toward the dead animal, the rest of the skittish herd spotted them, and that was enough to cause them to flee, racing across the opening and crashing into the forest.

"Run, Forrest, run," Bill muttered. Meri gave him a strange look, to which he replied, "Old movie." She nodded, accustomed by now to his odd cultural references she didn't get.

The goat was small, so Bill just bled and gutted it. Rather than get his uniform dirty by slinging it over his shoulder, he cut a small sapling to which they tied the goat's feet, then lifted it over their shoulders and carried it back to camp. This time, though, Bill had slung his PDW and carried his rifle.

Karen looked up as they walked into the camp. "Home is the hunter, home from the hills." She had them to use forked sticks set up on either side of the fire and get the goat on a spit.

Bill noticed that only two hammocks were set out. He gave Karen questioning look. "We figured you two honeymooners need as much time together as possible, so we're letting you use the *Guppy* as your personal honeymoon suite for the next several nights." Karen had clearly watched a lot of reruns and old movies in her youth. Once again, though, the old Earth reference went right over Meri's head. As Bill glanced over at the canoe, he saw a new carving on the bow, enhanced with charcoal.

"Really? *Guppy*?" he asked in amazement, looking at the two.

"Karen's idea," Ben said with a grin, waving his hand at her. Karen grinned like the proverbial Cheshire cat.

"What's the *Guppy*?" Meri asked.

"It's from an old TV show, probably even before our parent's time, about a small group of castaways on a tropical island. Their boat was the *Guppy*." Karen said, laughing.

"Seems appropriate," Meri said.

"I thought so," Karen said softly. She cleared her throat. "Well, stop gabbing, everyone. Get supper ready and then hit the rack. Bill, you've got first watch, Meri second, me third and Ben last."

Bill was disappointed that he and Meri didn't get to stay up a while together, but Karen reminded them they still had at least another five days before they crossed through the Strait of Gibraltar. "You'll have some free time together before then," she told the two.

Gibraltar

The next morning the crew awoke to colder temperatures than the day before, with a stronger wind from the north. Bill and Meri, sleeping without the benefit of a hammock tent, were awakened by a few fat raindrops hitting them in the face.

Ben already had breakfast ready, another stew, along with a cup for each of them of the dwindling instant coffee supplies. "Enjoy it while you can," Karen said, sipping the hot brew.

After breakfast and once all the equipment was packed and lashed down, they set out for another river that Bill had selected further south along the coast. He explained that it was where Barcelona, Spain, was located on Earth.

"It's a full day's sail, but there's another river about halfway down if we decide to pull in," he told them.

The south wind pushed them along the coastline at a faster rate than the day before, and within thirteen hours they were pulling onto the beach just south of the mouth of the Llobregat River. This time Bill and Meri set up camp and got a fire going while Karen and Ben went hunting. They had seen several geese and ducks on the river, so they were hoping to bag a couple. Both took rifles and Karen carried her PDW.

It wasn't long before Bill heard shots from the smaller PDW in the near distance. Fifteen minutes later, Ben and Karen returned to camp carrying two fat geese by the necks.

Boiling the geese to assist in removing the feathers wasn't an option with their limited cooking equipment, so Ben and Karen plucked their kill as best they could. They plucked the large tail feathers one by one, pulled out clumps of body feathers with their hands, then used knives to scrape the down off. Bill and Meri collected the tail feathers for use as arrow fletching.

After plucking, they chopped the heads off with hatchets and gutted the fowl. The two birds were spitted and strung over the fire, which had burned down to coals, though, after supper, the fire would be brought back up to flames to serve as a deterrent to wild predators.

Meri took over the cooking chores, occasionally turning the spit, keeping the birds cooking evenly. She had made a small brush from some branches, swiping the fat drippings from the bottoms of the birds, before it dripped into the fire, back onto the tops.

Meanwhile, Karen and Ben elected to wash their soiled undergarments and take rinse showers. After they were done, Karen took over cooking so Bill and Meri could shower. When he was clean, Bill walked along the edge of the beach looking for edible plants. Seaweed was an option, but not his favorite. Eventually, he found some nettle and sorrel. Gathering the nettles was fun (not!), as they caused his hands to sting, but Bill knew that if he moved fast enough back to camp, he would be able to remove the oils from his skin by rubbing them vigorously with sand and his bandana. Goodland had taught them during survival training that the best way to get rid of potential pain from poisonous plants, such as nettles, poison ivy, and poison oak, was to use friction to remove the oils. Nothing else worked as well.

When he returned to the fire, he separated the leaves from the stems, tossing the leaves into a pot of boiling water that Meri had set up. Knowing what he was up to, she also had a pot of cold water set aside. After a minute, Bill poured the boiling water out, making sure to hold the leaves in the pot with some sticks turned into makeshift tongs. As soon as most of the water was drained, he dumped the leaves into the cold water. Now they were ready to eat.

To say that supper was a tasty, but greasy affair, was putting it mildly. The food tasted like a gourmet banquet to the hungry crew. Rather than waste soap, though, the four cleaned their hands by rubbing sand on them and then rinsing off.

As they ate, the four talked. Karen estimated that it would take another nine or ten days to get to Gibraltar at the rate they were going. She told Bill to plan out a route that would allow them to RON at safe harbors with rivers.

"When we get to the Strait, we'll spend a few days there hunting and collecting greens. We've each got our multivitamins, but I'd like to hold off using those until we have to.

"Also, let's see about turning some of the hides into moccasins or sandals. No sense wearing boots on the Guppy and getting them damaged by salt water. And I don't want people stubbing or breaking toes, either. So no barefootin'."

Once again, Bill and Meri retired to the Guppy while Karen and Ben slept ashore.

The next nine days were spent sailing down the east and then south coast of the Iberian Peninsula. The first stop was in the large delta of the Ebro River, where they managed to kill several more large waterfowl and repeated the previous night's feast.

During the day they would sail and work on projects, such as basket weaving and practicing the art of navigation while sailing.

At each stop, Bill would tell the others what major city on Earth existed in their RON location. Some of the names were familiar, such as Valencia and Malaga, but most were not. On the seventh night, they stopped in the Andarax River, where the town of Almeria was. Of course, all that existed in Planet 42 was a river, trees, and some tasty goats.

Bill elected to get some water and took two small pots with him. As he bent over to fill up the first pot, he saw a glitter of something in the shallow riverbed. Looking both ways to ensure nothing was planning on making him a meal, he set the full pot down next to him, reached into the water, and pulled out a heavy rock. It was a small, water-worn gold nugget. He didn't stare at it too long before he put it in his shirt pocket, filled the second pot and made his way back to the fire.

Not saying a word to anyone, he put the pots on the fire to boil. Meri was off hunting with Ben this time, so Bill had the opportunity to explain his thoughts to Karen and seek her help in his plan. She wholeheartedly agreed and offered to help, but told him to wait until they got to Gibraltar.

Finally, they made their last landfall in Eurasia. As they sailed around the Rock of Gibraltar, they stared at it in awe. For the Earthers, it was a place of legend — the gate to the Mediterranean, the place where the Brits held off the Germans during World War II, and a sore point for the Spanish.

"I thought it was an island," Ben said, disappointed, as they sailed around it into the Bay of Gibraltar. Despite having been on several surveys, including one other Initial Survey, this was Ben's first time seeing the Rock.

Finally, they beached the *Guppy* at the mouth of a river at the north end of the bay. Karen sent Ben and Bill out hunting while she and Meri set up camp. Bill carried his PDW and rifle while Ben just had a rifle. As always, both men carried all their primary survival equipment, along with their backpacks.

An hour's walk upriver yielded numerous rabbits and a couple of wild goats. Both types of meat wound up in the evening's stew, along with more nettle and sorrel the women had gathered. Not all the goat was used, so the remainder was turned into jerky, with the skins being set aside to make leather. Ben brought the head back this time; usually they left it to save transport weight. This time, however, they needed the brains for tanning the skin to make into leather.

The next morning Karen sent Ben and Meri on a plant hunt to increase their vitamin C supplies. "Try over on the cliffs," she said, pointing toward the Rock, which was about eight kilometers distant. "There's a plant called rock samphire, which is supposedly loaded with it. Take a couple of baskets with you."

The baskets were made to be strung across the body from the shoulder and rest on one hip, leaving the back and hands free for other things, such as a backpack and rifle. "We'll work on tanning these hides and jerking more meat."

After the two had left, Karen turned to Bill and said, "I managed to get the size. Now we just need to make a mold and fire it. Did you see any clay in the river when you were hunting yesterday?"

Bill had, so the two headed off to collect. A short time later they were back in the camp and had molded it in the proper form. Karen had Bill hide the mold and said, "Let it dry. We'll finish up tomorrow. In the meantime, let's get some prep work done."

To tan the hides meant scraping all the hair off them, something they had done in survival training. A quick review of their survival books and they were ready to go. The first thing they needed to do was get a smooth log to work over, which necessitated cutting down a small tree, about six inches in diameter, and then peeling the bark off it. Once that was done, they laid one end on the canoe and the other on the ground, then draped one of the goat skins on it, hair side up.

Bill took a block of wood that he had cut from a limb and jammed it on the point of his survival knife, effectively turning it into a drawknife, and used that to scrape all the hair off the goat skin. Turning it over, he fleshed the skin, removing all the excess meat and fat, then repeated the process with the second skin.

Karen worked the brains of one of the goats into the first skin. She had previously mashed the brains in water, then warmed the mixture over the fire. "We'll have to all work these once the brains are in," she told Bill. "We can smoke them tomorrow."

It was late afternoon before Meri and Ben returned to camp, baskets stuffed with rock samphire.

"You were right about this stuff," Meri said to Karen after giving Bill a quick hello kiss. "It's all over the cliffs. You want us to go back tomorrow?"

"Yeah, I'd like to see us with as much as possible. I'll smoke this stuff tomorrow while you're gathering. Did you find any sea lettuce?"

Ben replied that they hadn't even looked, focusing on the rock samphire.

After breakfast the next morning, Meri and Ben set out again with empty baskets slung over their shoulders. Bill set up racks over the fire to smoke the newly tanned hides. The smoking was the final step in the process. Afterward, they could cut the tanned hides for sandals or moccasins.

After he got things going and cleared the smoke-induced tears from his eyes, he saw that Meri and Ben were far enough away on the beach heading toward the Rock they wouldn't be able to see what he was doing. He pulled the clay mold out of its hiding spot. It was pretty gritty; he set it at the edge of the fire to harden, leaving it there while he and Karen sought out more plants to harvest nearby.

A couple of hours later Bill turned it so the opposite side would face the fire, then returned to his gathering duties.

At lunchtime, he and Karen returned to the fire and inspected it.

"Looks good to me," Karen said.

"I think it's good to go, too." Bill used a pair of sticks as tongs to pull the mold away from the fire.

He took the gold nugget from his pocket and placed it over the impression in the mold. Then he pulled a small, orange butane lighter from his pack. He flicked the lid latch with his thumb, flipped open the spring-loaded lid, and pressed the starter.

The piezoelectric starter clicked and a blue flame shot out of the nozzle. Bill was amazed that it still worked, considering all other unprotected electronics that were in the plane when it was electronically fried by the EMP bomb. He applied the flame to the gold and soon it was glowing with heat. In less than a minute the gold had melted completely into the mold's cavity.

"Guess that'll have to do," Bill said, somewhat disappointed that the gold hadn't completely filled in the cavity.

"Let it cool. We'll break it out of the mold before the others return," Karen said.

Bill put the lighter away, and the two of them returned to their gathering tasks. This time they sought out some sea lettuce in the waters nearby, filling several baskets. They decided to try and dehydrate the seaweed, so they hung it over the smoking fire along with the goat skins.

By late afternoon, Bill started looking down the beach for Meri and Ben. He soon spotted them and called out to Karen.

"It's time," he said.

"Yep, I think you're right."

Picking up the now-cooled mold, Bill cracked it against a rock. It chipped but did not break. He did it again, harder. This time the mold broke in two, exposing the now-formed gold. Bill tugged on the gold until it was completely free of the clay, rinsed it off, and carefully inspected it.

He silently handed it over to Karen who also inspected it, and then tested it against the original model. It appeared to be exactly what Bill was aiming for. She handed it back to Bill who promptly tucked it away in his pants pocket.

Soon Meri and Ben were back at the campsite, baskets laden with rock samphire. Karen and Bill set them out to smoke.

Supper consisted of smoked goat, smoked sea lettuce, and smoked rock samphire.

As the four were finishing up, Bill turned to Meri and said, "Y'know, despite all the legal stuff, it still doesn't feel like we're really married."

"How so?" Meri asked, looking puzzled.

"I don't know. It just seems like something's missing." He looked down at her hands, which were still holding her eating pot and spork.

Her eyes followed his. "Well, other than a ring, I haven't the faintest idea."

"A ring! Exactly!" Bill exclaimed, snapping his fingers. "That's what's missing."

With that, he stretched his leg out, reached into his pocket, and pulled out the gold form. He took the pot out of Meri's left hand, set it on the ground, then took her hand in his. Sliding the small, handmade wedding band on her finger, he said, "There, now it looks right."

Meri stared at Bill in amazement while Ben and Karen clapped their approval. It was quite apparent from her bear hug that she was quite pleased.

"How did you do this?" she asked after coming up for air from the kiss she gave him. Bill explained about the gold, but then had Karen describe her role.

"Remember when I had you try on my wedding ring?" she asked Meri, who nodded. "Well, that was Bill's way of finding out if we could use my ring as a model. Seems it worked out fine."

Bill could see Karen's look of sorrow as she glanced at her own ring. She was a married mother of a two-year-old son, who was waiting for her back on Hayek. Being so pointedly reminded of that had Bill feeling some of her sorrow.

After a moment, Karen cleared her throat and announced, "We're pretty much set to go, but I think a couple more pieces of prep are in order. I've been thinking about the fact that we've had pretty easy sailing so far. It ain't gonna last. And, right now, we've only got one mast. If that breaks, we're SOL. So, before we set out, let's cut down a couple more. We can lash them to the net between the canoe and the outrigger."

Her crew gave her nods of assent for her command.

"Another thing. Any of you give any thought on where to land? I'm open to suggestions."

"East coast of Ti'icham is our best bet," Bill said. "Especially if it's not too far north or south. Mid-Atlantic region is my choice."

"Why there instead of the Rio Grande or the Isthmus?" Karen asked.

"Couple of reasons," he said. "First, it's hurricane season. I don't know about you guys, but I'd like to spend as little time on the ocean as possible especially in the Gulf. Second, if we do it right, we'll be using rivers, rather than walking. We can head up one of the rivers, cross the Appalachians, and then go down a river until we get to the Mississippi, the Ohio, or the Tennessee. From there we take the Mississippi upriver to the Missouri and then head west. That way we'll be on water most of the way, which means we won't die of thirst and there should be plenty of game. Any other route and we're spending more time on the oceans and crossing deserts. Wandering in a desert in the middle of summer, not knowing where the next water is gonna come from doesn't sound like my idea of a good time had by all."

The others nodded. "He's got some good points," Ben said.

"Okay, so, we can try to sail up the Rio Bravo, but that'll put us in a desert after a long ocean crossing; or we can try to go to the Mid-Atlantic regions and follow rivers and cross mountains," Karen summed up. "I see two other options: head for a more northern access point and not cross so many mountains, or head straight for the Mississippi and take that all the way up. Thoughts?"

"Both options leave us on the ocean longer," Meri said, "which means more danger from storms. And they both also mean more time on rivers. If I recall correctly, the Mississippi meanders a lot, which means we'll spend more time going east and west than north. I say we go with Bill's idea."

"If we do, we gotta make sure we're far enough north. Won't work to wind up not being able to float down the Ohio or Tennessee," Bill remarked.

"Okay. Your task before we set sail tomorrow is to identify all the possible rivers," Karen told Bill. "Make a list of them and jot down their lat-long in a notebook. I'll want everyone to have a copy of that. Once we're on the water I don't want those tablets out of their waterproof homes."

Bill nodded.

"I'm thinking the furthest north we'll want to go is the Chesapeake, so make sure you've got the coordinates for that," Karen said to Bill. "And just to be safe, identify all the coordinates of river confluences, like where the Ohio connects with the Mississippi, and where the Mississippi ties in with the Missouri."

"I'd suggest looking at the easiest way to get to the New River," Meri said.

"Why's that?" Karen asked.

"Well, it's the oldest river in Ti'icham, even older than the Appalachians. That means that it cut through the mountains as they rose. It's the only river that runs east to west and through the mountains and hooks up with the Tennessee. Otherwise, we'd have to hike over some pretty rugged mountains."

After supper, Bill began plotting out the coordinates of each suitable river. Following Meri's reasoning, he narrowed his choices down to the Roanoke River at the southern limit and the Susquehanna River to the north. Looking at the options, he considered his two favorites to be the James or the Roanoke. Both required land crossings to get to the New River, but the Roanoke would be the one with the shortest travel time involved. He then spent several hours identifying the latitude and longitude of all the major river confluences.

The last night the crew spent on the Eurasian continent went quietly. No animals attacked and the weather remained calm.

Bill was on final watch, and he got to see the morning rays of the sun light up the tip of the Rock of Gibraltar. *If nothing else,* he thought, *at least I'm getting to see some beautiful sights.*

THE ATLANTIC

Trekker

Leaving Gibraltar

As dawn morphed into daylight, Bill stoked the fire to get water heated for coffee and to warm up the leftovers from the night before, then roused the others. As they drank and ate, he described what he had been doing.

"It looks like the shortest and easiest route would be if we went up the Roanoke River as far up as possible, and then hoof it over to the New River. From there we can canoe or raft down to the Ohio, and that'll get us to the Mississippi."

"How much hoofin' are we talking about?" Ben asked.

"About twenty-five to fifty klicks, depending on water depths. That's still a whole lot better than hundreds of klicks in the desert," Bill said. "We'll also be gaining about 300 meters of elevation, so it shouldn't be too bad."

"What's our best route there?" Karen asked.

"Well, we could try to sail straight west, but that wouldn't be the best plan, due to the wind and ocean currents. If we sail south a bit, on the Canary Current just west of Africa, we can catch the trade winds. And with those, the equatorial current. Combined, those two'll push us across the ocean faster. First landfall will be in the Greater Antilles in the Caribbean Sea, which means we can possibly resupply with food and water. We can sail along the islands north to Ti'icham. If I'm correct, we'll be able to sail right into Pamlico Sound at the mouth of the Roanoke."

"How long?" Karen asked, a worried look on her face.

"About ten thousand klicks. Straight line is seven thousand klicks, but ain't no way, no how, we're gonna be able to sail straight across. Winds and currents wouldn't be with us. As it is, we'll be lucky to hit hull speed and gain an extra klick per hour with the ocean currents. If we're really lucky, figure we'll hit the Caribbean in around two weeks, give or take."

"Two weeks we can handle," Karen decided. "For now, let's get those spare masts and get this show on the road."

"Don't you mean 'on the water'?" Meri asked with a grin.

Groans from all greeted that comment.

Breakfast finished, they began the process of packing up for their journey across the Atlantic in a carved wooden boat. All personal equipment was packed, stashed, and lashed down, along with all food and spare water containers. The solar still was removed from the inflatable raft kit and set for deployment. Karen informed the others that she wanted as much fresh water as possible as soon as possible, and even then they'd be on short rations until they made landfall.

After identifying two suitable candidates for masts, Karen had Bill and Ben cut them down while she stood guard and Meri finished the packing process.

Both cut trees were limbed, then the men carried each to the beached outrigger canoe where they were strapped to the net between the canoe and the outrigger. Only after Karen was satisfied that both were secure and the equipment stowed and lashed down did she announce that they were ready to set sail.

As Meri was the smallest and lightest of the four, Karen had her get in the canoe and take control of it so the others could push it off the beach. Nobody wanted the boat and all their equipment to sail off into the sunset on its own. She climbed aboard the vessel, whose bow was grounded on the beach, and made her way to the back, grasping the tiller.

Ben untied the canoe from the tree it had been anchored to and strapped the rope around his shoulders, while the other two stripped down and threw their uniforms into the canoe. Bill took the rope while Ben stripped and deposited his uniform with the others. The three then began pushing the canoe into the gentle waves of the Bay of Gibraltar. Once it was fully afloat, they scrambled aboard, with Bill bringing up the rear.

Picking up their rough-hewn paddles, the three began paddling backwards, away from the shore, while Meri used the tiller to turn the craft so it was facing seaward. Within minutes the boat was facing toward the mouth of the bay, at which time they stopped paddling. Karen and Ben deployed the sail made from a spare parachute.

It was still morning; the land had yet to heat up, and there was a light onshore wind that helped push them out to sea. Once the wind caught the sail, Bill set his paddle on the deck in front of him.

Karen ordered all to get dressed and put their life preservers on. These were inflatable Mae West types salvaged from the downed Monarch's life raft.

"I don't want anyone getting totally sunburned, and if you fall overboard, I want a chance of saving your ass."

Looking back at the beach they had just left, Bill saw movement near their former campsite. Looking closer, he swore it looked like a small group of humans. "Hey," he called out to the others, directing their attention to the beach.

Karen pulled a small monocular from her pocket for a closer look.

"Holy shit!" she exclaimed, lowering the monocular. "Freakin' humans!"

The others clamored to use the instrument; she handed it to Ben. He looked through it, then passed it to Bill in the stern.

"I don't think they're humans," he finally said. "They look more like Neanderthals."

"Let me see," Meri called, and the monocular was passed forward to her.

After looking at the group gathered around their campfire, some of whom were pointing out to sea at the canoe, Meri said, "I think Bill's right. They don't quite look like *homo sapiens*, but close. I'm betting on Neanderthal, too."

"Great!" Karen said. "Just what we needed. Witnesses. Well, let's hope they can't follow us."

Stashing the monocular back in her pocket, she went on, "Well, ain't a damned thing we can do about it, so let's just get the flock outta here."

The canoe rose rhythmically as it crested the small waves, making its way toward the mouth of the bay and the final stretch between the Mediterranean and the Atlantic Ocean. After an hour they had left the hominids far behind, clearing the Bay of Gibraltar and entering the Strait. It soon became apparent when they were no longer in the bay as the swells increased in size and chop, causing the small outrigger to slap up and down.

Bill informed the others that they should expect a slow ride as they passed through the Strait due to the current flowing into the Med from the Atlantic.

"If I recall correctly, it's because the Med has a higher rate of evaporation, and the water coming in is replacing it," he said, almost yelling to get his message to Meri in the back.

True to his word, it became evident that they had slowed down, with their speed reduced almost by half. Fortunately, there was no fog, and the winds and tides were with them.

Four hours later, Bill announced that they were passing the southern tip of the Iberian Peninsula, and were finally entering the Atlantic Ocean.

"With any luck at all, we'll be able to catch the Canary Current and start heading south tomorrow."

Meri joined Bill in the bow, and the two sat quietly, watching the land pass on either side.

Bill retrieved his rough paddle from the well of the canoe, pulled out his pocket knife, and began carving on the canoe. He figured they had a couple of weeks to kill, so he might as well make the paddle as best he could. After a couple of hours of carving, he set his paddle down. It was starting to take shape nicely, but his hand was starting to cramp. Anyway, no need to complete it right away.

While Bill was carving Meri had conferred with Karen and was in the process of obtaining their lunch and dinner — fish. Rather than a typical fishing rod, Meri was using a device called a Cuban yo-yo reel. It was a circular piece of plastic, much like a pulley wheel, with heavy-duty fishing line wrapped around the outside groove. Tied to the line was a metal leader with a hook. Meri had attached a small piece of meat to the hook and was trolling over the port side of the Guppy, opposite of the outrigger.

Bill had been surprised to find what all was included in the life raft survival kit. It included means of making fresh water, catching fish, and cooking them. Along with the inflatable solar still and several yo-yo reels, there was additional fishing tackle, a large hand-pump-operated desalinizer, almost half a meter long, a smaller hand-pumped desalinizer, and a collapsible solar oven with a simple grill and pot that fit inside. Bill suspected that they would be using everything in short order.

Throughout the day the four got used to sailing the Atlantic versus what they had experienced in the Mediterranean. The swells were the first obvious difference, being larger and further apart. And the further west they went, the further the land receded. Soon there was no land in sight; they were now at least seventeen kilometers from shore. They also saw several large groups of whales breaching the ocean toward their west. The Earthers stared at them in wonder, coming from a planet where most whales had become extinct due to man's insatiable appetite for their blubber.

It wasn't long before Meri announced she had a fish on the line. Reeling it in was a pretty simple affair, technically. All one had to do was wind the line around the yo-yo. The actual doing was something else. This was mainly due to the fact that the object on the other end of the line didn't particularly want to be reeled in, and it appeared to also be rather large, giving Meri a run for her money.

Eventually, she managed to fight the fish to the side of the canoe. Ben, sitting behind her, bashed it over the head with a wooden club that he had carved specifically for the deadly task. He dropped the club back into the canoe, reached over, and hauled the fish aboard. It was a tuna and easily weighed thirty kilos. Plucking the hook out of its mouth, he handed it to Meri, who finished reeling the line in, and set the hook in a small groove on the side of the yo-yo.

While Meri stashed the yo-yo away, Ben took his knife, lifted the gill cover, and cut through the gill arch. This let the large fish bleed out. Once the bleeding stopped, he proceeded to gut and clean it. All the offal went overboard, to either float or settle in the wake behind the boat. Rather than fillet the large fish, he cut long strips from its sides, which he draped them over the netting between the canoe and the outrigger. Not all of the strips made it to the net; he handed a few out to the others, asking, "Sushi, anyone?"

Eventually, one side of the fish was cleaned of all its flesh, and Ben asked Karen to hand him the solar oven and grill. "Time to make some lunch," he announced, unfolding the compact insulated box. Setting it so the opening was facing south, which was still to port, he put the grill insert in and then loaded the grill with flesh strips. Taking the tempered glass cover out of the oven's carry bag, he carefully secured it to the stove.

"Give it a couple hours and we'll have some cooked tuna."

"Make sure they're done before nightfall," Karen said. "I want everything packed up and secured before it gets dark."

"Roger, that," Ben replied. Removing the glass, he drizzled salt water over the fish, then replaced the oven glass. "That oughta give it at least a little flavor."

The next several hours passed uneventfully. Bill continued to sit in the bow, turned around so he could talk with Meri and Ben. Ben monitored the solar oven while Karen napped in the aft.

At what they guessed was noon local time, Bill dug out the sextant and "shot the sun": took measurements of the sun's location relative to them. This allowed him to determine their latitude. They hadn't moved too far south, yet.

Looking at his chronograph, he did a quick calculation on their longitude, recognizing that it was only a rough calculation, as he wasn't sure of the exact time. This was due to the stability, or lack thereof, of his platform: the canoe.

He told the others their approximate location, summing it up with, "close enough for *Corps* work."

As the three sat there, with the swells causing the vessel to bob up and down and the wind keeping the parachute sail taut, the talk turned to home.

The four had gotten to know each other fairly well during their initial survey of Planet 42, but most of the time it was talking from a distance. Ben would usually be in the pilot's seat, or napping; Meri in the co-pilot's seat, or napping; and Bill and Karen buried in their remote sensing workstations further back in the plane. Or napping. A week at a time airborne didn't leave a crew of four much time to do anything but work and nap. Sleep, as in a full eight hours straight, without interruption, was not on the agenda when flying an Initial Survey.

The week off was usually spent apart from each other — well, except for Bill and Meri, who shared a small apartment on Sacajawea Base. Ben lived in another small apartment on the *Corps'* main base, but he was seldom in it, spending most of his time off exploring Hayek and dating a variety of non-*Corps* women. Karen lived on base with her husband and two-year-old boy, Jeff, whom she called Jeffy (and whom her husband, Tran, referred to as "the mutt" due to his mixed Vietnamese-English heritage and her Norwegian heritage). Tran was another Explorer, a flight instructor operating on Bowman Field, the main airfield on Sacajawea Base. Bill had learned that the *Corps* policy was to ensure no children were left orphaned, so every Explorer couple had at least one parent remaining in a nondeployed role.

Now that they were crammed into a smaller vessel than the Monarch, and with a lot more time on their hands, the crew opened up to each other more.

Bill had known that Ben and Karen were from Earth, but he didn't know much about their backgrounds. Ben was from somewhere on the Chesapeake Bay in Virginia but had gone to school in North Dakota. It was supposedly a great flight school where Ben earned his bachelor's degree in Aeronautical Science.

Karen was another refugee from the military, having been in the U.S. Army working with geographic information systems. She was seconded out to the National Geospatial Defense Agency where she got more involved in remote sensing systems.

Ben told them of growing up in the small town of Quantico, south of Washington, DC.

"Yeah, it was a pretty nice town, but it went from a small town to a bedroom community of DC, and that pretty much destroyed its character," he lamented.

"When I was a kid it was mainly farms and fields, but as I grew up, they became crowded tract homes. My dad says it was even better when he was growing up back in the '80s. It just got worse and worse as the population grew."

Like many other Explorers from Earth, Ben was escaping the crowded conditions, pollution, overpopulation, and the increased regulations and the government controls that had come with the War on Terror and the Iranian War.

Ben had known that Bill graduated from the University of Washington with a degree in geography, which is where he learned GIS and remote sensing, but he was surprised to find out that Bill had grown up all over the place.

Bill explained how his widowed father, a lieutenant colonel in the U.S. Air Force, had been moved from base to base every two years. That's probably what got Bill interested in geography. That, and the fact that the *Corps of Discovery* was actively recruiting those who specialized in GIS and remote sensing, along with a whole host of other specialties necessary for the exploration of parallel planets.

Bill rattled off the list of locations he had lived; he had them memorized in order. It was a common question. With the exception of northern Virginia, when 'The Colonel', as Bill thought of him, was stationed at the Pentagon, all the other locations were air bases that housed fighter squadrons.

Meri was different than the others, not only because she was the only native-born Hayeker on the crew, but because her father, now Bill's father-in-law, was the Commandant of the *Corps of Discovery*. She was also the only one to have graduated from one of Hayek's universities, earning a degree in Exploration Science.

As they sailed, Meri told them some of the stories her father had told her about his time as an Explorer conducting surveys over twenty years ago.

"They didn't even have much in the way of digital data — almost everything was actual film and photographs," she said in amazement. Bill had trouble grasping that fact, considering he had grown up in the digital age and regarded a terabyte as a small amount of storage.

"He's the one who actually designed our rifle," she told them. "It was based off of a concept called the 'scout rifle' by some Earther. But, from what I hear, Dad's version is a whole lot better."

The two men agreed.

Meri told them how her father would be gone for weeks at a time, and, since her mother had died in childbirth she had been raised mainly by her aunt and uncle, neither of whom were in the *Corps*. Her uncle was in the construction business and had built a number of the buildings in Milton and Tahoma.

"Of course, when Dad was home, I stayed with him. It wasn't

until I was almost a teenager that he took over as Commandant, and I lived at home with him until I graduated."

"Why didn't you live on campus?" Ben asked, puzzled.

"Oh, campus living is limited, and restricted mainly to those who have to travel in from the hinterlands. Since I lived on Sacajawea, it was only a short ride on the sky train to campus."

Karen woke up during the conversation, but sat there listening. Eventually, she reminded Ben of the cooking tuna. Sure enough, it was ready to eat, and Ben had each Explorer get one of their canteen cups. As the cup was passed to him, he would grab a piece of fish and quickly put it in the cup. After each piece, he would dip his hand in the ocean to cool off the fingers, then repeat the process.

Karen had Bill dig into one of the handmade baskets and pass out pieces of rock samphire.

"Let's not play old time navy and get scurvy," she said. "Everyone eat something green." Looking directly at Ben, she emphasized, "and that don't mean your boogers."

"Why are you looking at me?" he asked, shoving an index finger up his nose to the "Ew's" and "Gross" from the others, before washing his hand in the ocean with a grin on his face.

The crew ate quietly, using the sporks they usually kept in their pockets. As they chewed, Meri remarked on how good a job Ben had done, especially salting the fish with ocean water.

"That really adds a nice touch," she said.

Ben took the compliment in stride. "Well, I do come from a long line of short cooks," he quipped.

Naturally, that got him groans from the others.

After supper, Karen had the crew clean their cups and utensils with salt water, but made sure they kept everything within the confines of the boat with the exception of the cup used to scoop water. The only way to sanitize anything was with the solar oven and the decision was made to not bother.

"Just make sure you've licked all the food off and then rubbed it off with salt water," she cautioned.

Drinking water was rationed, and any used was immediately replaced by either the solar still or one of the hand-pumped desalinizers. Karen made the executive decision to retrieve and extract all fresh water from the solar still before nightfall. There was no reason to leave a solar-powered still deployed when there was no solar energy to fuel it.

The first night sailing, Karen had the crew resume the two-on six-off schedule. It was similar to the watch schedule they had been running ashore since crash landing. Nobody would actually get a full straight eight hours of sleep, but it would be close enough.

Bill was given the first watch, to begin at sunset, and he would pass it on to Meri, two hours later. Special care had to be taken to mark the start time as his chronograph, as were Ben's and Meri's, was still set to Alpha time, the local noontime in Milton, while Karen's was set to local noontime at their crash location, so they could accurately determine longitude while sailing.

They were still far enough north that despite it being late June, the nights would cool off. Each crew member dug out their individual summer sleeping bag to use with a poncho, which they would wrap around them to keep spray and water that pooled in the bottom of the canoe from soaking them. Before deploying their poncho/sleeping bag combos, the crew used their canteen cups to scoop out what little water was in the canoe.

Karen also made sure that everyone understood that for safety's sake they would all be required to keep a rope tied between them and the boat at all times at night.

"I don't want anyone disappearing overboard at night. I don't care how uncomfortable it is, you wear it. Even taking a dump or leak. Got it?" she asked pointedly.

All agreed, and Bill made a comment that would continue for the rest of the journey. "Don't like it? Suck it up, cupcake."

"Exactly!" said Karen.

As the sun set over the western horizon, the stars started making their appearance. Bill had a rudimentary astronomical knowledge, having studied sufficiently to qualify for a secondary duty as Navigator with the *Corps*. Of course, the first star he looked for was the North Star. He definitely didn't want to put the SS Guppy on a reverse course by mistake. As long as he kept the North Star off the starboard side, he figured they'd be fine.

Soon Bill was alone, the rest snoring quietly — or not so quietly, in Ben's case. Bill sat and enjoyed the solitude, gazing with wonder at the heavens above him filled with a multitude of stars, unlike anything he ever saw from Earth. Even on a week-long backpacking trip to Philmont Boy Scout Ranch in New Mexico, he never saw skies like this. The Milky Way wasn't an ephemeral wisp, as seen from Earth, but a wide ribbon of diamonds cutting through the night sky. It was something he had only seen since migrating to Hayek barely a year ago.

The next two weeks passed uneventfully. After turning southwest after the first night, they sailed toward the equator for another five days, then turned east when they hit the trade winds at around 20 degrees north. From there it was a straight shot west, being pushed along by both the winds and the North Equatorial Current.

The days became hot. The sun beat down on them, the only relief being the occasional cloud or brief squall. The squalls, while wild and windy, were always welcome, giving the crew the opportunity to bathe with something other than salt water and lessened the incessant heat.

Dolphins came up to the boat often and surfed in its small wake. It seemed that the oceans were teeming with wildlife, from fish to mammals.

Each day was pretty much the same. One of them would fish in the morning, and whatever was caught was cooked in the solar oven. Bill's favorite turned out to be red snapper, which they caught plenty of once they turned west. Meals usually consisted of fish and either rock samphire or sea lettuce, until the greens ran out; then it was just fish and their daily multi-vitamin, which Karen was adamant about them taking. It was the only way to get a sufficient quantity of vitamin C into their systems to prevent scurvy.

They spent the days chatting or sitting quietly staring off to the horizon, carving their paddles or working on the bows and arrows they intended to use once they made landfall. Sometimes one would climb out on the net to sprawl out and escape the narrow confines of the canoe. The biggest hurdle facing them now was boredom and the unrelenting heat and humidity of the shadeless tropical ocean. They didn't even get the luxury of having the wind in their faces, as the wind was pushing them, and could hardly be felt.

Karen, thinking of the future, had them working to create salt by putting seawater into their mess kits. They kept adding water and letting it evaporate until each had a pan full of salt. This would be used for meals and salting hides for clothing.

Going to the bathroom proved to be an exercise in diplomacy for all. With no restroom stalls, they developed a method of climbing out onto the net and hanging off the rear, supporting themselves by hand on the outrigger and safety rope attached to the canoe. The limited toilet paper retrieved from the

Monarch was used sparingly, and only for certain activities (the concept of a saltwater douche became very in vogue for all). Privacy was obtained by those in the boat facing away from the participant.

Meri, despite her red hair, managed to tan, while Karen, with much fairer skin, sported a perpetual sunburn and peeling nose. Bill was fortunate in that his base tan was strong enough that he browned more than he burned.

On the sixth day at sea, they ran out of the coffee from the Monarch's small galley. All the coffee that remained was in the few flight rats and the field rations they had packed. Karen vetoed opening the rations just so the crew could get coffee, so for the next two days, everyone suffered through caffeine withdrawal. Ben and Bill were hit the hardest, both winding up with migraines. Bill had heard of them but never experienced one before. He hoped never to do so again.

Finally, ten days after turning west, land was spotted. Ben was the first to see it, noticing the clouds on the horizon with underbellies tinted green.

"Land ho!" he yelled from the bow.

"Where?" Karen asked.

"Yonder," Ben replied, pointed to the southwest.

All heads turned and then Bill saw what had drawn Ben's attention. As all they could see were the clouds, Bill knew that they were at least twenty kilometers from land, and probably closer to fifty. *With any luck at all, we'll be there in two or three hours,* he thought.

Meri, at the tiller, started turning the vessel without any command from Karen. None was needed. They all knew that the first land they spotted would be where they made landfall, if for no other reason than to get out of the cramped quarters for a day or so.

Trekker

Caribbean

Bill was correct in his guesstimate, as mountains were finally spotted an hour later. They approached the unknown island after less than two more hours had passed.

"I'm thinking this is either Hispaniola or Carib," he said. "I'll know more once we land."

As they approached the island, they sailed along it looking for a spot where a river fed into the ocean, eventually finding one in a small sheltered bay. Karen ordered the crew to sail toward it. Once they were within one hundred meters Karen had them drop the sail and take up paddles. They paddled the remaining distance, finally beaching the outrigger to the side of the small river.

Karen ordered Bill and Meri to get their rifles out while Ben secured the craft to a nearby palm tree. The boat bobbed in the gentle surf while the two complied and Ben waited. Finally, the two were armed, rifles loaded and at the ready. Only then did Ben jump out of the vessel into the surf.

Wading ashore, he tied the rope to the biggest palm tree within reach.

"Looks like the tide's coming in," he announced after looking around. The prior high tide had left a line of flotsam, with dry sand between it and the water.

"Bill, you and Meri keep watch, one from the boat and one from the shore," Karen said. "I'll hand Ben our equipment. Let's see about setting up camp and getting some fresh food and water. And keep an eye out for any signs of people. I want to avoid contact if there are any here."

Bill slipped his handmade moccasins off, then his pants, and with rifle in hand, jumped over the side into the shallow water. Wading ashore, he kept his rifle at the ready and head on a swivel. New planets and new lands were always a hazard.

While the two kept watch, Karen handed equipment and supplies out to Ben. Soon all the equipment and the diminished supplies were ashore in a pile. Karen grabbed another rope attached to the middle of the canoe and handed it to Ben to tie to another tree.

"Don't wanna lose our only ticket out of here," she said.

Once all the supplies and people were ashore, Karen outlined the plan of action.

"First, let's fill our water supplies and then get clean. Meri, you and Bill are already pulling guard duty, so you'll get to do so for a while longer. Ben, you and I'll fill all the water containers and then we'll bathe and do laundry. And don't forget the soap!"

An hour later, all the water containers had been filled, with several of them stashed aboard, and the four Explorers were truly clean for the first time in over two weeks.

"Man, I forgot what it was like to wash with soap and water," Meri commented. Fortunately, nobody had developed any saltwater boils, bedsores, crotch rot, scurvy, or any of the sundry other problems that could have developed from a long ocean voyage on short water rations. The worst that they had suffered was some sunburn and loss of muscle mass due to the lack of activity in the cramped quarters of the canoe.

"I almost forgot how nice you smelled clean," Bill said.

Meri gave him a dirty look. "What, you don't like my natural scent?"

Bill stammered a reply that it didn't bother him, but wasn't it great to be clean?

The others got a chuckle out of Bill's discomfort.

The talk turned to plans for their stay on the island.

"If this is like just about every other timeline we've been on, there shouldn't be any real predators to worry about here," Karen said, referring to the island's ability to prevent migration of large animals. "Regardless, we set up as usual: fire and trip wires. Each night two of us'll spend the night on the *Guppy*, trading off." This caught Bill's attention, and he looked over at Meri who was looking back at him with a grin.

"It ain't for your personal honeymoon," Karen told the two. "It's so we don't lose the boat. But Ben and I'll stay ashore tonight," she added with a knowing grin. "Anyhow, we'll spend a couple of days here enjoying the fresh water and getting back into shape with some hunting, walks on the beach, and a bit of swimming in the bay. After that, we head north to Ti'icham."

She directed Bill to determine their latitude. They would determine their longitude the next day using local noon as a reference.

"Depending on which island we're on, Cuba or Hispaniola, determines where and how we sail next."

Karen had the crew set up camp and then she and Ben went on a foraging expedition to find fresh greens. Before leaving she told the newlyweds to try and catch a fish or two for supper.

Within an hour the two foragers returned with plenty. Meri had been successful fishing while Bill stood watch, managing to bring in a couple of red snappers.

Bill then took a break from watching for threats, dug out the sextant, and shot the sun. After more than two weeks at sea taking constant shots, he had become quick at it and soon determined their latitude.

Pulling out one of the tablets from its waterproof home, he activated it and pulled up a map of the Caribbean. Comparing his calculations with the map, he estimated they were on the island of Hispaniola, near what was the town of Puerto Plata on Earth.

"I'll have a more accurate assessment tomorrow after noon," he told the crew. "If we can maintain our regular speed, we're only about three days from our destination."

Later that afternoon the fish was grilled over an open fire, the smoke adding a flavor that had been lacking while cooking with the solar oven. The greens were a welcome addition after so many days without. Bill could feel the saliva pooling in his mouth as the food was served.

The tropical night came early, heralded by a flame-red sunset that lit up the sky. The clouds abutting the mountains gave a surreal look to the last of the day, and twilight, then dark, rapidly descended.

In an effort to give the two a small bit of privacy, Karen told Ben that they would take the first two watches, with Bill and Meri taking the last two. The newlyweds were quite happy to retire to the canoe early and tried hard not to make any noise.

Ben awoke Bill near midnight, told him all was quiet, and then retired to his hammock, strung at the edge of the beach. Bill, rifle in hand, added some driftwood to the fire and briefly watched it as the flames caught hold of the wood. Turning away from the growing fire to preserve his night vision, Bill scanned the surrounding forest. It wasn't hard to stay awake as the mosquitoes seemed to find him quite tasty. Occasionally he would glance up at the sky and observe the stars. While not as clear as seen from the middle of the ocean, they were still quite bright, lighting up the moonless night. Bill had to make sure he looked around rather than fixate on the stars, otherwise he might be in for a surprise.

The hours passed slowly, and then it was his turn to wake Meri and get some more shuteye before the dawn. Crawling into the canoe and draping his summer sleeping bag over himself to prevent the mosquitoes from continuing their feeding frenzy, he thought, *I can't wait to get a full night's sleep* as he drifted off.

When he awoke later in the morning, he was bathed in sweat. The sun had risen higher into the sky and beat down on his covered body. He pushed aside his sleeping bag cover, feeling the air immediately begin to cool his skin. *Not quite like Yakama, is it?* he thought as the sweat refused to immediately dissipate as it would have in the drier climate at Sacagawea Base.

Climbing out of the canoe, he found the others already partaking of breakfast.

"Oooh, yummy. Fish for breakfast," he said, rolling his eyes.

Meri grinned and handed him her canteen cup, which emanated heat from the liquid inside. He took a sip, then grimaced. "What the hell is that?"

"Hemlock," Meri replied with a straight face. "Don't you like it?"

Bill immediately spat out whatever moisture remained in his mouth.

"Ha, ha, ha. Seriously, though, what *was* that?"

"Periwinkle tea," Meri said. "It's supposed to be a bit bitter, but so is regular coffee if you don't add sugar," she completed.

One of Meri's many skills that Bill was awed by was her vast knowledge of edible and poisonous plants. It was apparently required training for those earning a degree in Exploration Science from one of Hayek's homegrown universities. Meri had taken more than the required number of classes just because she was interested in the subject, so she had a greater knowledge than the other three combined.

"We figured since we ran out of coffee we'd try a substitute. What do you think?" Karen asked him.

"Tastes terrible. Think I'll just continue going sans stimulants," Bill replied.

"Your loss," Meri said, taking the cup back from Bill and taking a sip, grimacing as well.

While Bill grabbed a piece of fish off the grill, Karen began planning the day's activities. This involved a bit more hunting and gathering, and most importantly having Bill determine their longitude so they could determine the best route for the next leg of their journey.

"We'll take the rest of the day to walk, swim, and get ready, but I'd like to be out of here tomorrow, so keep that in mind," Karen told the group.

She volunteered to determine local noon so Bill and Meri could do the morning foraging. Bill elected to carry his PDW while Meri brought her rifle. Each had the remainder of their primary survival kits with them along with one of the handmade foraging baskets used on Gibraltar. They were hoping to find some plantains or similar fruit. Karen told them to stay close to the beach, with minimal forays into the brush.

"And watch out for snakes or other critters," she warned them as they headed out.

The two made their way down the beach, following in the tracks Karen and Ben had made the previous day. When they saw footprints going into and coming out of the jungle, they continued on for another klick, then stepped into the jungle and began their search for food in earnest. Bill, walking in front, kept his head constantly moving, looking up, down, left, right, and occasionally turning to look behind Meri. One of the many things he remembered from survival training was that predators would strike from any direction, and one way to get their prey was to stalk them, just like Bill had done on numerous occasions.

While watching for threats, the two kept an eye out for edible plants, eventually finding some. Cassava appeared to be relatively plentiful in the sandy soil near the beach. The tubers could be turned into flour for bread or baked like a potato. They also found a soursop tree that was fruiting and plucked a number of the spiny green fruits.

It was early afternoon as the two made their way back to camp. Both were hot, sweaty, and covered with jungle detritus and bug bites. They couldn't wait to divest themselves of their gear and gathered food.

A half hour later they were in camp, backpacks dumped and food baskets set near the fire. Karen was keeping watch while Ben was swimming in the small bay.

"You might as well join him. You two look like you need it," Karen called to them.

They didn't need any further encouragement. Stripping out of their survival gear, they set their weapons down on top of the pile, peeled off their sweaty clothes, and waded into the water. They were barely knee deep into the water when Meri abruptly fell face first into the water. Bill's first thought was that she had stepped in a hole, but then she raised her face, shook her head, and exclaimed, "I needed that!"

Bill decided to do the same, but rather than just fall face first he did a shallow dive into the water.

The water was cooler here, due to the fresh water flowing in from the river. Bill felt immediate relief from the heat. He raised his head above the water he turned over onto his back and scrubbing to remove the detritus from his arms and chest.

As Bill drifted on his back in the gentle swell, he was shocked by the sound and concussion of a rifle firing.

"Out of the water. Now!" Karen yelled, then shot out to sea. Meri bolted from the water toward shore. Bill scrambled to his feet and began running awkwardly through the water toward shore, as fast as he could.

Meri grabbed her rifle as Bill rushed to his PDW. They turned and faced the direction Karen was firing.

Ben was still frantically swimming toward shore. Bill saw the threat: a fin slicing through the water toward him. Bill and Meri joined Karen in firing at the shark. Waterspouts rose all around it as bullets peppered the water.

The distance between the two closed, and then the fin disappeared. Less than a second later Ben rose up out of the water as if pushed from below, then dropped back into the water with a shriek. A red stain blossomed in the water around him.

Ben waved his arms as he sank further into the water. Then he was jerked under, disappearing into the widening stain.

As the three watched helplessly, another fin, and then a third, approached the blood-stained waters. Soon, the water where Ben was last seen was frothing, but only for a minute. All knew that there was no hope that Ben survived the shark attack.

Karen dropped her weapon to her side as Bill realized the futility of shooting at the sharks. It was a waste of precious ammunition. They had reacted to the situation well, as they had been trained to do so, but it wasn't enough. Now, one of their number was dead and gone. Further shooting wouldn't bring him back.

Bill stood limply, gun by his side, looking out to sea. The red stain slowly fading away, turning the ocean back to a bright aquamarine. The fins disappeared. All evidence that his companion existed disappearing with them. He was numb.

What the fuck? Seriously, what the fuck? This can't be happening.
The same thoughts kept repeating over and over, much like
somebody trying to pray their way out of a bad situation, but
can't get past the "Hail Mary, full of grace" line of the prayer.

He felt the gut-dropping feeling of anxiety, like being kicked
or falling rapidly from a great height. His fingertips tingled
with hypersensitivity, then numbness. An overwhelming,
crushing feeling overtook him. He couldn't tell if it was shock,
sadness, grief, the feeling of being lost, despair, or a
combination of all of them. Tears slid down his cheeks. He was
too numb and too much in shock to even wipe them off as they
traced tracks down his face, through his beard stubble, to finally
drip off his chin to the sand below.

The whole trip to this point had been an adventure. They
were all going to make it. They had their shit together. But that
wasn't the reality. They could have their shit together, packaged
in pretty paper and tied up with a bow, but the reality was that
they were just four, now three, people stranded on a hostile
planet thousands of kilometers from any help, and nobody and
nothing on this planet giving a damned about them. All it took
was a moment's inattentiveness or just plain bad luck and they
could become a meal.

A flashback of a propeller cutting through a cockpit,
decapitating his instructor pilot, and covering him with the
pilot's blood appeared so vividly, so real, it caused him to gasp.
A shudder ran down his spine, transforming into a whole body
shudder. Bill could feel the wet, viscous fluid covering his face.

He blinked, and he was back on the beach, staring at the calm
waters of the ocean, still in a daze. The post-traumatic stress
disorder that he had managed to keep at bay with counseling
and being busy made a full-on return, leaving him paralyzed.

It wasn't until he heard Karen cursing and sobbing that he
came out of his daze. She held her rifle in front of her and

swearing inarticulately. Tears streamed down Meri's face as well, rifle forgotten in her hands as her arms hung down.

Bill walked over to Meri and her a one-armed hug. After a minute, Meri left Bill and went to Karen, giving her a hug. Nobody said anything. There really wasn't anything to say.

Eventually, the trio got their emotions under control.

"We leave here tomorrow," Karen said bitterly, turning away from the beach and the site of the death of one of those under her command. It was a heart-wrenching moment, one Bill wished he had never experienced.

Supper that evening was a desultory affair. The three almost forgot to keep watch, but Karen kept them on task. Meri made a stew with the fresh food she and Bill had brought in, but nobody really tasted it.

As they ate, Bill asked Karen if she had managed to determine local noon and mark the time. She dug out her notepad where she had marked the time according to her chronograph. She told Bill that she had checked it against where he thought they were and he was correct: they were on the beach he identified on the island of Hispaniola.

Bill dug one of the tablets from its waterproof case and turned it on. Within minutes he had a course plotted.

"As best as I can tell, our best course is to sail northwest, through the Bahamas, and then take the Gulf Stream up to Cape Hatteras. From there we go into Albemarle Sound and up the Roanoke River."

"Okay. The faster we can get off this damned island, the happier I'll be," Karen said. "High tide should be around nine tomorrow, so let's get the boat loaded, get up early, and get outta here."

Ever practical, Meri asked, "What about Ben's stuff?"

"We'll bring it with us. We're gonna be in boats most of the way, so if we don't have to leave something behind, I don't want to. Go through it tonight and see if there's any personal stuff. If we make it, his parents might want it." The sound of resignation in Karen's voice did nothing to improve their situation.

After supper was complete Karen had them load up all necessary equipment, including the two strung hammocks.

"Sorry, guys, but I'll be crashing in the *Guppy* with you tonight."

Karen gathered up Ben's uniform and primary survival gear, which was still on the beach where he had discarded them prior to swimming, and took them to the fire. First, she went through his uniform pockets, and then through his equipment. Anything of a personal nature was set aside and the rest repacked. There wasn't much set aside. Flipping through his wallet, Karen found a laminated photograph of Ben wearing a cap and gown with an older man and woman on either side of them. There was a Saint Christopher's medal in the wallet, which she showed to the others.

"I didn't know he was Catholic," Bill said, looking at the medal.

"What's it mean?" Meri asked.

"Catholics have patron saints that they hope will protect people," Bill said. "For example, Saint Michael, who was a warrior, is the patron saint of soldiers and police officers. Saint Christopher is one of the patron saints of travelers. I bet his folks gave it to him. It was probably the closest saint they could find for an Explorer."

The only other thing Karen kept from Ben's wallet was his *Corps of Discovery* identification card and a small gold coin. The ID card contained all of Ben's personnel and medical information, along with his banking information. The rest of the wallet was just the usual stuff people carried. Ben's contained a library card from his hometown on Earth, a student ID from his college, and a debit card for a bank on Earth. Karen threw those into the fire. The three watched another part of Ben disappear before their eyes.

"No sense carrying something that ain't worth nothin'," Karen said as the plastic melted.

The wallet she tossed into the jungle. The picture and *Corps* ID went into her wallet and the coin and medal into her pocket. She got out her notebook and pen and jotted a note.

"Just writing down what happened, along with the inventory and what was destroyed, and where," she told them. "If I don't make it, be sure this notebook does."

Both nodded, saying nothing. Losing one of their number was hard enough; neither could bear the thought of losing another.

The night passed slowly. Without Ben, each Explorer was required to stand two watches. Unsurprisingly, when dawn finally arrived in a blaze of red, everyone felt tired.

Karen had the final watch and woke Bill and Meri just as the dawn was breaking. Bill climbed out of the canoe, strapped his rifle over his shoulder, and headed off to the other side of the beach to relieve himself. The sky was shot with red; Bill remembered an old sailor's rhyme, *Red sky at night, sailors delight. Red sky in morning, sailors take warning.*

After washing his hands in the saltwater of the bay, he joined the women at the fire.

"I'm not too sure we should be sailing today," he said, reciting the poem.

Karen considered it briefly, and then said they would be sailing anyway.

"Let's face it, tropical sunrises are always vibrant and red," she said. "Regardless, I want out of this area, so let's finish up and get out of here."

Karen made sure all the equipment was properly packed and lashed, and that the spare masts were still in place on the netting between the canoe and the outrigger. The only things kept unpacked were their life preservers and primary survival equipment, the latter of which would be packed and stored once they got underway.

The tide was still coming in, so they held off for several more hours. During that time the wind picked up a bit, but not to a level that would cause alarm.

Shortly before nine o'clock, they pushed the outrigger off the beach and into the bay. The waves were small, and with the wind coming from land, they were muted a bit. Raising the sail, which snapped taut once up, they turned the boat north and headed out of the bay. In less than five minutes they had cleared the mouth of the bay and were once again in the open ocean.

Karen, sitting in the bow, ordered Bill, at the tiller, to turn the boat so it was traveling northwesterly, toward the islands of the Bahamas. Their first passage, expected early the next morning, would be between Little Inagua Island and West Caicos Island, about 300 kilometers away, or, if they were lucky, fifteen hours of sailing. Bill figured that the 45 kilometers spacing between the two islands would be plenty wide for any passage, even if they hit a storm.

Karen had each of them stow their primary survival equipment, ensuring that the rifles were protected from the environment. They each kept a canteen available and Bill deployed the solar still. Other than that, all that wasn't packed were the three Explorers, their clothing, and their survival knives which were strapped to the belts holding up their pants. Bill was glad of the latter, particularly the ventilated wide-brimmed hat the *Corps* issued to all Explorers. Not only did it shade his face, neck, and ears from the brutal tropical sun, but the ventilation allowed his head to remain cool.

Two hours into the voyage the wind began picking up even more, with high scattered clouds developing overhead. Bill watched the clouds scudding rapidly across the sky and began to get worried. He tightened the drawstring on his hat; Meri did the same. The gentle swells had started to throw some spray, developing into small whitecaps, and warm rain started to fall. Recognizing the futility of keeping the solar still deployed, Bill reeled it in and handed it over to Meri. She deflated and packed it away, after pouring out the water inside: as the wave action had mixed the distilled and salt water making it non-potable.

By an hour before sunset, perhaps five o'clock local time, the wind had become more than a breeze, it had developed into a full-scale gale. Bill estimated it to be Force 8, or about 65 kilometers per hour. The wind-created waves had become relatively large, higher than six meters, judging by the view of the mast tip to a wave crest when the canoe was in a trough. Fortunately, the waves weren't breaking above them, but it still worried him.

Looking forward, he could tell that both women weren't happy with the situation. Every time Karen or Meri turned around, he could see their faces taut with worry and fear. Meri's knuckles were white as she gripped the gunwales. It was a good thing all three were tied to the boat and wearing life preservers.

What worried Bill more than the large waves was the possibility of grounding on an island they couldn't see at night. He crawled forward to his wife and yelled his concern in her ear, asking her to pass it on to Karen. Karen looked back at Bill and gave him a thumbs-up and nod.

By nightfall, Bill estimated there were less than halfway to the passage between the two islands they were aiming for, so he passed on the suggestion to Meri that they should secure the sail and deploy a sea anchor and wait out the storm. Karen wanted to keep moving, but she agreed to reduce the sail even more, making it a storm jib in effect, and deploy a sea anchor. This was nothing more than an empty parachute pack. This action kept them going in a northwesterly direction slowly while still giving them control over the vessel.

By now the wind speeds had increased, approaching Force 10, almost a full-blown hurricane. The waves were now over ten meters tall and the sea was a froth of foam. The three were constantly bailing the boat. Bill forgot what it was like to be dry.

Nobody would be getting any sleep that night, as the wind, waves, and rain kept them all on edge. The boat would climb precipitously up a wave, then come sliding down it, the three crew hanging on for dear life. Groans and creaks from the boat were felt more than heard; nothing could be heard above the howling of the wind and the crashing of the waves.

By midnight, there was still no let-up in the storm. The waves, unseen but felt through the rainy, lightless night, continued to throw the *Guppy* around, just like the original *SS Guppy* in the first episode of *Gilhooly's Island*.

Suddenly, there was a loud snap, and Bill heard something crash onto the boat. He yanked out his flashlight and turned it on. The mast had snapped in half and was dragging in the water. Karen and Meri shone their flashlights around, illuminating the scene.

Bill, at the tiller controls, could do little but watch as the women figured out what to do. He could see the two women talking, but couldn't hear what they were saying over the roar of the wind. Then, Meri, closest to the mast, crawled out to try and resolve the dangerous situation. No way could they leave the broken mast attached to the canoe — it might cause it to capsize, especially in these high seas.

"We gotta cut it loose," he yelled as loudly as possible.

Meri nodded, dug into a bag, pulled out a hatchet, and shoved into her belt. Making sure the rope holding her to the canoe was secured, she pulled on the rope and parachute sail, trying to bring the broken end of the mast closer to her. It wasn't an easy task, doing all this by the light of flashlights held by Bill and Karen while the wind and waves caused the mast to sway and move erratically. At one point she stumbled and fell back into the canoe.

Struggling to her feet, she tried to reach the mast a second time.

A large wave caused the boat to suddenly rise up, tossing Meri overboard.

Bill was stunned. In the light of his and Karen's flashlights he could see the pale figure of Meri's arm sticking out of the churning water. Just as he was rising to save her, Karen's hand snaked out and grabbed Meri's wrist.

Bill dropped his flashlight and joined Karen. As she pulled on Meri's arm, Meri's other arm popped up. Bill grabbed and pulled with all his strength.

Meri's head popped up, and was immediately covered with the foaming water.

Bill leaned forward and grabbed Meri under her armpit, giving him more leverage. Karen did the same on her other side. Leaning back, they pulled her out of the water and into the boat. She collapsed on top of him, coughing and sputtering.

"Give me a sec," she yelled, panting.

"Get back to the tiller," Karen yelled. Even though she was only a couple of feet away, Bill could barely hear her. But he did, and giving Meri one last look, picked up his flashlight, then turned and crawled back to the tiller.

Karen watched Meri, until the younger woman nodded. Again, Bill couldn't hear what was said, but seeing Karen's tight-mouthed look and nod, he suspected Meri was going to try it again.

After a minute, Meri made a second attempt at the sail, this time managing to grasp it. Once she got the tip of the broken mast within arm's reach, she held onto one end, drew her survival knife, and cut the rope near the tip. This allowed the sail to separate from the broken part. She reeled in as much of the sail as possible while the end of the broken tip floated away. Unfortunately, the mast hadn't sheared. It was still hanging on by some wood fibers, which needed cutting.

Soon she had most of the sail in the canoe, and then began cutting the broken tip away. Meri climbed up the mast until she was almost at the level of the broken section. Holding onto the mast with one arm, she pulled the hatchet out of her belt and began hacking on the piece of wood holding the mast together. After several whacks, the mast came loose, but it swung around and slammed into Meri, causing her to lose her grip and tossing her into the violent sea a second time. The hatchet went flying, also landing in the water.

Yelling, "Man overboard!" Bill dropped his flashlight and lurched forward frantically, grabbing his wife's safety line and pulling with all his strength. Fortunately, Meri wasn't knocked unconscious, so she was able to swim toward the boat while Bill pulled. Kneeling in the canoe, he reached over and grabbed her under her arms as soon as she was alongside the boat. With strength borne of fear, Bill yanked Meri out of the ocean and plopped her in the boat. She was coughing and spit up salt water.

She held up her hand to Bill while coughing, indicating that he should not slap her back or do anything else.

After the coughing spell was over, she leaned over and yelled in Bill's ear, "I'm okay. Save the sail!"

Bill began bringing in the sail, which had been partially dragged back into the sea. He soon had the sodden mass in the canoe, and, after giving Meri a quick kiss, returned to his position at the stern of the craft. He picked up his flashlight, which was rolling around in the water at the bottom of the canoe, casting an eerie light through the water, and turned it off. *No sense keeping it on when there ain't nothin' to see* he thought.

The wind continued to blow until late into the night, when it suddenly stopped without warning. One minute it was blowing the rain and surf sideways, then the next it was clear.

Bill looked up and saw stars shining brightly. It then dawned on him what he had been subconsciously thinking all night.

"Hey, I think we're in the eye of a hurricane," he said.

A bedraggled pair of women looked at him uncomprehendingly.

"What?" Karen asked, bewildered.

"Hurricane. We've been riding through a hurricane," Bill replied. "And right now, I think we're in the eye. Should we try and rig up a quick storm jib with what remains of the mast?"

"That's probably a good idea. We'll handle it; you stay at the tiller just in case."

Moving as rapidly as their spent bodies could, the two women turned the soaked parachute sail into a small storm jib. This time Karen got to climb the mast. Using a length of rope, she created an eye to draw the sail's line through so they could raise and deploy it. This took longer than they had hoped, and Karen was forced to descend and climb the mast several times, just to rest, before it was completed. She finally got the storm jib up, climbed down from the mast and then collapsed in the bow of the *Guppy*, not even caring that she was lying in water.

As they were finishing, the storm returned with a vengeance. One minute it was calm, the next minute clouds were sweeping over them along with the rain and Force 12 winds. The three hunkered down in the canoe, only sitting upright to bail.

Again, the wind and storm lasted for hours, keeping them awake. But this time, rather than increasing in intensity, the storm's fierceness abated until, by dawn, they were floating on a choppy sea with only a mild gale pushing them. The modified storm jib had held, but just barely.

With bleary eyes Bill looked around and saw both women curled up, sleeping in the bottom of the canoe. He continued to bail until there was only a thin film of water left.

There was no land in sight. Bill dug the sextant out and took a sun shot. He calculated the latitude, then, based on their expected speed during the storm and the numbers Karen had generated the day Ben was killed, he roughed out their approximate longitude. He took into consideration the northeasterly direction of the hurricane and their reduced speed when figuring it all out. He guessed they had come approximately 200 kilometers since setting out the day before, which would put them approximately sixty to eighty kilometers south by southeast of the larger islands of the Turks and Caicos Islands, a bit more than halfway to their target passage.

Being extra careful, he pulled a tablet from its waterproof bag, activated it, and pulled up the imagery for the stretch of Planet 42 that they were sailing across. Zooming in on the imagery, he saw several smaller islands, or cays as he recalled them being called on Earth, between his estimated position and the larger islands.

I'll have a better idea where we're at around noon, he thought, putting the tablet back.

Using the sun as a compass point, Bill lined up the bow to face northwesterly in hopes of making landfall soon.

Bill let the others sleep while he sailed the vessel toward what he hoped would be a safe harbor. That got him thinking of a song his dad would often play on the old-fashioned CD player he kept in his car. *There's this one particular harbor....* kept playing through his mind. *Yep, that's what I'm looking for* he thought. *That one particular harbor.*

Recognizing the need for fresh water, Bill got out the solar still and deployed it. He drank from his canteen until it was almost empty, and then used one of the smaller hand-pumped desalinizers to refill it. It took him almost an hour of hand pumping to fill the canteen. By the end, his arms were sore and he was sweating enough that he dunked his hat in the ocean to cool off.

A couple of hours later Meri stirred. Sitting up, she wiped the sleep out of her eyes and gave Bill an owlish look. He still couldn't get over how blue her eyes were, despite the redness from lack of sleep and an overabundance of salt water rinsing.

"Hey," he said softly.

"Hey, yourself," she replied. "Where are we?"

"Well, I'm not entirely sure, but we're probably several hundred klicks north of Hispaniola and between fifty and a hundred klicks south of the larger Turks and Caicos Islands. If I'm correct, we should start seeing some islands soon."

Meri looked at Karen, making sure the Survey Commander was breathing. Once she verified that Karen was still alive, she turned back to Bill.

"So, what's the plan?"

"We continue sailing northwest until we can find land. Beach the boat, repair the mast, then continue on."

The mast was less than half its original height. The modified storm jib was full, but there was room for more sail.

"Should I let out more sail?" she asked Bill.

"Yeah. It'll help our speed if you can."

Meri gathered in some of the sail near the bottom of the mast, sat on it to hold it down, and then untied the bottom line holding the sail to the mast. She let out some of the sail until Bill told her to stop, then she re-tied it.

The additional sail increased the speed of the *Guppy* a little, but enough to be felt.

Soon the craft entered shallow water, and the two could see coral reefs below them.

Meri woke Karen to tell her they might be near land. A short while later she spotted a couple of small islands, neither more than half a kilometer across, barely above the ocean, with wide, sandy beaches. Bill guided the broken craft toward the left-most of the two, sailing over water that was clearing from the recent hurricane, hoping not to run aground on any coral heads.

They finally beached the boat, and all three jumped out and hauled it onto the beach as far as they could. Being heavy, and laden with all their possessions, and especially lacking Ben's help, that wasn't too far.

There were no real trees on the small island, so they tied the dugout to a couple of the smaller bushes, hoping that would work to keep it secure.

"I doubt we'll have another storm real soon," Bill said once the boat was secured.

Due to Karen's foresight to carry two spare masts, they were nowhere near as bad a situation as they could be. The first hour was spent removing the old mast, followed by several hours prepping and installing a new one. It was a couple of hours shy of nightfall by the time they were finished, so they elected to remain beached for the night.

Bill and Karen brought most of the equipment on to shore while Meri fished from the waterborne stern of the canoe. What could be spread out to dry was done on the beach and over some of the low-lying shrubs. The two found enough driftwood that was dry to get a fire going — just in time, as Meri had managed to land a couple of groupers. Before night fell, the three repacked and reloaded all the equipment into the canoe.

It was a mostly dispirited group that gathered around the fire that evening.

"I'm beginning to hate this fucking planet," Karen said angrily, pounding the ground with her fist. "First the Monarch, then Ben, now this fucking hurricane. What next?"

"Maybe that's it," Meri said hopefully. "I mean, we're almost to Ti'icham, so we don't have all that far left to go."

"Not all that far?" Karen asked incredulously. "It's another two thousand klicks to the Roanoke, and then another five thousand to the IP, and that's in a straight line. News Flash! Ain't no such animal as a straight line when traveling on rivers! And I'm not even counting the mountain ranges we've gotta cross!"

In an effort to calm her down, Bill mentioned that they had already come over 10,000 kilometers. "Yeah, we lost Ben, and we had some problems, but think about it! When have you ever heard of anyone trekking ten thousand klicks and living to tell about it? We've already done more than anyone else, and for the most part, we're still in pretty good shape."

Karen thought about it . "Yeah, I guess you're right. Even Janice only had to cross one continent," she said, referring to Janice Goodland's trek. Even so, Karen still seemed gloomy.

After supper, the crew packed up the gear, whether dry or not, and reloaded the canoe. Karen had them sleep on the boat, this time without a watch. Her rationale was that the island was too small to host any predators, the boat was tied up, and the hurricane was past. Even if the lines broke and they drifted out to sea, the change in motion would wake them.

Before going to sleep, Bill shot the stars and determined their latitude. Reviewing the data on one of the tablets he determined their possible location as a bit southwest of the passage they were aiming for.

For the first time in a month, everyone got a full night's sleep. Bill awoke as dawn was breaking, and saw Meri already on the beach brewing some sort of concoction she would probably call tea. After his last experience with her tea, he decided to forgo it.

He climbed out of the canoe and did his morning ablutions on the side facing away from Meri. Despite all the time spent in survival training and on this trek, he still held a small modicum of decency and didn't particularly like waving things around in front of the women while he relieved himself. Washing his hands in the salt water afterwards, he joined Meri at the fire.

"Yum, eggs Benedict with fresh-squeezed orange juice and croissants!" he said when he saw what Meri had on the grill.

"Shut up and eat your breakfast," she said, smiling as she handed him a warmed filet of leftover grouper. Bill took the offering, giving her a nod of thanks.

"Want some tea?" She held out a canteen cup of the heated beverage.

That got her a resounding negative nod of his head while he continued chewing.

Bill swallowed his first chunk of fish. "Should we wake Karen up?"

Karen announced from the boat, "I'm awake. How the hell do you expect anyone to sleep through all that chattering?" It was obvious to the two on the beach that she was joking.

Karen joined them for fish and tea, and, looking around at the flat, barren island, said, "As soon as we're done, let's get this show on the road."

Once breakfast was done, the three released the ropes holding the canoe to the shrubs, climbed aboard the *Guppy*, and pushed off, paddling away from shore until Meri could raise the sail up the new mast.

Bill stowed his paddle and grabbed the tiller, turning the boat which had now caught the wind in a westerly direction away from the island. Soon they were passing the small island and cruising through the shallow waters.

"Look for any water that looks like it's going over rocks, that'll be a coral head," Meri told Karen

Within an hour the *Guppy* had cleared the shallow water and was back at sea.

TI'ICHAM

Trekker

East Coast

After four uneventful days, they finally approached Ti'icham. Passing through a gap in the Barrier Islands, they pulled into Pamlico Sound. No longer was worrying about their longitude an issue, but they still needed to get into Albermarle Sound and find the mouth of the Roanoke River.

Karen had them beach the canoe on the Pamlico Sound side of one of the low-lying sandy islands so Bill could get the most accurate sun shot possible. "Make it fast, 'cause I don't want to be out in this boat any longer than necessary," she told him, as he scrambled out of the canoe, sextant in hand. In the meantime Karen took out a tablet and activated it.

"Can't take a shot until noon," Bill said, holding up the sextant. So, the three waited.

At noon, it only took Bill a couple of minutes to determine their latitude.

"According to my calcs, we're at about 35 degrees and 15 minutes north."

Karen looked at the imagery on the tablet, with lines of latitude and longitude overlaying. "It looks like we're just south of where we need to go. Another ninety klicks or so oughta put us there. We need to get to 36 north and 76 degrees 30 minutes west. That'll put us right up the river. Let's just get moving. We should be able to tell when we're getting into the right sound, as the shoreline will go further east."

Bill handed the sextant to Karen, then pushed the canoe back into the sound. As soon as the bow was fully afloat he climbed aboard. On his way back to the tiller he gave Meri a quick kiss with a smile and a quiet, "Well, we made it." Meri returned both the kiss and the smile.

It was approaching mid-afternoon before the land began visibly receding to the east. Karen had Bill turn the *Guppy* west into what they thought was Albermarle Sound. They passed a bay to their south, and then the land began closing in on either side. Another couple of hours and they came to the confluence of two river estuaries.

Karen ordered them to take the southern river, which had an east-west orientation.

"That's it for the day," she said, telling Bill to steer toward the northern shore. "We'll crash here overnight and take a proper fix tomorrow."

Once again, they beached the big outrigger, this time tying it to the low-hanging branch of an old cypress tree.

That evening marked their final day on the *SS Guppy*. The river had become too narrow to navigate the bulky outrigger, so it was beached for the final time.

"Let's pull this bad boy up as far as possible," Karen said, as they landed. "On the off chance we make it back, this thing'd be awesome in the *Corps'* museum." The museum on Sacajawea Base chronicled the history of the *Corps of Discovery* and contained numerous artifacts, including a smaller outrigger canoe, from prior trekkers' journeys. Bill and Meri were glad to hear the old Karen return.

Karen ordered Meri to keep watch, so before the canoe was dragged ashore, Meri retrieved her rifle and took position on the beach.

Using ropes, Bill and Karen managed to get the vessel completely out of the water. It was a tight fit between the large trees, the majority of which were cypress.

"Here's the plan," Karen began, once the boat was grounded and life preservers tossed into it. "We're gonna make another dugout, only this one'll be smaller. As far as I can tell, other than the life preservers, and maybe one of the smaller desalinizers, there's nothing from the life raft we'll need anymore. So, while one of us works on the dugout, the other two will go through the equipment and eliminate anything we don't need.

"First things first, though. Let's get camp set up, and then we'll find a good tree for the dugout."

The three unloaded all the equipment from the *Guppy*. *Again*, thought Bill. The first things they unloaded were their rifles, survival vests, belts, and packs. The belts and vests were donned immediately, while the packs were left on the ground. Rifles were held at the ready. A campfire site was chosen and the hammocks hung around it. Karen then strung the trip-wires around the camp while Bill collected firewood and Meri kept watch.

After establishing the camp, Karen ordered all to shower and clean their salt encrusted uniforms.

"No swimming, though. I don't know if we're far enough inland for sharks, and who knows if 'gators range this far north here."

Collapsible bottles were filled and left in the sun to warm up. Salty uniforms were stripped off and rinsed in the river water, always with an eye toward the river and shoreline for any predators. An armed person remained on watch at all times.

A fire was started after clothes were clean and hung to dry. Each person then used a couple of the collapsible bottles with the shower attachment to wash off a week's worth of salt and sweat which was a great relief. *No more sticky feeling for a while, at least,* Bill thought, not even noticing that he was stark naked, as were the two women, other than the rifle each held while on watch.

Once the camp was established, the three began a circuit around it looking for a suitable tree. They were fortunate, finding one less than 30 meters away. It was a cottonwood tree that had been crowded out by surrounding cypress, and, as such, was stunted. Its diameter was only a meter, which was more than adequate for what they needed.

Looking up at the branches intertwined with the larger cypress, Bill asked, "So, how we gonna cut this thing down if it's being held up?"

Karen looked at him with a grin. "Looks like we get to play monkey woodcutter."

"Huh?"

"We're gonna have to climb up and cut the branches before we cut the tree down," she replied. "But, ain't no sense in starting now, especially after getting nice and clean. So, we'll come back tomorrow and take it down. In the meantime, let's mark it so we won't have a problem identifying it tomorrow." Karen took her hatchet from her belt and began hacking at the tree, creating a half-meter-long white blaze down its side. "There. Easy to spot from a distance."

The three returned to the campsite, where Bill 'volunteered' to try and catch supper.

"Yeah, volunteer my ass," his bride said with a grin. "You just want somebody else watching while you fish."

"Any harm in that?" he asked her, grinning himself. He pulled out his fly-fishing gear, something he hadn't done since leaving Eurasia, and got back into the *Guppy*. Standing in the stern of the canoe, he cast upriver and watched the dry fly float downriver, making sure to mend his line as it got close to the boat. Soon he saw a ripple around the floating fly, and then the fly disappeared into the river with a splash. Pulling back hard, he set the hook. For the next couple of minutes, he fought the fish, eventually landing it.

"Okay, that's enough playing," Meri said fifteen minutes later, after his third fish. "You caught 'em, you clean 'em."

The night passed uneventfully, and after a quick breakfast of pemmican, Karen had the trio return to the chosen tree to cut it down.

Meri was given the task of removing the intertwined limbs. Wrapping a length of rope around her waist and the trunk of the tree, she shimmied her way up, just like a power utility lineman would.

As she came to a limb, she used her hatchet to cut a V into the bottom of it. Then she shimmied her way above the limb, and, still being supported by the rope, used her ax to cut the top portion of limb above the bottom cut, until the limb eventually bent and cracked from gravity and the loss of wood.

As each limb began to break, Meri hollered, "Timber!", alerting Bill and Karen to get out of the way. After a half hour of limbing, Karen ordered Meri down and took her place. Then it was Bill's turn.

Eventually, enough limbs were cut that Karen was confident that the tree would fall without being snagged by another. She did the initial back-cut and then had Bill finish cutting the front. The tree came down with a crash and landed with its top near the river. They cut the tree into three parts and decided to use the center section as the canoe.

Once again, Bill got to wield the adze, cutting away the interior of the dugout while Karen and Meri took turns working on shaping the ends. While two chopped, the third kept watch.

Rather than take the old method of burning the interior to soften the wood, they elected to do the same as they had for the Guppy, directly cutting away the interior with the adze. While more difficult, it was actually faster, but still took several days of chopping. As the work was hard, and the weather hot and muggy, the three usually worked wearing only a minimum of clothing. Their portable showers got a daily workout at the end of the day, as did the portable clothes: a lightweight dry bag with bumps inside to assist in agitating the water.

The canoe was designed to fit all three Explorers, along with their equipment. It differed from the Guppy by not having a sail nor an outrigger, and it was considerably shorter, barely seven meters long.

Roanoke River

Before beginning the journey upriver, Karen ordered Bill to maintain watch over the equipment while she and Meri took the canoe upriver for a test run. Both women climbed into the canoe, which had been pushed into the river and tied to a cypress. They put their survival belts and rifles in the bottom of the canoe and donned life preservers.

Bill released the rope. The women, using paddles, made during their journey from Eurasia, back-paddled to move away from shore, and then moved upriver, cutting through the morning's mist. Bill turned his attention to the forest, alert as always for threats.

Occasionally he would look upriver to check their progress. One minute they were in sight, the next around one of the many meanders the river offered. It was quite a few nervous minutes before the dugout reappeared, easily slicing through the water on its way downstream.

Before too much longer, the canoe approached the riverbank. Meri tossed Bill a rope which he grabbed in mid-air and pulled the canoe to shore. He quickly tied the rope to the cypress.

"It works!" Karen said with a grin. Meri had the same grin.

"Now that it's ready," Karen went on, "let's sort through the gear and decide on what goes and what stays. We'll put whatever remains in the *Guppy* and cover it with brush."

The women took off their life preservers, replaced them with their survival belts, and took rifles in hand.

The first thing they went through was the Monarch's life raft and its equipment. The only thing they decided to keep was one of the smaller desalinizors and the adze. Other than the one parachute sail used to cross the ocean, all the other parachutes were tossed on the "ain't going with us" pile. Ben's pack and survival gear were also rifled through. Other than ammunition, food, food gathering gear, and socks, all that remained of Ben's existence was tossed on the pile. It was Bill's suggestion to keep Ben's socks, knowing full well that they would be one of the first clothing items to wear out.

The rifle ammunition was divvied up between Meri and Karen while Bill got all the PDW ammo. The rest of the equipment was split up evenly among the three. The remains of the pile were loaded in the *Guppy*. Bill and Meri cut brush and covered the abandoned boat.

"Now, let's get it loaded and get going," Karen said. "Meri, you're the best with a bow, so I want you up front with yours. You see anything worth taking, do so. I'm tired of fish.

"We'll sit on our packs. Until the river gets shallow enough to stand in I don't want anyone wearing their belts — put 'em on the floor in front of you."

Once more the trio broke camp and loaded their equipment. Meri placed the bow, quiver, and arrows she had made on the ocean voyage near the front of the boat. Putting on their life preservers over their survival vests, they then slung rifles over shoulders. Bill kept his PDW in his hand and didn't set it down until they had boarded the canoe.

Bill was ordered to the stern, once again, while Karen sat in the middle. This time Meri untied the rope from the cypress tree, while the other two maneuvered the boat to remain in place while she climbed into it.

They began paddling upstream. Despite the relatively strong current, Bill was glad to see that the canoe moved easily through the water. He estimated they were moving about half as fast as they could walk, about one to two klicks an hour. *At this rate, it'll take us forever to get home. Then again, it's still easier than having to carry everything.* He still remembered hauling all the equipment from the Monarch to their first river rafting trip in Eurasia, and how even using a travois to haul the gear wasn't easy.

Lunch was a short rest on a sandbar, consisting of pemmican and water. Bill wanted to fish but didn't dare ask Karen. Her comment earlier in the day had pretty much put any kibosh on that, at least for the next couple of days.

While Bill and Karen paddled almost continuously, Meri would occasionally set her paddle down across the bow and look upriver and to the sides, hoping to spot a feeding deer or some other wild game she could take.

It was approaching late afternoon when Meri set her paddle down and slowly held up her hand. Bill followed her gaze and saw a lone tapir on the riverbank, getting a drink. It was Bill's first time seeing a tapir outside of a picture. It was bigger than he expected. Meri motioned the two to paddle toward it, which they did,. slowly inching closer. Meri raised her bow, arrow nocked, then took her shot.

The tapir, surprised when the arrow struck it in the side, turned and ran into the forest.

"Keep paddling," whispered. "He's not gonna go far. I know where that arrow went."

Once they grounded the canoe, Karen ordered Bill to stay with it while she and Meri went after the tapir. They replaced their life preservers with their survival belts, donned their packs, and with rifles in hand began slowly tracking the animal.

Bill tied off the canoe to a nearby tree, then sat, trying not to worry too much, rifle in hand. Of course, being on a planet occupied by a variety of predators with no fear of humans didn't make that too easy.

An hour later, the women returned, Meri first, with Karen in tow. Karen carried her rifle at the ready while Meri dragged a travois loaded with meat.

"We'll overnight here," Karen announced. "Bill, you continue to keep watch. Meri, get a fire going while I set out the tripwire."

As Bill continued to stare into the forest, Meri scrounged up some dry wood and got a fire going. In the meantime, Karen had dug the trip wire lines from her pack and had set them out.

In less than a half hour, a fire was blazing, hammocks were strung, and a pot of tapir stew was started. The two women had managed to forage some greens and other edible plants on their way back from retrieving the tapir.

While waiting for the stew to cook, they sliced the remaining meat for jerking. The tapir strips were lain over a makeshift grill over the fire.

Dinner was a bit more animated than the previous days. Perhaps it was the act of moving upriver, fresh meat for the first time in a long time, or that they were becoming used to Ben's death and the lack of his presence. Regardless, the small group definitely had a more upbeat feel, Bill noticed.

The next several days followed the same pattern. Rise early, break camp, canoe upriver at a snail's pace, break for lunch, canoe some more, and stop for the evening. The group subsisted mainly on the tapir jerky and whatever animals they managed to snare during their overnights. Hunting was put on the back burner while they were paddling, mainly because all three were needed to get the canoe moving against the current.

As they traveled, the width of the river decreased, as its depth and flow. They were able to move a bit faster the further upstream they got, probably because they weren't fighting so much moving water.

It took almost two weeks of paddling before the trio made it to their first inland water obstacle: rapids formed by the division between the piedmont of the Appalachian Mountains and the coastal plain that they had been traveling through. They had an advance notice of the upcoming feature when they spotted several large rocks sticking out of the otherwise flat river. Passing the rocks, they arrived at a fork in the river. They took the wider fork, then paddled through a river meander. The sound of rapids became audible, and after coming out of the curve in the river they saw the first of the white water.

Paddling up to the rapids, Meri, still in the bow, called back to the others, "I don't see an easy way through. There's a beach up on the left. Should we beach the canoe there?"

Karen yelled over the sound of the rapids, "Yeah. We'll portage over there."

Within minutes the canoe was grounded on the small sandy beach and quickly tied off to a small tree.

Once on dry land, they exchanged life preservers for survival vests and belts and kept their rifles handy. Karen and Meri walked upriver, scouting the best route to take the canoe while Bill remained behind.

When they returned Karen said, "I think the easiest way is to tow the canoe through the water. It doesn't look too rough. Just rough enough to prevent us from paddling, though.

"Grab your packs and paddles. The only things I want left in this thing while we're towing it are those we can live without."

Backpacks were thrown on backs, and paddles were strapped to the packs. Meri offered to keep watch while Karen and Bill towed the much-lightened canoe upriver. It didn't take long before they were over the rapids. *That wasn't too hard,* Bill thought when they had finished and were loading back up to continue their journey.

Over the next fifteen kilometers, they repeated the process numerous times. Some of the rapids were more like actual falls, albeit small and taking the canoe through the water was not an option. In those cases, they dragged the canoe upriver on land, which wasn't as easy as they hoped it would be. Unlike a modern composite or aluminum boat, the wood canoe was heavy, weighing several hundred kilograms. Dragging it uphill took all three of them.

After three days of navigating and portaging the rapids, the crew were finally above the fall line, out of the flat coastal plain and into the hilly piedmont of the Appalachian Mountains. The water, while still relatively flat and calm, had become just noticeably swifter due to the slight drop it experienced in its progress through the hills. It wasn't fast enough to appreciably slow them down; just enough to tire them out faster.

The volume of the river decreased, and the hills to either side of them grew larger until they were passing through small mountains. When the water got shallow enough that the paddles were scraping the riverbed, they switched to poles. Usually, one would pole, standing up, while the other two sat, bows in hand, keeping an eye out for any unwary game that could be converted to supper. They had fresh meat just about every night, with leftovers and jerky the following day.

Eventually, they got to the point in the river where exposed rocks were difficult to navigate around and the water was too shallow for the canoe while they were sitting in it. As the plan was to drag the canoe from the Roanoke River to the New River, they had to make a decision: continue upstream to the chosen takeout spot, or leave it and make another when they arrive at the next river. They elected to tow it upriver as far as possible. *Thank God! I didn't want to dig out another damned canoe,* Bill thought.

Two days later, Bill wasn't so sure that had been the best choice. They had reached the headwaters of the Roanoke, and the water was now too low to even tow the canoe. The vegetation was crowding the area of what had effectively become a small creek, to the point where it was difficult walking through it. After several hours of struggling through branches and being splashed in the face by water kicked up by walking, all while pulling a heavy canoe in the summer heat and humidity, Karen said "Let's stop and set up camp. I want to revisit the whole 'drag the canoe 20 klicks overland' thing." She looked pointedly up at the mountains hemming them in.

They established camp, strung hammocks, and set out the standard trip-wire. So far, it hadn't been set off by any animals since they arrived on Ti'ichem, but that didn't mean it wouldn't be in the future.

Because they had been walking and towing a heavy canoe for the past two days, their hunting opportunities had been limited. Bill offered to supplement the dwindling meat supply with fish.

"Heck, these types of rivers are what fly fishing was made for," he said, strengthening his argument.

Karen relented, agreeing to stand watch while both Bill and Meri fished. The two found some small pools well within eyesight of each other and proceeded to cast into them. It didn't take long before Meri had a fish on, followed by Bill. Within a half hour, they had a sufficient quantity of fish for supper. They had also managed to capture several crayfish to supplement their meal.

Karen offered to start the fire and suggested Meri and Bill use the small river to wash up in. They took advantage of the break to get the day's mud off them and wash their sweaty clothing. After changing into dry clothes, Bill took over the watch duty to allow Karen to wash up and do laundry. When Karen was done, the fire had burned down to coals, ideal for grilling the night's meal.

The talk over the fire that evening centered on the next river's journey, and the question of towing the dugout from one river to another. All agreed that towing it upriver in a small stream was hard enough, and trying to get it through the forest and over rough terrain would probably be too much for them.

"So, what are our options?" Meri asked. "Another dugout?"

"I don't know about you two, but I'm kind of tired of digging out canoes," Bill said. "What about a regular canoe with bark or skin?"

Looking around the small clearing, Meri said, "Just sayin', but I don't see any birch trees hereabouts."

"I agree, no birch trees," Karen said. "That means skin, which we're pretty much out of. So, how much time would it take to hack out a new dugout instead of killing enough game and curing enough skins, and then making a skin canoe?"

"Hmm, couple of days to soak the skins, a couple of days to tan, and maybe one to smoke," Bill said. "Figure a couple of days to build the actual canoe. About a week. Same as making a heavy dugout. On top of that, we'd get a lot of food out of it, not just wood chunks."

Karen looked thoughtful. "It probably makes sense to haul everything over to the New River and then do our hunting over there. Even though we've pared our equipment down, we've still got a bunch of stuff to haul as it is."

"You think one travois will suffice?" Meri asked.

"I do," said Bill.

"Me, too," agreed Karen. "So, tomorrow, let's make a single travois, load it up, and head cross country to the New River."

"What if we see something along the way, like an elk or deer?" Meri asked.

"Only shoot something large if we come across it. Otherwise, the plan is to get to the river ASAP. We'll set up base and do all our preps there."

Trekker

Upper New River

It took them the better part of two days to make it from the Roanoke River to the New River, most of it through old growth forest and rough terrain. Occasionally they would come to an open spot, and at one of these glades, Meri managed to down an elk with her bow. The skin was thrown on the travois, which Bill was dragging, along with enough meat to sustain them for another day. Wrapped inside the skin was the animal's brain, to be used to tan the hide.

Man, am I glad we decided not to drag that boat this way, Bill thought, as he struggled to drag the travois through the forest.

They finally arrived at the New River a couple of hours before sunset. By now they had been trekking for a bit over two and a half months, so setup went quickly. Hammocks, trip wire, fire. Supper consisted of elk stew, which Meri made while Karen began soaking the elk hide in the river. She did so by setting the skin in the river and covering it with large rocks.

"If it floats away, we'll just kill another elk," she said, inspecting her handiwork.

The evening's discussion was on how to best do everything. They needed to hunt, but they also needed to cut down enough wood to construct the frame. Any of these, by themselves, wasn't an issue. The issue became who would remain watchful while the others did the work. While they hadn't been attacked by anything since leaving the Caribbean, that didn't mean threats had gone away.

"It kinda makes no sense to have somebody at camp building stuff if the hides aren't ready in the first place," Bill said. "I'm thinkin' we should all hunt together. Once we've got enough hides soaking and tanning, we can build the frame."

"Bill's right," Meri said. "We're struggling enough just keeping watch. Splitting up and trying to get everything done would just become crazy. Especially with the kinds of dangerous animals we're facing here. Ti'icham's got several types of bears, cats, and wolves. And that's not even counting the venomous snakes we need to watch out for."

"It's settled, then," Karen said. "From now on, we stick together. But anytime we leave this campsite, we take all our primary and secondary survival gear. The lifeboat stuff can stay, but I don't want any of us caught out there needing something that might have been left behind. Is that clear?" she asked the others. Meri and Bill nodded.

Hunting began in earnest early the next morning. The trio donned all their survival gear and headed out, leaving the campfire smoldering. Nobody was worried about a wildfire; rather, the concern was that some wild animals would come into the camp and take the one skin they had.

All three carried bows that had been made during the Atlantic crossing, but Bill's was slung over his shoulder while he carried his rifle at the ready. The team traveled in an inverted V-formation, with Meri and Karen in front and Bill trailing behind them. His job was to provide security, so as they moved, he was constantly looking forward, to the sides, up in the trees, and behind them. Fortunately, the two women were walking slow, in the method they learned during survival training as "still hunting." Each of them would take a couple of slow steps, gently placing their foot down and putting their weight on that foot. After two or three steps they would stop, slowly move their heads around to look for game, then proceed in the same manner.

They had been at it for some time when they finally approached a large clearing. Bill could see charred stumps of trees; the clearing had been made by fire. Grass in the clearing and a lack of burnt wood smell meant that the fire had happened a year or two ago. *I'm betting this was a lightning strike fire last year*, Bill thought.

Across the clearing, they could see a small herd of elk, headed up by a monster bull with an amazing set of antlers. They rivaled the ones that Bill had seen on the Roosevelt elk he had been used to seeing on Earth. Though, nobody here cared about the antlers.

Karen whispered a quick plan to Bill and Meri, then she and Meri began the stalk. Bill made sure the tree above him was predator-free before leaning against the giant bole, biding his time while the women made their way closer to the herd.

The stalk was slow and silent. Occasionally, one or another elk would raise its head and look at one of the women. When the women saw an elk head start to rise, they would freeze in place, barely even breathing. It took almost a half hour, but finally, Meri and Karen were in place.

Bill slowly raised his rifle and sighted down it while the women slowly brought their bows up and drew the strings back. Bill made sure to keep both eyes open so he could see at least one of the women while also keeping an elk in his sights. As soon as he saw Karen loose her arrow, he fired.

The elk Bill had chosen dropped like a rock. The rest of the herd, startled by the shot, stampeded into the forest away from him. Immediately after firing, Bill took his rifle off his shoulder, charging it in the way he had learned during Explorer firearms training: bolt handle slammed up, bolt drawn forcefully back, a quick glance down to see the spent casing eject and a fresh cartridge move up to load into the barrel, forceful action of pushing the bolt forward, and a final action of slamming the bolt handle down, locking the bolt in place. All of this was done in less than a second and without a conscious thought.

Bill looked around, conducting a quick threat assessment, then finding no threat near him, did the same for the women. Once satisfied that all was good, he left his position and started making his way across the clearing to where Meri and Karen were standing.

It only took him a couple of minutes until he had joined the women.

"How'd it go?" he asked.

"We've got two blood trails. One looks like it's lung-shot, and the other might be a heart shot. We'll know more in about twenty minutes" Karen said. "In the meantime, let's get this one skinned."

The two women worked to skin the dead animal while Bill maintained watch. It didn't take long, particularly since they were only after the skin and brains. Meat was secondary. Afterwards, the women helped each other wash blood off their hands with their canteens.

Meri grabbed the rolled-up skin with the brains tucked inside it and strapped it to the outside of Bill's pack. "Let's go get the others."

They carried their rifles: the need for safety superseded the need to save ammunition. Unstringing their bows, they stashed them on their packs. The bowstrings went in their pockets.

The second elk they found was the one that was shot through the heart. It hadn't gone too far before bleeding out. As with the first, it was only a matter of minutes before it was skinned and the brains collected. This time Bill had the pleasure of cleaning the game with Meri while Karen stood watch.

After cleaning it, he wrapped the brains in the skin, and strapped the load to Karen's pack.

They backtracked to the clearing to track down the final kill. Finding the third elk took some time, as it traveled quite some distance. They followed the drops of frothy blood it left on the ground, the grass, and leaves of low-lying bushes. Finally, after more than a half hour, they came across the body of the elk. Unfortunately, it wasn't alone.

An American lion, larger by one-third than Earth's comparable African lion, was gnawing on the kill. As he spotted the humans, he laid his ears back and issued a throaty grumble.

"Crap. Big and mean, and on our kill," Karen muttered.

"We need that skin," Meri said in a quiet voice, aiming her rifle at the large cat. In fact, all three had their rifles aimed at the lion.

"Hold on. Let's do this a little different. How're your peeder skills, Bill?" Karen asked, referring to his shooting ability with his PDW.

"What are you thinking?"

"Can you take him out with a head shot?"

"Yeah, I think so," he said.

Keeping her rifle trained on the growling creature, Karen said, "Do it. We'll provide cover."

Holding his rifle in one hand, Bill shrugged out of his pack and set it on the ground. With his free hand, he unstrapped the PDW. Setting his rifle down on the pack, all the while eying the lion, he checked the PDW to verify it was loaded, extended the stock, then brought it up to his shoulder.

Taking careful aim through the low power scope, he sighted

in on the large cat's eye. He quietly said, "On three." When he got to the number, he shot.

The bullet went exactly where Bill aimed, into the lion's eye, through the eye socket, and into the brain. The poor beast never knew what hit him, and dropped dead instantly. All three Explorers breathed very audible sighs of relief.

"Looks like we've got another skin," Meri said. She turned to Bill, she said with a huge smile. "You caught it. You clean it."

The four elk and one lion skin proved more than sufficient to clad the canoe. Branches were lopped off nearby trees and carved to form the ribs, and the tanned hides were applied over the frame. Pitch from nearby pine trees was used to seal the holes from where the hides were stitched together. To Bill, it seemed the pitch was also used to cement his fingers together. Only with vigorous rubbing with sand, which also took away some skin, was he able to remove it.

A week had passed, and finally, the canoe was ready. It was now late August, still summer in the piedmont, but it was slowly fading into fall in the mountains. Through gaps in the trees caused by the river, Bill could see the leaves on the tops of nearby mountains changing. As he helped load the canoe for their journey down the river, Bill said, "Looks like summer's just about over."

Meri and Karen followed his gaze.

"Well, at least we'll be done with the heat, humidity, and mosquitoes soon," Karen said, as a bead of sweat dripped off her nose.

Bill was more worried about the coming cold than he was about mosquitoes. According to his reckoning, they still had over six months of travel ahead of them, the last three taking place deep in the continent where sub-zero temperatures could be expected to last for weeks during the late winter. He scratched his chin and thought, *Well, at least my face'll stay warm with this fuzz I'm growing.*

The equipment loaded, the Explorers boarded the canoe and continued their westward journey.

"It seems strange to be moving into the mountains and not fighting the current," Bill said. The others agreed, looking at the rising terrain around them. Their seating arrangements were the same as the trip up the Roanoke — Meri up front with a bow, Karen in the middle, and Bill steering from the stern. Karen and Meri both had their rifles slung over their backs, while Bill kept his PDW close to hand, slung across his chest. His rifle was strapped to his pack, which, like the other packs, rested in the bottom of the canoe, strapped down in the event of a capsize. All three wore their survival belts, vests, and life preservers.

Bill was surprised at the different handling of the skin and frame canoe compared to the dugouts. He could feel its nimbleness and with each stroke of the paddle, its lightness. It was also slightly tipsier, he noticed. But still, it rode well and practically leaped forward when he dug his paddle into the swift waters. It was nice traveling downriver. Not only was it easier, despite the muscles they had built up rowing against the Roanoke's current, but faster. The landscape seemed to rush by them as they made their way westward, cutting through mountains.

A bit over four hours later they had entered the cut between the first range of mountains. They stared in amazement at the steep mountains towering hundreds of meters above them. *Not quite like the Alps,* Bill thought, *but still, intimidating enough.*

The land around them was steep, and the current picked up, so Meri set her bow down, retrieved her paddle, and helped control the canoe.

They went through two more steep ridge cuts before entering an area of more scattered hills and mountains, with some flat land near where streams fed into the river. It was at one of these flat areas that Meri saw a small herd of deer. She motioned the other two to maneuver the canoe closer while she traded her paddle for her bow. Once within range, she loosed an arrow, bringing down a small doe. The other deer saw the animal fall, then noticed the approaching canoe and fled into the forest.

Meri said with a smile, "Venison for supper."

Again, Bill thought, somewhat sourly. He was fast becoming tired of eating mainly meat and was beginning to crave real vegetables.

"Too bad we don't have any carrots or potatoes to throw into the pot," he said.

They grounded the canoe and Meri hopped out first, rifle at the ready. Grabbing the canoe with her free hand, but looking around to maintain awareness, she pulled it further ashore so Karen could climb out. The two then pulled the canoe even further, enabling Bill to get out without having to jump into the river.

The area they landed was a flat piece of ground on a meander between two small streams, with a hill between them. *I bet there's a town here on Earth,* Bill thought.

Meri went to the downed doe and began cleaning her kill, while Karen identified where they would establish camp. Bill kept watch while Karen set out the tripwire lines. Once they were set, she gathered fuel for a fire. Using his foot, Bill cleared a small area for the campfire. Karen then gathered some stones from the river's edge and created a small stone ring in the clearing.

By the time Karen was done getting the campsite established, Meri had cut up enough of the deer to make a hearty stew.

Casting about, she found some edible plants to include in the meal.

Once the fire was going, the need for Bill to remain on watch was lessened, so each Explorer set up their own hammock.

They were camped under some large oak trees, so Karen had them collect acorns. "Might as well leach them tonight. That way we can use them tomorrow."

After supper, the three settled into their evening routine of personal hygiene, care of equipment, and trading off sleep for standing watch.

Morning dawned clear, which Bill was grateful for. With the narrowness of the river's channel and the steepness of the mountains surrounding them, if there was substantial rainfall the river's flow would increase dramatically. The last thing he wanted to do was deal with the rapids of an unknown river at flood stage.

It was only a matter of a few minutes before the hammocks were taken down and packed away, and a breakfast of grilled venison with dandelion greens devoured.

The day's journey was an easy drift downriver with a few Class I and II rapids. Not being familiar with the river, Bill had no idea if this would be the extent of the rapids or if they could expect worse, so he brought the subject up.

"When we break for the night, see what you can pull up on the tablet," Karen said.

Bill estimated that they made twenty-five klicks that day, thanks to a fairly swift stream flow combined with paddling. The location they pulled out was another of the rare flat spots along the river, this one on the south side.

After setting up camp, and while Meri prepared the evening meal, Bill pulled out his tablet and began reviewing the data on the river.

"From what I can tell, we've got plenty of whitewater before we hit the junction of the next river," he said after a few minutes. "Not sure what type of rapids, but we should probably stay on our toes, and get off this river before any rain swells it."

"Good idea. I've seen rivers go from Class II to Class IV rapids overnight with a heavy rain," Karen said.

Of course, once stated, the prophecy was fulfilled.

Not long after climbing into his hammock after second watch, Bill heard a spattering of raindrops hit the fly. *Man, I hope this is just a shower*, he thought. His hopes were dashed as the rainfall became heavier. Soon it felt like Bill was inside a drum. It didn't stop him from sleeping, though.

When he awoke several hours later, it was still raining. And warmer. Looking out from under his hammock's fly he could see the ground around him was soaked, and the light was muted by the clouds and rain.

He retrieved his boots and put them on. He also dug his poncho from his pack and, carefully exiting the hammock, he put on the poncho as quickly as possible. He couldn't avoid getting wet, though; by now the rain was a steady downpour. Grabbing his rifle, he made his way over to the smoldering fire, where Karen sat on a log, also dressed in a poncho.

The river had risen overnight; it was rapidly rising over the flat area where they had landed, and the current was moving swiftly.

"What's the plan?" he asked Karen, as he sat next her on the log.

"We can either wait it out or get on the river as fast as possible and hope we don't hit anything worse than yesterday. If we wait, it might rise high enough to force us off this site and up onto the slope over there." Karen pointed to a steep slope at the edge of the campsite.

"Not much room to pull the canoe up," he noticed.

Karen nodded. "Yeah. Looks like we're between a rock and a hard place."

"More like a rock and a wet place," Bill said with a grin, trying to lighten the mood. Karen just shook her head and muttered, "Why me, Lord? Why?"

Meri climbed out of her hammock. Donning here poncho, she joined the two. "So?" she asked.

"I'm thinking downriver," Karen said. "If I'm correct, this is a tropical depression we're dealing with, which means we'll be getting even more rain. The faster we can get someplace safer, the better we are. So, let's break down camp. Breakfast will be on the river." She looked directly at Bill. "And that doesn't mean fish!"

Ten minutes later the camp was broken down and the canoe packed. Everyone wore their primary survival gear under their PFDs and had rifles slung over their backs over their ponchos. If the main gear was lost in a capsize situation, they would at least have some survival equipment.

Karen made sure that the packs and remaining survival equipment were lashed to the bottom of the canoe. "Hopefully, we won't lose anything," she said, looking at their handiwork.

The three climbed into the canoe in their usual positions and started down the river. Almost immediately Bill could feel the difference in the water flow. When they had landed last night, it had been swift, but not like this. In seconds they were pulled along by the current, faster than before.

While Meri and Karen worked to keep them from bashing into any rocks, Bill struggled to steer the canoe from the rear.

The rain came down in sheets, oftentimes obliterating their view. Bill felt the sweat pouring off his body, the moisture trapped between him and the poncho. It was like having to swim in a warm tub, increasing his level of discomfort.

The river was impressively powerful, and they began to encounter larger and larger rapids, mostly in the Class IV and V level — much too intense for them.

"Hey, Karen," Bill shouted above the storm, "this river's too rough."

Karen nodded, then shouted, "Meri, keep your eyes peeled for a safe spot to pull in. Let's get off this river."

The three continued to fight the river, desperately seeking a flat spot to land on.

Suddenly, Meri turned back to the others and screamed "Falls!"

For a second, nobody responded. Then Karen yelled, "Pull over port!" The three paddled as hard as they could and managed to reach the steep shore. Meri jumped out and held onto the canoe, which started to swing stern first downriver. Bill continued paddling to try and remain in place while Karen scrambled to the front and over the side onto land. She grabbed ahold the canoe, which was rocking in the churning waters. Bill could hear the sound of the falls just downriver.

Karen and Meri both grasped the canoe, stabilizing it somewhat.

"You'll have to jump out and drag the tail end to shore," Karen yelled.

Bill dropped his paddle in the bottom of the craft and gingerly stepped out of the canoe on the landward side, the fierce current tugging on his legs. As he tried to reach the shore, his foot slipped on the moss-covered rocks, and he fell face first into the water. The shock caused him to lose his one-handed grip on the canoe, and he was immediately swept away.

He heard Meri yell, "Bill!", but it was too late. The current had ahold of him and was sweeping him downriver, feet first and face down.

Face up, feet first, he recalled from his training, and tried to turn around so his face was up. Just as he did, he went over a waterfall, cracking his head on a rock as his feet went over the edge.

Sharp pain caused his mind to flare, and then, nothing.

Trekker

"Yeah. Shit. Sucks to be us. On a positive note, at least it wasn't the tibia and it didn't break through the skin, so we don't have to worry as much about infection."

The pain meds soon kicked in and Bill drifted back off to sleep.

Bill was awakened by the sound of somebody singing softly. Meri now sat where Karen had been the night before, rifle draped across her crossed legs. There was a dull ache in his leg, but nothing that he couldn't bear.

"Hey," he said.

Meri stopped singing and looked his way. A smile rapidly grew on her face and she reached over and gave him a kiss, rubbing her hand through his hair.

"Hey, yourself," she said after pulling back. "How you feeling?"

"Better than the first time I woke up, that's for sure."

"Good. Want something to eat or drink?"

"Yeah, but I need to go to the bathroom first."

"Then you might need this." Meri picked up a handmade crutch. It was a simple forked stick, the fork padded in leather and the bark peeled off.

It took a bit before Bill could stand. First, he had to flip over onto his stomach, then push himself up onto his knees. Once on his knees, he was able to use his good leg, along with the crutch, to rise to a standing position. He was a bit shaky but soon settled down. The pain in his leg was still there, a dull drumbeat with every heartbeat, but not enough to cause him too much discomfort.

Supporting himself with the crutch, he looked around. Meri pointed him to a slit trench latrine on the far side of the camp.

Bill hobbled over to the latrine, making sure to minimize the amount of weight he placed on his broken leg. He knew from his medical training in Survival School that one could walk with a broken fibula as long as there was some form of support, such as the makeshift splint he was wearing, but he didn't want to chance damaging it any more than necessary.

Once at the latrine, he felt grateful be a male who could pee standing up. *Yeah, squatting down for a shit's gonna be real interesting.*

Finished, he hobbled back to the bed and with a bit of struggle, and a lot of help from the crutch and Meri, flopped down on his sleeping bag.

Meri held a canteen out for him to wash his hands. He managed to keep most of the water out of his bed. With more of her assistance, he got dressed. She removed his splint while he pulled his pants over his legs, and once his pants and socks were on replaced the splint. He decided to keep his boots off for the time being.

"Hungry?"

"I could eat."

She handed him a small pot filled with stew. A spork was already in it, so it was just a matter of digging in and eating his first meal in days. It didn't take long before the stew was gone.

Meri took his pot and utensil and cleaned them with sand and water.

"Don't get used to this domestic lifestyle where I do all the cooking and cleaning," she joked as she poured boiling water over the spork and into the pot, sterilizing them.

"Promise I won't. But can I enjoy it right now?" Bill asked with a grin.

Karen crawled out of her sleeping bag, holding her rifle in one hand and covering her mouth with the other as she yawned.

"Hey, look who's finally awake," she said. "How you feeling?"

"A lot better than the other day, that's for sure."

"Good. You feeling well enough to travel?"

Bill thought about it for a moment. "As long as we take it easy. No way I'm gonna be carrying a pack or doing anything really physical for a couple of weeks, at least."

"More like a couple of months," Meri said.

"Here's what I'm thinking," Karen said. "You ride in the middle, I'll be in the stern, and Meri stays in the bow. That way we'll have somebody who can actually use a bow in the premier spot, somebody who can move with at least some small degree of agility in the back, and we'll use your strong back in the middle."

"Hmm. Strong back, weak mind thinking going on there?" Bill asked with a touch of humor.

"You said it, Sparky, not me," Karen said with a grin.

"Yeah, I think that's manageable," Bill said.

"Great. You up for leaving now or do you want to give it another day to see how you're feeling?"

"Gimme a day to figure out how to use this thing," Bill said, pointing to the crutch.

"Sounds like a plan," Karen said. "We'll head out first thing tomorrow. In the meantime, take it easy but try using that thing so you're not so helpless. Last thing we need is to have you eaten or something."

Reaching behind the pack Bill was resting on, Karen pulled out his rifle and handed it to him.

"Here, you might want this," she said.

Immediately, Bill saw there was a problem. The rifle scope was broken. The tube was crushed and cracked and the front lens was missing.

"We think it hit the same rock that gave you the concussion," Karen said.

"No sense keeping it on," Bill said and unlatched the quick-release lever holding the scope onto the picatinny rail. "Guess that's why the *Corps* keeps the iron sights on."

"Yep, two is one and one is none," Meri said, referring to the *Corps* attitude toward redundancies and backups.

Damaged scope in hand, Bill wondered what to do with it. He didn't see the sense in carrying dead weight, but he also knew the *Corps* didn't like leaving too many artifacts lying around in the event another hominid species existed on the planet under exploration. And since they'd already seen Neanderthals on Planet 42's Eurasian continent, he was particularly concerned about discovery.

As if reading Bill's mind, Karen said, "Just smash it some more with a rock and throw the pieces in the river. They'll eventually get covered up with sediment."

"Here, give it to me. I'll do it." Meri held out her hand.

While Meri was at the river, Bill inspected the rifle. He could tell it had been cleaned, as there was no rust or dirt on it. Looking at Karen with a raised eyebrow, she raised her chin in Meri's direction.

Bill nodded, then turned his attention back to the rifle, inspecting the chamber to ensure it was loaded. It was. He then ejected the magazine: it was full. He replaced it, tapping the bottom upward into the rifle to ensure it was seated properly.

"I guess I'm good enough to stand watch if either of you need some more sleep," he said, as Meri came back into the camp.

"Naw, we're good," Karen said. "Well, other than a broke ASS, that is," she finished with a grin.

"Ass?" Bill asked, raising both eyebrows.

"Ain't that what you are, an Aerial Survey Specialist, or Ay Ess Ess?" Karen replied, laughing.

Slapping Bill on the thigh of his uninjured leg, she said, "Take it easy for the rest of the day. I'm sure tomorrow's gonna be a bitch for you."

The chatter of the awakening forest woke Bill before the dawn. The birds, in particular, were noisy. This was especially true because of the sheer number of them. Back on Earth, Bill would see flocks of birds, but nothing like what he had experienced on Hayek, Zion, and now Planet 42. Passenger pigeons were quite loud as they fed on the mast of the surrounding chestnut and oak trees surrounding the campsite. It wasn't the cooing of doves that he was used to; rather these birds made shrieking, clucking, and chattering sounds. Bill was amazed that Meri and Karen could sleep through it. *Then again, after all the time they spent swapping watch and taking care of me while I was zonked out, no wonder they're dead to the world.*

The fire was still smoldering, so Bill decided to add fuel to it. After a couple of awkward minutes getting on his feet, he was able to grab a couple of sticks stacked near the fire and set them atop the glowing coals. *That oughta keep the nasties away.*

Taking care not to stare into the fire and lose his night vision, Bill grabbed his rifle and made his way to the latrine where he managed, yet again, another successful toilet.

Returning to the campfire, he got a pot of water set above the fire on a stick that had been set up for that purpose. Bill didn't know where the fixings were, but he knew that Meri had found some sassafras to make tea with: a far better success then her initial attempt at concocting a hot brew for them. Scrounging around, he finally found the sassafras roots, but they were only partially dry. *Guess this'll have to do*, he thought. Grabbing his knife from his web belt, which was on the ground next to his sleeping bag, he cut the roots into slivers, dropping them into a pot.

By the time dawn was in full swing, Bill could hear stirring from the two hammocks. Soon he was joined by the women, both of whom were suffering from bedhead and bad breath. By now the tea was brewing. Rather than risk trying to stand and pour hot tea, he convinced Meri to pour a cup for each of them.

As always, sipping the brew reminded Bill of coffee, or the lack thereof. Along with the lack of any type of sweetener.

"Hey, any thought of trying to raid a honey bee nest?" he asked.

"No thanks," Meri said. "I'm already taking care of one sick, lame, and lazy guy. Don't feel like taking care of another." She tempered her comment with a smile.

"Not me," said Karen. "Not up for getting stung multiple times."

"We could smoke them out," Bill said.

"Yeah. No," Karen said. "Besides, we've got enough to do without trying to find something to satisfy your sweet tooth needs."

Bill shrugged. "Just a thought." He took another sip of the bitter tea.

Karen suggested pigeon for breakfast.

"Bill, you keep an eye out. We'll use our slingshots and take a bunch of them out quietly."

Bill felt it was sacrilegious to kill any passenger pigeons, considering they had gone extinct on Earth over a century ago. The logical side of his brain argued with the emotional side until the logical side finally won. There were billions of passenger pigeons on Planet 42; they wouldn't be going extinct any time soon. Besides, he was getting tired of venison stew for just about every meal.

Bill stood up and held his rifle at the ready, scanning about, while the women retrieved their rifles and slingshots and went hunting under the nearby trees.

Within minutes they each had several birds, which they brought back into the campfire. Bill helped dress them out and spit them. It wasn't long before the passenger pigeons were roasting over the coals of the fire.

While the birds were cooking the three went about preparing to load the canoe. Bill was able to help, but not as much as he wanted to; it was difficult for him, with only one hand. The other was holding on to his makeshift crutch. He finally resigned himself to standing watch while the two women did all the packing.

It didn't take long for Meri and Karen to collect the trip wire, and then pack up the hammocks and sleeping bags. The packs and rifles were stacked together while the three donned their web belts and survival vests.

"Keep the peeder packed," Karen told Bill. "If we've only got one person armed and ready to shoot at a moment's notice, I want them armed with a rifle."

Bill complied.

"Now, let's get the packs and canoe over to the river and get this show on the road."

Karen and Meri dragged the canoe back to the water and pushed it in, stern first. While Meri held onto the bow, Karen removed her socks and shoes and rolled her pants legs up, then loaded the packs. Then she pushed the stern so the vessel was parallel to the shore.

"Okay. Let's see if we can get you loaded without having you fall in the river," she said to Bill. He handed the rifle to her and she put it in the back of the canoe.

Bill, using Karen and Meri as supports, was able to step into the canoe. Sitting was a struggle, but the three of them managed it. Bill sat on his pack, broken leg stretched out in front of him, his rifle in his lap. Karen handed him a paddle before climbing into the rear of the canoe.

Before pushing off, the three put on their life preservers.

"After last time, I don't think I'll ever go on the water without one of these," Bill said as he struggled into the PDF.

Karen pushed away from the shore with her paddle while Meri continued to hold onto the bow.

As the canoe's rear started to swing into the current, Meri climbed into the front and began paddling backward, pushing them further into the river's channel.

In just a minute the trio was making their way down the New River, westward bound once again.

It wasn't long before they were engaged in fighting the river again. Even though the water level had dropped dramatically several days after the storm, they were in an area of numerous rapids. The mountains closed in on them, the river narrowed, and the rapids kept coming one after the other. Most were Class II, fairly easy to negotiate in the canoe, but some were Class III, and there were even a couple of Class IV rapids that got Bill's attention.

As the canoe bucked and rolled through the rapids, he hoped that they would end soon and that the canoe wouldn't be too damaged. Water sprayed up in their faces, and it was a struggle to keep their hats on, despite the draw cords. After just six hours on the river the trio called uncle and pulled up to a flat stretch of land. They were exhausted, despite it being only early afternoon, so they decided to set up camp.

Once again, the majority of the work fell to the women while Bill kept watch. After the camp was established and a fire started, Bill did some fishing while Karen took over the watch and Meri began hunting for edible plants to supplement their diet and get some much-needed vitamin C.

After supper, Karen gave Bill the first watch after he said he had recovered enough to at least do that. The night passed uneventfully.

The next day they were back on the river just after dawn. This time, even though the water level had continued to fall, the river had more, and tougher, rapids. There were more Class IV, and even a couple that Bill thought were Class V. *Damn, I'm glad I've got this life vest on,* he thought as they passed through one particularly rough one, soaking everyone.

It seemed like forever before the gorge they had been traveling through widened and the rapids ceased to buffet them, but it was barely past noon. They finally reached the fork where the New and Gauley Rivers merged, forming the Kanawha River, and the water smoothed out. The added flow from the Gauley increased their downriver speed, which made everyone happier as they waited to dry out in the warming day.

Trekker

Kanawha River

Traveling down the Kanawha River was the easiest part of their waterborne journey since the time spent rafting down the Rhône River in Western Eurasia. The river was wide and mostly smooth, without the elevation drop they'd had coming out of the mountains. After the rapids, rough water, and falls of the New River, the Kanawha was a pleasant respite.

It wasn't long, though, before they heard the sound of more rushing water, louder than the rapids they had been running all morning. Deciding that discretion was the better part of valor, Karen ordered the craft beached. This time, they were careful to pull the canoe in parallel to the shore and exit on the shore side.

Grabbing her rifle, Karen told Bill, "You stay here while Meri and I go see what we're dealing with."

While Bill sat guard over the canoe and equipment, the two women walked downriver. They were gone less than five minutes.

"Another set of falls," Karen said upon their return.

"So, what's the game plan?" Bill asked.

"We portage. Meri and I'll take the equipment down while you tag along. Once we've got everything down, then we'll portage the canoe down."

Bill felt useless, lacking the ability to do anything more than sit on his ass and watch while the women did all the work. A small, misogynistic part of him thought morosely, *Well, at least I get to see women working*. He promptly shut down that line of thinking, realizing he was being an asshole, even if only to himself.

Each woman grabbed her pack, shouldered it, and headed downriver. Karen took the lead while Bill hobbled along behind Meri. The two women, being hale and hearty, were able to cover the ground faster than Bill with his makeshift crutch, so it was no surprise that they started widening the gap between them and Bill. He thought about moving his rifle from the ready sling position to slinging it over his back when he caught sight of some movement in the trees above Meri. He stopped and focused on the movement, which had also stopped.

It took him a moment for his brain to register what his eyes were seeing, but once it did, he shouted "Down!"

Dropping his crutch, he brought his rifle up to bear as the two women hit the ground.

As Meri landed, a mountain lion jumped on her back and bit down. Bill took aim through the ghost ring sights of his rifle, fired, dropped his rifle to the ready position, ejected the spent round and chambered another.

Bringing the rifle up, he saw the lion was writhing around on the ground on the other side of Meri. He didn't have a clear shot.

Karen came to her feet, rifle up, and shot the lion from only a couple of feet away. The writhing ceased and the big cat lay motionless, obviously dead.

Bill grabbed his crutch and hobbled down the slope as rapidly as he could, rifle still held in his right hand. His heart was pounding and he was filled with fear.

God, let her be okay, he prayed as he slowly raced toward Meri.

Karen was already checking for injuries, her hands moving around Meri's neck. Meri was unconscious, not moving.

"Help me get her pack off, but don't move her," she said as Bill arrived.

The two managed to undo the buckles of her pack straps, and Karen removed the pack and set it aside. Once more she searched for injuries, but couldn't find any. No blood was visible anywhere, except on the big cat.

Kneeling back on her haunches, Karen said, "I don't think she's got any neck injuries, but I don't wanna take any chances. I'll stabilize her neck while you roll her over on her back. We'll use a field expedient collar until she comes around."

Bill managed to get down on his knees and position himself at his wife's side. *Thank God, she's breathing*, he thought as he saw her back rise and fall.

Karen wrapped her hands on either side of Meri's head and held on tightly.

Bill positioned himself so that one hand was on Meri's shoulder and the other on her far leg.

"On three, roll her towards you," Karen said. He rolled Meri while Karen kept her head aligned with her body and shoulders.

"Put something under her neck," Karen said.

Bill grabbed Meri's pack and extracted a T-shirt. Making sure it was snugly rolled, he slid it under Meri's neck so that her head remained aligned with the rest of her body.

Karen carefully released her hold on Meri's head and the two worked together to make a somewhat more secure neck brace using more clothing from her damaged pack. They also took her summer weight sleeping bag and draped it over her, in an attempt to treat her for shock.

Bill could see a bruise forming on Meri's forehead. Other than that, he didn't see any signs of injury.

"Okay," Karen said. "We gotta make sure she doesn't move until we can check her out further. You keep an eye on her and I'll get our stuff together and set up camp."

Picking up her rifle, she headed back up the slope to where the canoe and the remainder of their gear waited.

Bill, holding his rifle, alternated his view from his supine wife to the surrounding area, paying particular attention to the trees. *Cougars are solitary critters*, he constantly reminded himself, not expecting to see another one. *But, they ain't the only killers that hang out in trees.*

Karen soon returned with Bill's pack, dropped it on the ground next to him, and went for the rest.

Meri still hadn't moved or awakened by the time Karen returned with the last of the equipment.

"Guess I'll get the canoe," she said.

This time Karen was gone longer, and if Bill hadn't heard her crashing through the forest as she made here way back to the camp, he would have been more worried than he already was. Soon he could see her coming down the incline, towing the canoe with the lead rope.

By the time she arrived, she was bathed in sweat, despite the cool temperatures.

"I'm gonna shower," she told Bill, dropping the canoe lead and going to her pack to retrieve her hygiene kit.

While Karen was dousing herself, Bill saw Meri's eyes flutter, then open.

"Don't move," he said to her. "You got attacked by a cougar and were knocked out, so we don't know if you've got any injuries other than a bump on the head. How do you feel?"

"Like shit. My head hurts, but that's about it."

Karen, naked and dripping, came over to the couple.

"Can you wiggle your toes and fingers?"

Meri wiggled her fingers, and then Bill could see her boots move.

"Okay, let's do a couple of tests. Bill, take off her boots."

While Bill was doing so, Karen ran her finger along Meri's palms. "Can you feel that?"

"Yes."

Karen put her index fingers in Meri's palms and said, "Squeeze my fingers."

Meri did.

"Okay, you can let go. Looks like your upper body's fine."

Moving down to Meri's exposed feet, she ran her finger up the sole, from heel to toe. It was obvious Meri could feel the touch, as she tried to pull her foot back from Karen's finger.

"Don't move," Karen said. "I want to check your spine. So far, everything looks good, but I don't want to take a chance."

Over the next couple of minutes, Karen ran her hands under Meri's back, feeling with her fingers and asking Meri what she was feeling and if there was any pain. Eventually, Karen worked her way from butt to skull, and Meri said she didn't feel any pain.

"Looks good," Karen said, looking first at Meri then at Bill. "Want to try sitting up?"

"Sure," Meri said. "But help me up, and let's take it nice and slow."

With Bill and Karen's assistance, Meri sat up. Gingerly moving her body around from the waist up, she declared herself to be physically okay. With some more assistance from Karen, she stood.

Once on her feet, she needed some support, as it was clear that whatever bonk she took to the head was causing some dizziness. Bill was afraid she would pass out and struggled to his feet to stand next to her and provide what little physical support he was capable of.

"I think I better lie back down," she eventually said and plopped back on the sleeping bag.

"Concussion," Karen said. "Here's the game plan. You stay awake tonight. One of us'll stay awake with you. We've gotta give this twenty-four hours, just in case."

"In case of what?" Bill asked. "There's no hospital. If she collapses, there ain't a damn thing we can do."

Karen paused for a minute. "You're right. Here's what we're gonna do. Meri, you get to sleep, but we're gonna wake you up every couple of hours and ask you some questions that should be pretty easy to answer. We've only got a limited amount of pain killers, so I don't want to use them on this. You okay with that?"

Meri nodded.

"Okay. That's it then. Bill, you keep watch, I'll set up camp. No sense having the sick, lame, and lazy get even more sick, lame, and lazy," she finished with a wan smile.

Karen took the time to skin and cut up the cougar, putting it over the fire to smoke before nightfall. "If nothing else, we get some good meat out of this."

The night passed slowly as Bill and Karen traded off watch, waking Meri every couple of hours. By dawn, it was apparent that she would be okay, but Bill was still worried, especially when the first thing Meri did with breakfast was to spew it into the forest. Despite that, she managed to eat some more and not regurgitate it.

Shortly after dawn they broke camp and were back on the water.

The next several days were relatively pleasant, mostly drifting, fishing, and occasionally taking game that was foolish enough to drink from the bank while they floated by. On the water, they felt more at peace than on shore, as the larger predators that would normally threaten them weren't all that adept at simultaneously swimming and attacking. Being on land was a different matter, though, and the three became more vigilant when ashore.

Bill was a bit worried about Meri, though, because even though it had been several days since the cougar attack, she still continued to get sick in the morning. Luckily, her sickness didn't last long, but it was becoming a daily event.

At one of their evening stops, Meri gathered in a bunch of crayfish from a pool and boiled the mini lobster-like crustaceans into a nice bouillabaisse.

On the final day on the Kanawha, they came to a large group of boulders and snags blocking the river. Again, they elected to portage around the blockage rather than take their chances.

It was at this point they entered the Ohio River, the largest of the rivers feeding the Mississippi.

"Smooth sailing ahead, folks," Karen grandly announced.

"Yeah, until we hit the falls," Bill said.

"Falls? On the Ohio?" Karen asked.

"Yeah. Don't you know about them? The river drops a chunk with a series of falls that last, oh, about two or three miles. On Earth, they're called the Falls of the Ohio. I don't think they're as bad as what we've already gone through, but then again, we weren't expecting some of this stuff."

"Where are these falls?"

"Uh, I think around Louisville."

"What's Louisville?" Meri asked.

"A city on the Ohio," Karen answered absently, apparently in thought.

Trekker

Ohio River

Bill was surprised at how large the Ohio River was. As they drifted along, he commented on this.

"Didn't you know the Ohio's actually got more flow than the Mississippi?" Meri asked.

Bill shrugged, his life vest rising with the movement.

"Hey, I may be a geographer, but that doesn't mean I studied a lot about physical geography. Remember, I'm a spatial analyst, not a physical geographer."

"But didn't they teach this kind of stuff at your school?"

Thinking back to his days in the Geography Department at the University of Washington, Bill was made aware, once again, by his more-educated wife, that the education he got was rather slim on geographical features, and long on analysis. Apparently, Hayek University was a bit more serious about geographic features and knowing places. Then again, she had a degree in Exploration Science while his degree focused mostly on cultural geography related to Earth.

"Not really. Guess I've still got a lot to learn."

Meri humphed and turned back to facing forward, keeping an eye out for something to kill and eat.

While they still had plenty of ammunition left, Meri continued to hunt with her bow, rightfully arguing that they didn't know what nasties might appear, and she'd rather use a rifle than a bow on an attacking Smilodon or lion (*or cougar*, Bill thought). Bill had taken to fishing off the side of the canoe. It was at this point he felt a bite and started reeling in the line on the YoYo. He had given up using his fly rod on the big river, not risking having it break with a monster catfish.

Sure enough, after a several minute fight, Bill brought a large catfish up to the side of the canoe. Being careful not to let its spikes poke him, he lifted the fish out of the water and into the boat, then hit it over the head with a heavy stick he kept in the vessel for exactly that purpose. At this, Meri looked back, saw the stunned fish, and promptly vomited over the side of the canoe.

"You okay?" Bill asked, after his wife finished wiping her mouth. She nodded and said "Yeah. Just having some stomach problems, that's all."

By now Bill was becoming a bit suspicious. "You sure you're not pregnant?"

Meri looked at him in surprise. "No." She shook her head. "Ain't possible. I'm on birth control. Remember?"

He turned to Karen. "You've been pregnant before. What are some other signs?"

Karen raised her eyebrows and placed her paddle across the canoe's gunwale. Meri looked back in shock. Leaning forward, Karen said, "Well, for most women, the first clue is skipping a period. But, since we're all on birth control implants, which can cause irregularities, skipping one wouldn't even be noticed. For me, it was tender boobs."

Looking past Bill to Meri, Karen asked, "Boobs tender?"

Bill turned back to Meri. Eyes wide, Meri nodded.

"It's possible," Karen said. "Wouldn't be the first time, and I doubt it'll be the last." Then she got a big, shit-eating grin on her face. "Congrats!"

Bill was in shock. Looking at his wife, he could see she was, too.

"I can't be pregnant," she protested. "I've got birth control implants," she repeated.

"Honey, those things are only effective 99.99 percent of the time. Looks like you're that rare point zero one percent," Karen said, resuming her paddling while maintaining her grin.

Bill continued to stare at Meri who had developed a worried look.

Slowly, a smile crept across his face. "Hey, we're gonna be parents."

It only took a couple of days to make it to the falls of the Ohio. During that time Meri continued to have morning nausea. They all finally, and in Meri's case, reluctantly, agreed that she was, indeed, pregnant. Bill was both secretly pleased and worried. He wasn't sure if he was truly ready for fatherhood, particularly if it involved being stranded on Planet 42 with no hope of rescue. But having a child with Meri also thrilled him, knowing that it was definitely a sign of commitment on both their parts, despite the unplanned nature of her pregnancy.

As they approached the falls, Karen decided to have them portage around them rather than risk any accidents. "One was enough," she said, glancing at Bill's broken leg.

Just like the prior portage, Bill wasn't able to do much other than hobble on his makeshift crutch. Fortunately, he was able to carry some of his primary survival gear along with his rifle. Of course, this didn't include his backpack, which was left at the takeout point for one of the women to retrieve. Once again, he provided rear security, but this time his shooting skills weren't needed, and they managed to complete the portage without incident. At the end, Bill was exhausted. Using the crutch while still maintaining security over three miles of rough terrain was more than his body was ready for.

While Bill rested with the canoe, Meri and Karen headed back to the takeout point to get Bill's pack. Karen, being taller than Meri, had left her pack with Bill just in case the two women didn't return.

Bill no longer felt nervous being alone in the wilderness. As he sat by the canoe, rifle in his lap, looking around for any threats, he wondered why that was so. He suspected it was a combination of his being an outdoorsy type growing up, along with the fact that he had managed to survive as long as he had during the extended trek. *Christ*, he thought, *here it is September. Three months and thousands of miles, and we've still got thousands more to go. Man, I hope we make it there before it gets too cold.* Bill's thoughts turned to the upcoming leg of the journey.

Okay, so if we go up the Mississippi, we can take the Missouri or the Platte. Which one will get us closer to the gate? The gate that allowed their survey craft to access Planet 42 was located on Bowman Field on Sacajawea Base on Hayek. That roughly correlated with the location of the little town of Selah, Washington, on Earth. *So, if we go up the Missouri, we can make our way up the Lewis.* At this point, Bill stopped thinking and chuckled to himself. *Just like Lewis and Clark in the 1800s. Ha.*

Of course, they would need to cross the Rocky Mountains in winter, most likely. He estimated it would take them until the end of the month at the earliest, but more likely late October before they made it to the headwaters of the Platte or Lewis Rivers, both of which began in the Rockies.

Cross the Rockies or stay on the plains? It was a question he wasn't quite prepared to answer. Luckily, it wasn't his decision; that fell to Karen, as the crew's commander.

Within a couple of hours, the women had returned with Bill's backpack. While they had been gone, Bill had also gathered some edible plants and started a stew with Meri's pot, using some of the cooked venison from the night before. Meri had wrapped it in leaves to preserve it as much as possible, but that didn't stop Bill from sniffing it before throwing it into the pot. *Bad enough Meri's barfing every morning*, he thought. *Last thing I need is to have her come down with food poisoning and be puking all the damned time.*

Upon their arrival back at the impromptu camp, Meri gave Bill a quick kiss and said, "Hey, look who can cook."

"Ha, ha," Bill retorted. "I'll have you know I've been cooking since I was a kid."

Karen looked around and said, "Yeah, we might as well set up camp here for the night. Don't know if we'll find another spot as good before we hit the Mississippi." She set out the trip wires, Meri set up hammocks, and Bill continued cooking and keeping watch.

It wasn't long before the food was ready. The three attacked it like ravenous dire wolves. Had this been home, Bill doubted he would have been able to eat so much, but the amount of energy they were expending on this trip was more than he was used to. "Y'know, I read somewhere that the guys from the original *Corps of Discovery* ate about five thousand calories a day and didn't gain any weight."

Karen looked down at her own body, then back up to Bill and Meri. "Considering how much weight we've all lost, I don't doubt it."

Other than having to tighten his belt a bit over the past several months, Bill hadn't really noticed any weight loss. As a matter of fact, he thought he had put some weight on, particularly on his arms, chest, and shoulders. And it looked like the two women had done the same.

"I don't think we lost weight, so much as lost any spare fat we had," Meri said. "Think about it. We're eating a lot, we're working a lot, but we've all packed on some muscle."

"Yeah, I guess you're right. I think most of the fat I lost was here." Karen gestured to her breasts.

"I'm thinking I'm going the opposite way, there," Meri said, looking down at her own chest.

"No doubt. Wait until you're near term, then they become huge."

"Well, I hope we're home long before then."

Nobody said anything, but Bill thought, *Me, too. I'm not sure I'm up to helping deliver a baby out here without a doctor.*

Morning arrived with the screeching of passenger pigeons awakening. The birds had flown in and settled in the surrounding forest the night before in swarms blocking out the sun so that sunset had been a rather hurried affair. Bill was on final watch, so he wasn't rudely awakened by the squawking and screeching, but the two women were.

As Meri climbed out of her hammock, Bill heard a noise just outside the trip wire, followed almost immediately by the sound of the wire being set off. A small flare burst several feet into the air, illuminating the scene. A befuddled looking bison was standing at the perimeter, looking at the small sun that was drifting down on its little parachute. Taking advantage of the opportunity for a large amount of meat, Bill shot the bison in the chest. He reloaded his rifle and had it ready for another shot just in case it was needed. The bison stood unmoving for about a minute, in which time Meri had retrieved her rifle and Karen made an appearance with hers. The passenger pigeons took flight from the shot, breaking branches as they took off en masse, and raising even more of a ruckus than they had before the shot.

Finally, just as Bill was about to take a second shot at the large bovine, it collapsed with a large groan, blood gushing from its mouth and nostrils. This was the first bison they had seen, and all three were stunned by its size.

Meri was the first to comment on it. "I think it's an Eastern wood bison," she said.

"Wood bison?" Bill asked.

"Yeah, cousin to the plains bison, only smaller."

"Well, it's certainly big enough," Bill said, looking down at the dead animal.

While not quite as large as the auroch they had killed in Eurasia, it was still big.

"You killed it, you clean it," his wife said, then promptly turned and vomited into the brush.

The rest of the morning was spent skinning and cleaning the bison and preparing it for smoking. Lunch consisted of bison heart and liver fried up with some wild onions and cattail stalks Meri had found near the river.

Karen and Meri gathered the sticks necessary to construct the drying racks, and soon after lunch, they had as much of the bison that could fit on the racks smoking over a fire. They estimated it would take a full day, so hammocks were left up and wild acorns gathered to replenish their flour supply. Meri discovered many berry bushes surrounding their camp, so the three also gathered as many as possible for pemmican.

Throughout the night, one of them tended the fire and kept watch while the other two slept.

Bill had decided to keep the bison skin and turn it into a coat. Winter would be upon them soon. The clothing they had, while barely suitable for winter conditions, wasn't up to the task of a potentially harsh winter on the Great Plains. Part of his training had emphasized planning for future conditions. The skin was staked out and Bill painstakingly went through the process of removing excess flesh and fat from the underside of it. After all the flesh was removed, he took some of the salt they had made while traveling across the Atlantic and spread it on the underside of the skin. Once it was coated, Bill rolled the hide up and set it against a tree trunk, with one end facing the ground. This allowed whatever remaining fluids in the skin to drip out onto the ground.

Mississippi

It took longer than they expected to resume the journey, but when they did so several days later, they had more travel food in the form of dried bison, ground acorn meal, and sundry other wild plants gathered during the course of their stay near the fall. Bill suspected they would be increasing their calorie intake, not just because they'd be paddling up a river, but also with demands created by cooler weather.

It didn't take them long to reach the confluence of the Ohio and Mississippi Rivers. Once again, Bill was surprised at the comparative sizes of the two rivers. Despite knowing that the Ohio had the greater flow, it was still unnerving for him to see "the Mighty Mississippi" smaller than the joining river. That got him thinking as to why the lesser of the two rivers was given the name of the conjoined rivers. He posited the question to the two women as they began paddling upstream. Both shrugged.

Talk tapered off as the act of paddling against the current wore on them. Fortunately, they had enough food that Meri didn't need to hunt, so all three were able to propel the craft along. They got into a steady rhythm, with two paddling while the third took a break. It allowed them to make steady progress without completely wiping them all out within an hour or two.

As he paddled, Bill realized he had come quite a far way from his beginnings on Earth. Even with all his time spent in scouting and fishing, he had never spent this much time outdoors, especially in a wilderness environment. Nor had he ever worked this hard in his life. Where once he was a slim, relatively in-shape young man, now he was a tanned, veteran Trekker, with callused hands, broad shoulders, and a slim waist. It reminded him of his former fiancée's comment about Captain America having a Dorito-shaped body — triangular with the wide part being the shoulders and the narrow part being the waist. *I wonder what she'd think of me now?* Then he thought, *Actually, who cares what she would think? She didn't want me gallivanting around on strange planets in the first place, and here I am, actually doing just that.*

At their first landfall on the Mississippi, after setting up camp, Karen called a mini-council, requesting input from the other two.

"Odds are, we're gonna be crossing the plains or the Rockies during winter. Staying put ain't an option, 'cause we'll likely die if we do. Thoughts on routes?" she asked.

Meri looked at Bill, raising an eyebrow.

Bill said, "We've got a couple of options. First is to float downriver to the Arkansas River, but that won't get us far enough west, which is why I didn't recommend that route months ago. Our best option is to continue upriver to the Missouri, and either follow that all the way to its headwaters, or we can take the Yellowstone or Platte.

"The Yellowstone will put us up around Yellowstone Lake, which is about 2400 meters up, and on this side of the Rockies. I haven't checked, but I think we'd be stuck at the Grand Canyon of the Yellowstone if we go that route. I've been in Yellowstone

National Park in the summer, and it snowed then. You can imagine what it'll be like in winter when even Yellowstone Lake freezes over.

"The Platte will also put us in the Rockies, at about 2700 meters in a valley surrounded by mountains averaging 3600 meters tall. I'm thinking crossing those bad boys in the winter wouldn't be such a smart idea, and since we're not planning on spending the winter here," he paused.

"That pretty much leaves the Missouri to its headwaters. Overall, it's pretty smooth, other than a couple of smaller falls and the great falls in Montana. Make no mistake, though, this'll be a long-ass trip. The river alone is over 3000 kilometers long, not counting the 300 or so we've still got here on the Mississippi. And that don't include the rest of the journey to the IP. At around twenty-five klicks per day, figure it'll take us about five months to get to the headwaters if all goes well. So, looks like we'll be getting there some time in February or March. And that ain't even considering the leg we'll have to take by land to get to the Snake River, which'll feed us into the Columbia River."

Noticing Meri's confused look, he amended his statement to reflect the differences in their geographic knowledge base. "I mean, the Nch'i-Wana."

"Ah, okay. Now I'm tracking," she said. "We'll take the Shawpatin down to the Nch'i-Wana, then up the Yakama."

"Yeah, that's about it," Bill said. "If I'm correct, we'll need to cross the Rockies and the Bitterroots, something that Lewis and Clark did two-hundred-odd years ago, before we can hook up with the Shawpatin."

Even though it was a warm September day, the thought of crossing the Great Plains and the Rocky Mountains in the dead of winter put a chill in all of them.

"Yeah, that's gonna be fun," Karen finally said. "So, we just continue paddling upriver until we can't, and then hoof it. Right?"

"That's pretty much it," Bill said.

"Okay, well, if the choice is walking thousands of kilometers or paddling thousands, I think paddling wins out. Just because it means we can carry more gear and keep it with us longer than we could walking," Karen said.

"There's another option to paddling," Meri said. Bill and Karen looked at her. "We can sail part of it."

"Sail on a river?" Karen asked.

"Of course," Bill said, slapping his forehead with his open palm. "Why didn't I think of that? It's not like we didn't do that crossing the Med and Atlantic. It's also what Lewis and Clark did."

Karen looked at him skeptically.

Meri nodded. "Exactly. We rig up a small mast, use part of the parachute for a sail, and when the wind is at our back, we raise it. We might even be able to get a couple of extra klicks a day out of it."

"Y'know, we've got room on this river to run an outrigger. That'll make it more stable, and really give us an opportunity to use a sail better," Bill said.

Karen raised her eyebrows thoughtfully. "Okay, let's make it happen. I want this thing ready to go asap, so while Bill's making supper, we can gather the necessary stuff and start working on it. Looks like we'll be here for a couple more days."

It didn't take long before sufficient dry wood was gathered for the gunwale and some suitable small trees for the outrigger and mast. As it was getting dark, Karen decided to hold off on cutting the saplings until the next day.

Between using small hand-held chain saws, hatchets, and knives, they were soon able to fashion mast supports, one for the canoe's bottom and one to fit across the gunwales. Rather than attempt to chop out the center holes for the mast, Meri marked the hole's location and then used a controlled burn to burn through the wood. The edges were scraped out using a survival knife.

It took a couple of days to get a canoe sail rigged and the outrigger installed. The mast had a single cross-brace at the top, allowing for a square sail. Ropes led back toward the stern, so whoever was riding behind the mast would be in control of the sail, and could either adjust the angle or roll it up. Meri's suggestion of having somebody use a paddle as a rudder meant that two people would be in the stern, one controlling the sail, and one handling the rudder. Bill, with his broken leg, was selected to the master of the sail (or, as Meri said, he could be "the sailor boy").

Looking at the small vessel, Karen wondered aloud, "What's smaller than a guppy?"

"A minnow?" asked Meri.

"Nah, minnows are bigger than guppies," Bill said. "What about a tadpole?"

"Tadpole's not a fish," Karen said.

"Yeah, but it both swims and goes on land, just like the canoe when we drag it ashore," Bill said.

"Good point. Okay, tadpole it is," Karen said. Raising her arms up, she intoned seriously, "I christen thee the *CDS Tadpole*."

"All right, let's get loaded up and see how this bad boy works," Karen said, turning and grabbing her pack.

In minutes the *Tadpole* was loaded and launched.

The morning air was still, so they paddled up the Mississippi. Shortly after noon, though, the wind picked up, and while not quite at their backs, it was close enough that they decided to test the sail. To Bill's pleasant surprise, it worked, and rather well.

"I think we're going faster than we were paddling," he said.

Karen, holding onto the paddle rudder, looked down at the rushing water. "I think you're right."

And, so it continued for the next ten days. Mornings would typically be spent paddling and afternoons sailing. Meri, bow in hand, would keep an eye out for tasty critters near shore as they sailed along. She also kept an eye out for nasty critters. On several occasions, she spotted bears and, based on the size of some of them, thought they were short-faced bears.

On the tenth day, they arrived at the confluence of the Missouri, the final river they would be traveling on this side of the continental divide. It was now mid-September, and while the days were warm, the nights were starting to get rather cool. Karen had given Meri and Bill orders to hunt specifically for another couple of bisons. "I don't fancy freezing out here, so let's make like the Injuns and make some seriously warm buffalo coats."

"Injuns?" Meri asked.

"Slang for Indians, what we used to call Native Americans on Earth before people developed a little sensitivity," Karen answered.

"You've got some weird habits on Earth," Meri said.

"Yeah, that we do," Bill said softly, thinking, *There's a reason I left.*

Lower Missouri

The trip up the Missouri River was just like the trip up the Mississippi, only a lot longer, with the three following the morning-paddling, afternoon-sailing routine. A week after entering the new river system, Meri spotted a small herd of bison on the north shore, so Karen ordered the boat aground. While Bill remained near the boat, she and Meri slowly approached the herd, which took no notice of them, especially since they stopped several hundred meters from the closest bison.

The two women went into the prone position, integral rifle bipods extended. They shot simultaneously, each hitting a different animal. While they were doing so, Bill kept an eye out for any threats from the edge of the river. Both bison dropped, and the remaining herd shifted around a bit, probably thinking that the resounding booms had been thunder. Their bovine brains didn't equate the two bipeds with the noise, so even when the women approached the downed bison, the rest of the herd barely shuffled about.

It took a couple of hours to skin the bison, mainly because they had to roll them over to complete the task. Rolling an animal that weighed over half a metric ton wasn't quite as easy as it looked in the instructional videos from survival training. Even the woods bison Bill had killed wasn't the same size.

While they were skinning the bison, Bill did triple duty: keeping guard over them, setting up camp, and preparing stakes for the skins. By the time the women were finished, it was almost dark. Bill had gotten a fire going in the campground, and hobbling around with his rifle at the ready position, kept an eye out for the predators that appeared to be following the herd. He had seen at least one pack of wolves, probably a Great Plains wolf, also known as the buffalo wolf. He wasn't sure, but he suspected he also saw a pack of dire wolves, somewhat larger than the smaller Great Plains cousins. Upon spotting them he had kept his rifle at the ready position, but fortunately didn't need it. He also called out to the women to warn them.

An hour after spotting the dire wolves, he saw a Smilodon, the big scimitar-toothed cat prowling along the herd's edge. Bill once again warned the women and kept extra care to watch the large predator, knowing just how dangerous it could be. The women stopped their tasks, picked up their rifles, and kept an eye on the tiger until it had wandered out of sight toward the rear of the herd. Fortunately, the Smilodon was more interested in bison calf than another obvious predator.

When the women returned to camp with their bloody, fuzzy trophies with the bison brains wrapped inside, Bill felt some relief. Giving Meri a quick kiss, he said, "Glad you're back. I was starting to get worried."

Meri gave him a wan smile, showing just how tired she was.

"Let's get these skins staked out. We'll need to scrape most of the flesh off them tonight," Karen said, dumping her bundle on the ground. "Bill, you think you can handle some scraping?"

Bill nodded. "Yeah, I think I'm a little less worn out than either of you."

The three spread out the hides and staked them down, and as Meri and Karen began making supper (*Oh, yummy. Bison for supper, AGAIN!* Bill thought sarcastically), he began the tedious scraping process.

He continued the project well into the night, working by the light cast by the campfire. As he worked, Meri kept watch, the two of the talking about the best ways of making the buffalo coats that should keep them warm in the upcoming winter.

Over the next several weeks the trio continued upriver, using paddles and the makeshift sail. Each evening was spent working on the bison hides.

As they had passed the Platte River, Bill had commented that if they wanted to get to the Front Range around Earth's Denver, the Platte would take them there.

"Just a thought," he said that evening, as they sat around the campfire, "but, have either of you wondered why we haven't seen any survey planes yet? I mean, we've been on this planet for damned near four months." Looking at Meri, he asked, "You grew up with this stuff. How long does it take to complete the Initial Survey and begin the aerial and ground surveys?"

Meri stirred the pot of bison stew, wrinkled her brow, swatted a mosquito from around her face, and said, "Lemme see. Forty to fifty days for the Initial Survey, which was just about a quarter of the way done when we crashed. So, that should have been done by late July. Give it a month or so to set up the field and logistics for the aerial surveys." She paused, thinking. "That puts us into September.

"So, the odds of seeing anything any time soon are pretty slim," she concluded. "In case you didn't know, it takes a while to run a survey, covering a swath maybe three klicks wide each pass. Remember how much territory we covered throughout Carib on Zion? Figure on three to five passes per flight each day, that'll push the survey out maybe ten, fifteen klicks. Probably average twelve klicks a day, so, about three hundred sixty klicks a month. We're still more than two thousand klicks from the IP, so figure if they started in September, they probably wouldn't reach this far for five or six months. Best guess, we might see them come January or February."

It took Bill a while to digest this news. He had always assumed that there would be a survey crew out further, looking for them, just in case.

What the hell was I thinking? he thought, bitterly. *I know the Corps doesn't send people out on hopeless rescue missions.*

He took a deep breath. "Well, looks like we'll be spending at least part of winter on the great plains. So, what are we gonna do about shelter along the way? I mean, the hammocks are great and all, and these new coats should work fine, but what about the sub-zero temps we can expect this winter? And, I ain't talking Celsius," he said, looking pointedly at Meri. "I mean, it's gonna get freezing ass cold, and we're gonna be in one of the coldest, windiest places outside of Siberia."

Even with the heat reflective liners, the hammocks weren't rated for temperatures that much below freezing. Both women sat quietly a moment, thinking.

Karen finally glanced up as she continued sewing a sleeve onto her bison coat. "Well, I figure we can do like the Native Americans did, and kill some more bison and make a wikiup."

"If we're gonna do that, we should probably gather wood for the frame now, before we get into the real prairie," Meri said, looking up from the pot. "And more bison skins," she said with a grin at Bill. He interpreted it as an evil grin, considering he would be the one most likely to do the flesh scraping.

"So, lemme get this straight. You guys hunt and I scrape?"

"Naw, not completely," Karen said. "Well, yeah, we hunt. At least, until that leg of yours is healed. So, yeah, I guess you're kinda have to do most of the scraping," she finished with a sheepish grin.

Bill just rolled his eyes and shook his head.

"You can also gather poles," Meri said. The soft smile she gave him was meant as a peace offering, which he willingly accepted.

The crew began gathering wood the next morning, despite Meri's comments about Bill doing it. There was plenty near the river's edge; they selected small Eastern red cedar saplings that were interspersed in the understory of the larger cottonwoods. Bill, with his broken leg, wasn't as mobile as the other two, so he did the cutting while the two women brought the small logs to the campground and began building a wikiup frame. First, three poles were lashed together at one end with rawhide, then raised, and spread at the bottom, creating a tripod. Then they laid poles upon the tripod, creating a cone-shaped frame structure.

The wikiup reminded Bill of the tipis he would see in some of the old classic movies, with the bottoms of the poles in a circle and the tops meeting above.

Once the frame was constructed, Bill realized that it wasn't tall enough for all three of them to stand in at any one time. He pointed that out.

"Well, it's your own fault you're so tall," Meri said, with a grin. Bill was pretty average height, not even close to being six feet tall.

"The goal's to be able to sit up, lie down, and have a fire inside," Karen said, looking at the structure, feet apart, and hands on hips. "Remember, this is a mobile wikiup, not a long-term thing. At most, we'll maybe spend a couple of days in it if there's a bad storm."

"Good start," Meri said. "Now we just need some skins and insulation."

"Where're you planning on getting insulation?" Bill asked.

"It's all around," Meri said, sweeping her arms wide. "Leaves, bushes, sod, whatever it takes. I'm sure we probably won't do too much insulating on the move, but if there's a storm coming in, I think it's best we plan on insulating, at least for the duration."

Over the last several months, the three had gotten pretty adept at reading the weather, so her comment wasn't out of place.

Once the last pole was in place, Karen had the three of them deconstruct it, lashing the tripod and other poles in place on the canoe's outrigger.

"We've still got plenty of daylight left, so let's get on the move. Keep your eyes peeled for a bison herd, 'cause I'd like to get those skins ready asap."

Within a couple of days, they spotted a larger herd of bison. Fortunately, many were near the water, drinking or rolling in it.

"Let's angle in so we're close, but not too close," Karen said. "Don't want to spook the herd and cause a stampede."

That's the last thing we need, Bill thought. *It'd suck if they stampeded our way.*

Since the daily wind hadn't kicked up too hard yet, the sail wasn't deployed. Not only did it make it easier to sneak up on the herd, with barely a ripple as they silently paddled near them, but it gave them a smaller profile, less likely to spook the herd. Bill imagined himself a bison, *Oh, no. Here comes a big scary thing to eat me. Run away, run away!*

They beached on a sandbar jutting from the shore. Slowly, they exited the canoe, dragging it further up the bar, until it was mostly out of the water. Luckily, it was still early morning and the sun was at their back; the bison probably wouldn't see them as they approached from the east.

Once again, Bill was relegated to standing watch while the women began stalking their prey. As they slowly slunk into the dust-filled air, raised by the herd's constant motion, Bill kept an eye out. It wasn't easy, as the land rose above the river, blocking his visibility. He awkwardly made his way up the small bluff, trying to move as slowly and silently as possible with the makeshift splint on his leg, rifle at the ready, and peeder strapped over his shoulder. Bill bit down on his rising anger at his situation. *Only a little longer and this thing comes off*, he thought.

At the top of the bluff he had a clear view of the area. Karen and Meri were getting into the prone position less than two hundred meters from the edge of the herd. He didn't focus his attention on them; they weren't a threat. *Well, not to me, anyhow,* he thought, keeping his eyes roaming over the landscape, turning around to make sure nothing was sneaking up on him. He glanced back at the women. They had their rifle bi-pods extended and were preparing to open fire.

Just then, flames shot out of their rifles almost simultaneously. It took a second for the sound of the guns firing to reach him. Two bison staggered, one collapsing to the ground.

As with the last herd, the bison looked around, surprised, then continued grazing. The second bison fell to the ground. Bill remembered reading about buffalo hunters from the 1800s standing all day, shooting bison, and the bison never moving.

Twice more the rifles sounded, and twice more a pair of bison dropped dead.

Only then did the women rise, rifles held in hand, and begin walking toward the herd, making noise and waving their free arms. This finally startled the bison, and they began moving away from the obvious predatory threat. As the hunters got closer, the bison broke into a slow trot, until the six dead bison were alone, surrounded by nothing but the tall prairie grass.

Meri approached the first bison cautiously, staring at the eye long enough to determine it was dead. Karen did the same with hers. Each animal got the same treatment: leave some space around it, watch the eyes, and if the animal didn't blink for an extended period, it was presumed dead. This was especially telling when a fly landed on the eye of the last bison they checked.

As the two began skinning the first bison, Bill's attention was drawn to a motion out of the corner of his eye. Slowly turning his head, he saw movement in the grass, heading toward the downed bison. Looking closer, he finally made out a Smilodon. Its tawny fur was engulfed by the brown, dried fall grass of the prairie. It was obviously in stalking mode, moving slowly, hunched down, its short tail sticking straight out, twitching lightly. The low-slung back reminded Bill of the hyenas they had fought in Eurasia.

Even though the big cat was almost three hundred meters away, and just about that far from the distracted women, Bill didn't feel like taking any chances. Getting down on one knee, he brought the rifle up, bracing the arm holding the forestock on his knee. Sighting through the ghost ring sights, Bill drew a bead on the deadly cat. He took a breath and slowly released it while tightening his finger pull on the trigger. At the end of the breath, when his body was most relaxed and not jumping around, he continued to squeeze the trigger until the rifle bucked in his hand with a loud report.

He immediately reloaded and brought his rifle back up to the ready position, all the while keeping an eye on the Smilodon. From shot to ready took less than a second.

The women were both on their feet, rifles at the ready. Bill stood and waved to them to indicate all was well. They were too far away hear even if he yelled, so he didn't bother.

He now looked to see if the dying cat had been traveling in a pair or pack. The grass swayed as several unseen animals moved through it, parting it like a speedboat on a windy lake. Fortunately, the unseen creatures, likely Smilodons, were making their way away from Bill and the dying animal, so he relaxed.

Hmm, I wonder what Smilodon tastes like, he thought. *I've heard mountain lion was the preferred meat of mountain men like Jim Bridger. Think I'll give it a try. Anything to break up the bison diet.*

Watching the still-thrashing cat, he thought, *I think I'll wait a bit. No sense wasting a real cartridge, when I can take him out with the peeder.*

It took a couple of hours before the bison were skinned. Bill had time to watch the dying Smilodon thrash its last, finally ceasing all motion. Once more, he had killed another animal. It wasn't something he particularly enjoyed. *You'd think I'd never killed anything before*, he thought. Of course, his wife and unborn child would have been the creature's meal if he hadn't.

When Meri and Karen finally returned to camp, each dragging a bison pelt, Bill had already gotten over his mild funk, mostly. Meri gave him a quick kiss and a brief, impassioned hug.

"Thanks," was all she said, before giving him another kiss, turning, and beginning the return journey to the remaining bison skins.

Once more Bill assumed his position on the bluff. The dead, skinned bison were becoming the main attraction for the local scavengers. Swarms of vultures gathered overhead, and Bill noticed coyotes circling. He wasn't too worried about either but still kept an eye on the 'yotes. If they appeared nervous, then

Bill figured he should be too, as something even more deadly than a coyote had to be out there. But the coyotes appeared calm, keeping their distance from the two women but dashing in to take bites from the fresh carcasses, then darting away to safety to swallow the bites. It became almost a comedy watching the small canines perform these feats of derring-do.

Eventually, Karen and Meri returned to base with the last two pelts. But their day wasn't done yet. Unlike the brain tanning they had done before, the preserving of these pelts was identical to the process Bill had performed on the woods bison back on the Ohio River.

Bill wasn't the only one flesh scraping; they all did, once the hides were staked out. Eventually, Bill dug out one of the leather sacks containing salt from the journey across the Atlantic. The three spread the salt on the insides of the pelts. Finally, the pelts were rolled up and leaned against the canoe, set to let the fluids drain and the salt work its wonders in drying out the skins.

There was still plenty of daylight left, so Bill convinced Meri to join him in seeking out the Smilodon he'd shot.

"Hey, don't you want a break from bison stew for a bit?"

"Yeah, but I'm not too thrilled about carrying another pelt back, as you can well imagine, oh great and mighty hunter," she replied.

"I'll carry it back if you'll carry my peeder."

That appeared to be the turning point for her. Grabbing her rifle, she joined him as he hobbled up the bluff to seek out the big cat.

Bill had his rifle slung this time, peeder at the ready. The small cartridge was powerful enough to take out any of the scavengers and predators hanging around for an easy meal. *And, if needed, I can put a bullet in the Smilodon's brain,* he thought as they walked toward the downed animal.

Eventually, the two arrived at the Smilodon's location. The animal was still alive, snarling as the couple approached. Both Explorers immediately raised their weapons, taking aim at the wounded animal.

It soon became clear, though, that the animal had a broken back. While it could move its upper body, it could only drag its lifeless rear legs behind it. Nevertheless, it attempted to charge the two, dragging itself with its front legs, long claws digging into the deep soil.

Bill, standing to Meri's left, raised his left hand, indicating that she shouldn't shoot. Taking careful aim with his peeder, Bill placed a shot into the cat's left eye, killing it instantly.

Lowering his rifle, Bill had a melancholy feeling wash over him, again. He hated killing, but he hating hurting thing worse. Both events transpired in one event to give him a feeling of complete remorse.

Meri reached over and put a hand on his upper arm.

"Hey, he was after me and our child. Don't feel too bad. I'm glad you saved me." She paused for a moment. "Again," she added, softly.

Bill shook his head as if awaking from a dream. "Yeah, I know. But, still..."

The two watched the Smilodon for a few seconds, making sure it was really dead this time. Eventually, they began skinning it, both for the pelt and the meat. This took far less time than the bison had, and soon the two were headed back to camp.

Bill decided to preserve the Smilodon's pelt, wondering if it would be like a wolf's hide. He had read that Native Americans used wolf fur around their winter parka hoods because the fur didn't frost over with frozen condensation when one breathed out.

They grilled the Smilodon meat over the fire on green sticks, angled and stuck into the ground.

"Don't expect this too often," Meri said as she cooked the cat. "Too much valuable fat is lost in the fire, but I figure you guys deserve a break from stew for at least one meal."

Once cooked, Meri yanked the sticks from the grill and passed them out. As the three began gnawing on the meat, they could hear coyotes howling around the bison carcasses.

Bill, took a bite of what he considered to be one of the tastiest pieces of meat he had ever eaten. The noise of the nearby yipping coyotes no longer freaked him out or raised the hair on the back of his neck. Night had fallen; the sky was ablaze with stars. The moon, expected to be full, had yet to rise in the east.

He turned back to the campfire and looked at his wife next to him. He was, once again, amazed by her beauty. The red glow from the fire emphasized her red hair, and despite the obvious exhaustion from the long journey, he could still see smile wrinkles at the edges of her blue eyes.

Leaning over, he gave her a kiss on the cheek. Not expecting such a relatively public display of affection from her rather reticent husband, her eyebrows rose up her forehead almost to her scalp. "That was unexpected," she said, turning to him.

"How about this, then?" He leaned over to kiss her on the lips, tasting the juice of her most recent bite of the Smilodon.

While the kiss didn't last long, it did enough to lighten the otherwise heavy mood that had settled over the small encampment, a mood that had been created by Bill.

Missouri Break

By late October, they had made it more than 1,200 kilometers up the Missouri. Bill estimated they were at the current location of Sioux City, Iowa, Earth when they pulled in for the evening. As they got out of the canoe, he wondered if this was the same bluff where Lewis and Clark had lost their only member to death.

Dragging the canoe up on shore, Bill thought, *Man, it feels good to finally be able to walk without that stupid splint*. The bone had finally healed enough that he could walk regularly, but he still needed more time to build up the lost muscle.

For the past couple of days, Karen had been complaining about stomach pain, but they all figured it was just something she had drunk or eaten, and expected it to pass soon.

It was only after camp was established and the wikiup set up that Karen suddenly vomited and collapsed to the ground, holding her belly. Meri rushed to her, placing the inside of her wrist on Karen's forehead. "Christ, she's burning up," she said to Bill.

Mere held Karen's hair out of her face. "Where's it hurt?"

"Lower right abdomen," Karen said through gritted teeth, then vomited again.

"Crap. Sounds like your appendix. I'll need you to lie down so I can check. Can you do that for me?"

With Bill and Meri's help, Karen was able to roll over and lie down. Meri undid her jacket, shirt, and pants, pulling her T-shirt up over the abdomen and her underpants partially down. Despite all the time the three had spent naked in front of each other bathing, Meri still tried to preserve some of Karen's dignity. Gently she began palpating Karen's abdomen, eventually making it to the spot over her appendix. As soon as Meri applied slight pressure, Karen almost bolted upright, screaming in pain. Bill, at her head, caught her and gently lowered her back to the ground.

With a grim look, Meri said, "Yep. Just as I thought. You've probably got appendicitis."

Karen nodded weakly. "Thought so," she whispered. "What now?"

Considering their location, over 2,000 kilometers from the Initial Point, but still without any hope of rescue, Bill figured Karen was a dead person talking. Looking at Meri, he raised his eyebrows.

"We've got two choices," she said: "hope you recover or I do an emergency appendectomy."

"What are the odds of recovery?" Karen whispered.

"Straight answer? Zero to none." Meri wasn't known for hiding the truth or sugar-coating things, so her blunt assessment came as no surprise to the other two.

"If the appendix ruptures, you've got twenty-four to seventy-two hours."

"Well, shit. Looks like you get to play a real-life Doctor McDoyle," Karen said, then gritted her teeth through another spasm of pain.

"Doctor McDoyle?" Meri asked, confused.

"Old television series from the '60s," Bill said. "*Star Venture.*"

"Ah." Meri nodded, clearly remembering Karen's fascination with classic television shows.

"Okay, let's get cracking," Meri went on. "Get a tarp out so we can put Karen on it and off this dirt. I'll get a first aid kit."

Bill spread the tarp on the ground next to Karen while Meri retrieved the first aid kit from Karen's pack. The kit contained more than just a couple of bandages and some pain relievers; it was a mini-medical kit designed to allow Explorers in the field to perform rudimentary operations, such as advanced wound treatment and basic surgery. While some of the material was disposable, such as the dressings and pain relievers, the actual surgical equipment was not. It was kept in sterile packaging until needed, and future uses required sterilization through immersing in boiling water or holding over an open flame (nothing anyone wanted to repeat more than once).

Bill and Meri gently moved Karen onto the tarp, and Meri began laying out the equipment and supplies she'd need for the procedure. As she did, she spoke softly to Karen. "First things first, we're gonna have to remove your clothes away from the surgery site. Then we'll sterilize the area and give you two injections. The first is gonna be morphine, followed by a local over the surgery site. We don't have means of giving you general anesthesia, so this is the best we can do. It should work."

On that last sentence, Bill raised his eyebrows again.

Meri returned his look and shrugged.

The morphine syrette was a needle with a squeeze tube containing a bit less than 40 milligrams of the drug. One applied it by injecting the patient and squeezing the tube, forcing the liquid into the body. It reminded Bill of a tube of Superglue or a mini-tube of toothpaste with a needle. His first-aid instructor in survival training told them that the syrette the *Corps* used was, for all intents and purposes, identical to those in U.S. military first aid kits during World War II.

Bill looked up at the clear sky. *At least it's not raining, and the wind's not blowing up a storm,* he thought.

Using care, the two removed Karen's clothing, draping her jacket over most of her upper body and her pants over her legs, leaving only her mid-section exposed. Meri swabbed Karen's leg with betadine, took the morphine syrette, and jabbed it into the recently cleaned skin. It only took a second for her to squeeze the tube between thumb and index finger, pushing the morphine into Karen's thigh muscle. Unlike in the movies, the morphine didn't kick in immediately. In about twenty minutes, it took effect, and Karen's face and body relaxed.

"You still got your lighter?" Meri asked Bill.

"Yeah." He pulled the orange lighter from his pants pocket and held it out.

"Keep it ready, and get your survival knife out, too. I'll probably want to cauterize the wound as I'm cutting in, just to prevent bleeding. Swab down and glove up." Meri tossed Bill an unopened alcohol swab packet and a sterile set of gloves in their sterile wrapping. "And come sit next to me. I'll need you to hand me the instruments as I need them."

Bill promptly moved to squat next to his wife.

After the two were gloved up, Meri handed Bill another syrette, this one containing lidocaine.

"Get that ready and hand it to me when I ask for it."

She opened the small plastic bottle of betadine and poured the sterilizing liquid over a cotton swab. Handing the bottle and cap to Bill, she then painted the betadine-soaked swab all over the area above the incision site, then tossed the used swab and wrapping to the other side of Karen. Bill capped the bottle and set it down on the sterile pad.

Holding out her hand to Bill, she said, "Lidocaine."

Bill removed the cap and handed the syrette to Meri, who

carefully jabbed the needle into the injection site, then squeezed, forcing the numbing agent into the flesh.

"There, that oughta prevent her from feeling some of this in a couple of minutes." She unwrapped a sterile pad and laid it on the tarp between her and Bill, then opened several other packages containing the instruments necessary for the surgery, along with gauze pads and dressings. Finally, the equipment was laid out and they were ready to operate.

Bill could tell Meri was scared, but he wasn't sure what to do.

"You ever done this before?" he finally asked, glancing down at Karen, who was off on her own little medicated world.

"You mean an actual appendectomy? Well, not really, but we did practice it on dummies in our field medicine class at Uni. But I guess there's a first time for everything," she said with a weak smile.

The two of them walked through the procedure, with Meri making sure Bill understood his role as the surgical assistant. "That means when I ask for something, you either do it or hand it to me immediately," she stressed.

Finally, it was time to operate.

Taking a deep breath, Meri said, "Okay, let's do this," and picked up the scalpel.

Carefully she made an eight-centimeter incision in Karen's abdomen at the point where Karen had felt the most discomfort during Meri's palpations. Blood welled from the incision. Karen didn't even flinch.

"Retractor," Meri said, holding out her hand. Bill placed the long end of the L-shaped instrument in her hand. Meri gently pushed the short leg of the instrument into the incision to slowly pull the skin closest to the navel up toward the sternum. "Hold that in place," she told Bill. He grasped the long end of the instrument and did so.

"Lidocaine," she said again. Bill handed the tube to her and she injected the freshly exposed layer of muscle. She handed the tube back to Bill.

Meri cut through the underlying muscle tissue, and once again said, "Retractor."

Using his free hand, he handed her the other retractor. With only two retractors, Bill suspected it was going to be a game of switch as Meri cut through each muscle layer, applying a fresh dose of lidocaine, until she entered the abdominal cavity. He was right. Each new cut was perpendicular to the prior cut. As she made the second cut, Meri tersely said, "You don't want all the cuts going the same way, as it might lead to further complications." While Bill held onto one retractor, Meri would hold onto the other while using the scalpel to slice open Karen's abdomen.

After the last cut, Meri placed the scalpel on the sterile pad, then inserted her forefinger into the incision. Feeling around, for what Bill thought was hours but was probably mere seconds, Meri muttered, "Gotcha, you little bastard."

Bill watched in morbid fascination as Meri wriggled a worm-like appendage out of the open wound. It was dark and inflamed, but to Bill's unprofessional eye, it didn't look ruptured.

"Hand me the surgical thread then take over my retractor."

Bill passed over the thread and, trying to keep his arms out her way, grabbed the second retractor and kept the wound open.

Meri took some thread and wrapped it around the base of the appendix, then did a second wrapping just above the first, separated by mere millimeters. As she tied off the second wrapping, she explained that the process was ligating, designed to cut off the flow of blood, much like a miniature tourniquet.

"Now we cut and cauterize. As soon as I've cut the bad boy, we'll need to heat up your knife and cauterize the wound. That means I'll hold the knife and you use your portable flamethrower to heat it. Got that?"

"Yep," Bill said. Sweat was beading on his forehead despite the cool temperature. Meri's forehead was also covered with a fine sheen of perspiration.

"And don't let go of your retractor," she cautioned. Bill grunted.

Bill picked up the lighter and flicked it open, ready to heat up the knife.

"Okay. Here goes." Meri picked up a small pair of surgical scissors and deftly cut the appendix between the two ligatures. Setting the scissors down, she picked up the knife and held it for Bill as he torched the tip on one side. As soon as the metal started turning orange, Meri pulled the knife away from the lighter and pressed it down on the exposed cut portion of the appendix. The wound sizzled and a waft of smoke drifted up. Bill almost gagged at the smell of burning flesh, but didn't let go of his retractor.

Looking closely at the cauterized wound, Meri said, "Looks good. Let's close her up."

The next several minutes were spent with Bill holding the retractors while Meri closed up each incision with neat rows of surgical thread. When it came time to close up the first incision, Meri worked hard to make it as good as possible.

"Don't want her embarrassed to wear a bikini," she muttered, while Bill sat back on his heels and wiped the sweat out of his eyes.

After the final stitch, Meri had Bill place a sterile dressing over the wound.

"There. Done," she said, wiping her own sweat as she watched Bill smooth out the dressing. "Let's not go through that again, shall we?"

"I agree." Bill leaned over and gave his wife a kiss. "You were awesome," he said when he pulled back, looking deep into her tired, blue eyes. Her red hair hung damply over her face. "Now, go get a shower. I'll keep watch."

After the surgery, the two of them moved Karen's still sedated body into the wikiup, placing her on one of the bison pelts and covering her with her sleeping bag, zipped open and laid flat like a comforter.

Within twenty-four hours, Karen began to return to normal. Her temperature dropped down to normal, and the amount of pain she was suffering decreased considerably. She still needed assistance, particularly in the hygiene arena, but Bill was glad to see her come back from the dead.

Meri had told Bill to expect a minimum of a week before they could resume the journey, so Bill decided to use that time to increase their food supply. Leaving a recovering surgery patient alone wasn't an option, so Bill had to hunt solo, something the *Corps* frowned upon, but they didn't have much choice. Bill decided to keep his hunting range short, not going more than a mile from the camp.

He carried his PDW at the ready, with his rifle slung. Bill figured that most threats would be from predators he could probably kill or wound with the smaller round. And considering that he could literally see for miles over the plains, he wasn't too worried about being surprised by a large cat or wolf. Of course, a stamping herd of herbivores would present a problem, but it wasn't something he bothered to worry about.

As he climbed the bluff above their camp, his geographer's training kicked in. Even though he had only had a single physical geography class in school, he recognized that the hill he was climbing was formed by loess, a wind-blown finely compacted soil that formed after the last ice age. Ten thousand years of grasses growing and dying on this landscape had made it into the fertile soil it was.

Taking a break at the top of the bluff, he slowly turned his head, covering the entire area around the camp, looking for signs of motion. He saw the smoke rising from the campfire, and Meri tending it. She looked up and waved at him. He waved back and continued his scan. The only thing he saw moving, besides the deep prairie grass and the leaves falling off the trees along the riverbank, was a large flock of Canada geese landing in the river, near the bank opposite the camp. The flock was so large that it created a shadow on the water below it.

As he was turning back to resume his ascent up the small bluff, motion downriver caught his eye. He stopped, turned, and stared at the spot, a distance of around a kilometer. He saw the wind moving trees, but the wind was blowing from the north, and the motion of the trees was defying the wind's direction.

Despite staring for several minutes, with occasional glances around to ensure he wasn't being stalked, Bill finally reached into his shirt pocket and pulled out a small, standard-issue monocular. It took him several seconds to zoom in on where he had seen the motion. Even looking right at the spot, and seeing the tree branches sway, it was still several more seconds before he identified what was causing the commotion.

Damn, is that a woolly mammoth or a mastodon? he thought. He saw an elephant-like trunk, covered with brown hair, rise up and wrap itself around the branch of one of the oak trees that still bore leaves, then saw the branch get stripped by the trunk, then disappear.

This was repeated, not just by the same animal, but by what appeared to be a herd. Eventually, one of them stepped into view. Now Bill could see it was a mastodon, the lack of a large head, and the shorter, less curving tusks differentiating it from its larger cousin, the woolly mammoth. Once he saw one, then others became visible to him, much like an optical illusion that reveals itself.

Judging the distance between the herd and the camp, he suddenly became worried. *If those guys are heading our way, they may just trample our camp.* With that thought, he put away the monocular and began heading back down the bluff in a combination jumping and running scramble. Each time he landed his pack would dig into his shoulders and his rifle would bang on his backpack's hipbelt and his thigh. *That's gonna leave a bruise*, he thought, as his rifle banged into his unprotected thigh for the umpteenth time.

As he came jouncing down the hill, he could see Meri looking up, rifle at the ready and a worried look on her face. He tried to wave to indicate it wasn't an emergency, but it was apparent she didn't understand him.

Within minutes he was back at the camp, gasping. "No immediate threat," he said between breaths, and pointing downriver, "but, there's a herd of mastodon heading this way. We should probably move, at least until they pass."

"Crap. Just what we needed, as if we don't have enough problems."

"I've got an idea," Bill said. "Let's move most of the gear uphill, out of the path, and set up an alternate camp. We shouldn't have to go too far, just far enough to get out of the way. We'll wait until the last minute to move Karen and the wikiup."

Meri thought about it, then nodded. "Okay. Let's get packed up and move the packs, food, and skins. We'll leave the fire going and I'll stay here with Karen until they come into view. If they get frisky, we shoot first and ask questions later."

Turning towards Karen, Meri asked, "You want to try walking or should we make a stretcher for you?"

"Forget the stretcher. Don't sound like we've got enough

time. And besides, knowing how clumsy that husband of yours is, I don't think I want to be dumped and roll down a hill into a herd of anything."

"Okay, walking it is." Turning back to Bill, Meri said, "We're also gonna need a flat area to lay Karen down. I don't want her sitting up much or rolling downhill."

"I somehow get this as one of those 'honey do' things," Bill said with a smile.

Batting her eyes at him, Meri said as coyly as possible, "Please, dear."

That broke the rising tension, with both Bill and Meri laughing and Karen smiling for the first time in weeks.

While Meri began the process of packing up, Bill hiked up the bluff again, this time to find a suitable spot for them. He finally found a relatively flat spot about halfway up the bluff, a small indentation in the hill. He set his pack and rifle down and then unstrapped his shovel from the back of the pack. Unlocking the tightening mechanisms, he set the blade at a ninety-degree angle and extended the handle. He then began hacking into the hill, cutting through the tall grass and thousands of years-worth of organic soil.

It didn't take long before Bill had a section cut out, just big enough for one person. He straightened the shovel and removed the loose soil, creating a level spot for Karen to lie in. After cleaning off the shovel blade, he collapsed the tool and attached it back to the pack.

Grabbing his rifle, he headed back down the hill, taking a quick look in the direction of the mastodon herd.

Hmm. Looks like they're definitely getting closer.

When he arrived back in the camp, he told Meri what he'd seen. She nodded. "Well, let's get the rest of this stuff up."

Meri was already wearing her pack, so Bill grabbed Karen's

pack and the two of them headed up the hill.

It took a couple of more trips to get all the hides and food moved, but soon everything, except Karen, was in place. The canoe was left on the riverbank.

"You ready to move?" Bill asked Karen when they returned for the final time.

Karen nodded. "Yeah, whatever."

Bill was a bit concerned, as this didn't sound like the take-command person he knew and had lived with for the past five months.

Meri and Bill grabbed Karen under each arm and helped her get to her feet. It was obvious she was in pain, but there wasn't much they could do about it. While Meri held Karen steady, Bill released her and rolled up the sleeping pad and bison pelt. He handed the pad to Meri and stuck the pelt under his arm, then returned to supporting Karen with his free hand.

Slowly the trio made their way up the hill until the finally reached the new site.

Once Karen was settled, Bill had a thought. "I'm gonna go down and throw more wood on the fire. Maybe that'll keep the herd away and not trash our wikiup."

"Good idea," Meri said. "While you're at it, bring some wood up here so we can have a fire, too."

Bill returned to the campsite and stoked the fire. Going inside the wikiup, he double-checked to make sure they had left nothing behind, then stepped outside and walked around the campsite, verifying that nothing had been left here either. Looking over at the canoe, he thought, *Can't do much about that other than hope they don't go near it.*

By now, Bill could hear the mastodon herd as it made its way to the campsite. He quickly gathered up a number of twigs and larger branches, along with a burning piece of wood from the fire, and for the final time, made his way back up to the secondary camp on the bluff.

He had barely made it when the first of the mastodons made their way into the clearing that had been the campsite. Up until then, the campfire smoke had been drifting lazily up. Now, the wind was picking up, and the smoke drifted toward the large animals. The lead bull stopped and raised his trunk.

As the three watched the mastodons mill about, Bill set down the firewood and handed Meri the still-smoldering piece of wood. He began breaking some of the twigs into smaller pieces.

"Let's get this fire going asap," he said, as he began to form a teepee with the broken twigs. "I'm thinking they don't like fire too much, so the sooner we've got one going, the safer we'll be."

He grabbed a handful of dried grasses, crumpled them up, and put them in the cavity of the twig teepee. As soon as he pulled his hands away, Meri inserted the glowing end of the smoldering stick into the dried grass. Leaning over, she gently blew on it. The smoldering end turned redder, then re-burst into flames, which then caught the grass on fire. Within seconds, the grass was burning and the twigs caught on fire.

As soon as the fire appeared strong enough, Bill added some larger twigs to it, then continued to do so with larger and larger pieces of wood until they had an actual fire going. Rather than drifting straight up, the wind blew the smoke around them, causing their eyes to sting and water.

Wiping the tears from his eyes with his shirtsleeve, Bill stood and took hold of his rifle, which had been over his shoulder at the ready slung position. Turning, he looked down at the still-milling mastodons and silently watched them.

It wasn't long before one of the outlying mastodons began making his way up the slope. He stopped and raised his nose, obviously catching a scent of something. Bill wasn't sure if it was the smoke from the small fire, or if the large animal had caught the scent of humans. *Probably never smelled a human before*, Bill thought.

Then the large herbivore spread his ears and began waving his raised trunk around, sounding off with a loud trumpeting sound.

The rest of the herd stopped their grazing, looked at the alarmed animal, then looked in the direction he was facing. A large bull mastodon, apparently the leader of the small herd, rushed toward the smaller bull and stopped beside him.

Bill could feel the large animal's eyes upon him as he stood, rifle in hand. *Crap, I hope he leaves us alone*, he thought, beginning to get a bit nervous.

But that was not to be. As soon as the thought passed through his brain the large bull, ears spread, trunk raised, and trumpeting loud enough to raise the dead, began a heavy-footed charge up the slope toward the small group.

Bill raised his rifle, taking aim at one of the mastodon's eyes.

Over the sound of the charging bull, Meri said, with some urgency, "Get in the prone position. You'll be less of a threat."

Immediately, Bill dropped, keeping the rifle on target.

Just as soon as he was down, the charging animal stopped. Head and large tusks raised up, eyes wide, trunk flailing around, ears spread, it was apparent the bull was protecting his herd, presenting as fearful a presence as possible.

"It's a false charge. He's threatening us, but probably won't attack if we don't threaten him back," Meri said. "Just stay down, but don't take your aim off him."

For several minutes, the large bull stood his ground, trumpeting and tossing his head and trunk around. The trio lay still, barely moving. Even Karen had picked up her rifle and held it across her chest, careful not to rest it on her abdomen. Bill could hear her muttering, "Fuck, fuck, fuck, fuck, fuck."

Eventually, the mastodon began backing down the slope,

bumping into the stationary young bull that had first spotted them. Getting back on level ground, the older bull turned to the herd and let out a series of smaller trumpets. Bill could feel the trumpets, along with a sub-sonic rumbling that he suspected was coming from the big bull's chest.

The herd began moving, circling around the still-burning campfire and the wikiup. One young mastodon got a bit too close to the wikiup, knocking down a portion of it, then scampering away with a squeal as that part of the tent came down with a crash. As the herd continued their journey upriver, Bill let out a sigh of relief.

"Whew, that was close."

"You ain't kidding," his wife replied, getting up an dusting the dry grass off herself.

Bill could still hear Karen muttering a series of "fucks," and it began to worry him. *I hope she's not losing it.*

An hour after the mastodons had gone, Bill and Meri returned to the campsite. Inspecting the wikiup, they quickly saw that everything was intact. A few of the support branches had been knocked out of alignment. It was only a matter of a couple of minutes work before they had the wikiup set back up.

Leaving their packs, they returned to their hiding spot and helped Karen back down. It was obvious that Karen was still in pain, and generally unhappy with their current conditions.

After they rebuilt the fire and settled down for supper, Bill said, "I gotta say, I wasn't too thrilled about how we handled that. I'm thinking we need to be prepared for anything pretty much all the time. Had those mastodons been moving a bit quicker, we might've lost just about everything."

Karen didn't say a word. She just lay there, seeming not really interested in the discussion. Meri looked over at Karen, then back to Bill. "So, what do you think we oughtta do?"

"Simple. Keep everything packed unless we're using it. We can afford to lose one or two packs, but not everything."

It became apparent to the two of them that Bill was starting to take the reins of control from Karen. It was something he was uncomfortable with, particularly since he had far less experience than Karen and less knowledge about wilderness survival than Meri, but then again, there it was.

Once supper was done, the pots and utensils were cleaned and stored.

With only two of them hale and hearty, and one of those four months pregnant, the concept of standing watch had faded into history. Now, the three Explorers spent the evening sleeping in the wikiup, relying on the fire to keep predators at bay.

As the sun set, the three of them settled down for the night. The wikiup door, a flap of bison hide, was kept open to let in fresh air and allow Bill and Meri to add wood to the fire as it dwindled down during the night. They had gotten used to doing that over the past several weeks, waking up as a sixth sense let them know it was time to rebuild the protective layer of flames.

It seemed that Bill had barely laid his head down when he heard wild trumpeting. It came from the direction the mastodon herd had headed the previous day. Groggily, he struggled to sit up, grabbing his rifle. In the dusky light cast by the campfire, he could see Meri also sitting up, the glow of the fire reflecting off the barrel of her rifle.

"Did you hear that?" he asked her.

"Yeah. Woke me up. Wonder what's going on."

"Beats the hell outta me, but just in case, let's get ready to haul ass."

The two stood up as best they could in the low structure, shrugged into their survival vests and suspender-supported web belts, then into their packs. Armed with rifles and PDWs, they stepped out of the small tent.

Out here, the sound of trumpeting, screams, and crashing through brush was even louder. Bill handed his pack and PDW to Meri. "Get back up the bluff. I'll grab Karen and her gear and join you."

Meri hurried off as Bill went back into the wikiup. Karen was awake, rifle in hand, still lying down, a look of fear on her face. "What's the plan?"

"We're gonna get you out of harm's way. Get ready to stand." Reaching under to shoulder, he said, "Up you go," and lifted her into a sitting position. Karen gasped in pain. The rifle rested in her lap.

"Fuck! That hurts!"

"Sorry, But we gotta do it. Okay, on three, let's get you to your feet."

Bill counted, and with his hands under her armpits, got Karen into a standing position. Without wasting any time, he draped her vest and then her suspender-held belt over her shoulders. Slinging his rifle over his shoulder, he picked up her rifle and slung it over his other. Her pack in one hand, and supporting Karen with the other, he began the tortuous journey back up the hill.

They barely made it. Karen collapsed into the dugout depression as Bill panted with the exertion of carrying her and all her equipment up the hill. Then the herd returned.

This time they weren't slowly moving and grazing; rather they were in stampede mode, tearing through the camp, trampling the wikiup and the campfire, scattering the coals and burning embers into the dry brush surrounding the camp.

One very young mastodon staggered into the light of the spreading fire. Bill could see three Smilodons hanging off it. One was latched onto the small herbivore's neck, holding on with its powerful front feet, driving its sharp, scimitar-like teeth into the young animal's neck. The second was holding onto the baby mastodon's rump, teeth sunk through the skin. The third was in a precarious position, hanging on to the belly. The predator was using its saber-like teeth to rip into the animal's abdomen and eviscerate it.

Bill and Meri kept their rifles trained on the death struggle, barely moving, trying not to attract attention to them.

As they watched, several more Smilodons jumped on the small mastodon, eventually driving it to the ground just below their position on the bluff. Despite the wind starting to kick up the fire spread by the stampeding herd, the Smilodons continued their assault on the screaming mastodon.

By this point, the rest of the herd had passed through the small encampment. They could hear it crashing through the brush downstream.

Bill glanced over to where the canoe was grounded on the banks of the Missouri River, but couldn't see it in the dark.

I hope they didn't trash our canoe, too, he thought.

It didn't take long before the baby mastodon was dead, its final death knell a small sound, between a wheeze and a keen. The Smilodon pack continued to ravage the animal, using their saber-like teeth to shred chunks of flesh. Bill could see their lower jaws practically unhinge, opening wide so they could use their large teeth. He could hear Karen whimpering behind him.

Unaware of the spreading fire, the big cats ate. Bill, on the other hand, wasn't as unaware of the growing ring of flames, beginning to spread up the bluff. Reaching over and tapping Meri with his hand, he pointed to the flames. She nodded then indicated Karen. "What do you think we ought to do?" she asked, keeping her voice down, but avoided whispering. The sound of whispering carries further than a low voice.

"We can't go up, 'cause that's where the fire's going," Bill said in the same low voice. The fire was advancing on either side of them, still below, but clearly on its way to flank them. "Best bet is down," he finally said.

"Are you crazy?" Meri asked. Her voice didn't rise in volume, but the inflection certainly came across.

"Yeah, like a fox. Here's what I'm thinking."

Bill then outlined his plan, all the while watching the fire grow and the Smilodons gorge themselves.

Meri heard him out, then agreed. "But you better hurry up. That fire's growing."

Bill brought his PDW up. Extracting the magazine, he took a quick glance to ensure it was fully loaded, then pulled out a second magazine.

"Just in case," he said in a quiet voice, setting it down on the ground next to him.

"Well, don't miss," Meri replied.

Getting into a prone position, he aimed the PDW at one of the Smilodons. "Get ready," he said, not taking his eye from the low power rifle scope.

Meri knelt, holding her rifle. "Ready."

Taking a deep breath, then slowly letting it out, Bill aimed at the point just behind the ear of the closest cat. Once all the breath was out of his body, and he was relaxed, he squeezed the trigger.

"Down," Meri said, keeping watch.

Bill immediately turned his sights on another Smilodon. This one had a confused look on its feline face, and had stopped eating to look at the now-dead Smilodon. Repeating the fire sequence, Bill shot the second cat just behind the ear, destroying the brain and immediately killing it.

"Down," Meri said again.

Bill shifted his aim to one of the big cats that on the ground between the dead mastodon and him. The cat was looking toward the sound of the gunfire, ears laid back. A shot behind the ears was out, so Bill took careful aim at the Smilodon's left eye.

Another shot and another brain-dead Smilodon.

By this time, the rest of the pack had become alarmed, and Meri took a chance to sow more fear into them. Standing up, she began waving and yelling.

It wasn't quite enough to start them running, but two more quick shots from Bill, these intended more to hurt than kill, caused the pack to give up its dinner and run away, the two wounded limping and howling in pain.

"Cover me," Bill said, standing up and slinging his PDW over his shoulder. He put the spare magazine in his pocket, then grabbed his shovel from his pack and ran downhill.

As he neared the fire, he could feel the heat wash across him, much like standing over a barbeque grill. He beat the flames nearest him with the shovel until they were out, then continued the process to either side until there was a path wide enough to safely transit.

Running back up the hill, he gasped, "Grab Karen's pack and head on down. I'll grab her."

Meri did so, making her way quickly, but carefully, down the hill, rifle held in one hand, Karen's pack in the other.

Bill slung his own pack on his back, then helped a cursing Karen upright.

"Una mas tiempo," he said, holding on to her waist, practically dragging her, as she slowly walked down the hill.

"Fuck it. Just drop me," Karen said. "I can't take this shit anymore."

"Bullshit. We've come too far to quit. Besides, you've still got a little boy waiting for you. Don't want him being raised by his dad, do you?" The last came out in grunts as Bill struggled to manhandle the pack and Karen down the slope.

As they passed through the gap in the fire, Bill gasped even more. The flames were picking up, the heat becoming unbearable.

Damn, had we waited any longer we might've been trapped up there, he thought, once clear of the burning line of grass.

"Let's head for the canoe," he yelled over the crackling of the flames. The fire was working its way up and down the riverbank, and trees were beginning to catch fire.

Bill was pleasantly surprised to see the canoe still intact.

"Help Karen in," he told his wife.

She dropped Karen's pack into the canoe, stepped in, then reached out to help the older woman. Karen was practically at the point of utter exhaustion. Once in the canoe, she collapsed in the bottom, shedding her rifle off her shoulder.

Bill stood outside the boat, near the point where it was tied to a tree branch. "Let's wait here. If the fire gets near, we can cast off, but I'd rather not do so if we don't need to. Who knows what's floating down that river that can slam into us."

Meri nodded. Karen was apparently too exhausted and in too much pain to even care.

Bill placed his pack in the canoe but kept his rifle handy.

Then he turned to Meri. "Why don't you rest? I'll keep an eye out. If things go bad, I'll shove us out and wake you."

"Not sure I can rest after that excitement," she said, stifling a yawn.

That brought a brief smile to Bill's lips. "Yeah, sure," he said, uttering the only known double positive to make a negative in the English language.

Soon both Meri and Karen were snoring, wrapped in their sleeping bags, the bison blankets having been left in the wikiup.

Bill watched as the flames made their way up the bluff and in both directions along the river. Fortunately, the canoe was in the right place, safe from the flames.

As the temperature began to drop, Bill retrieved his jacket from his pack, and put on a pair of gloves. As he breathed, frost formed in front of him.

Gettin' cold. That oughta at least slow down the fire.

Just as he thought that, he felt something cold and wet strike the tip of his nose. He wiped it off, then looked around. Snowflakes were falling. *Wow! Snow in October?* Within minutes, the snowfall became heavier and soon began extinguishing the fire. Bill placed a tarp over the sleeping women, so the wet snow wouldn't wake them.

Soon Bill was surrounded by darkness, with only the snow and his thoughts to keep him company. Looking about at the now snow-encrusted landscape near him, he began to worry.

If it's snowing this early, I wonder how bad the winter's gonna be. Shit, I've got a kid on the way. How am I gonna keep him warm? How am I gonna make sure we've got enough food. Sure as shit, Karen ain't gonna be able to do much.

It was at that point that Bill admitted to himself that he was now the one in charge of the expedition, or what was left of it.

As he pondered that turn of events, he gathered some nearby wood and got another fire started.

No sense in freezing or attracting a hungry critter looking for a tasty human for a snack.

Dawn arrived, muffled in falling snow. Fortunately, the ground hadn't been too cold, so it took some time before the snow started to stick and accumulate. By dawn, there were several inches on the ground, and it had begun to taper off.

Bill, who had remained awake the entire night, added more fuel to the fire. His eyeballs felt gritty as he looked around at the rapidly appearing landscape, utterly exhausted. He heard a stirring behind him, and turned to the canoe. Meri sat upright, the tarp covering her tossed aside, a puzzled look on her face.

"It's snowing," she said in wonder. Holding her hand out, palm up, she caught a snowflake, then watched it disappear as it melted from her body heat. Just looking at the wonder on her face made Bill's heart melt a little, too.

"Yeah. It put the fire out and seems to have kept the nasties away for a while."

"You must be exhausted." She climbed out of the canoe and shrugged into her jacket.

"Just a tad," Bill said.

She reached back into the boat, retrieved her rifle, and came to stand next to the fire. Holding the rifle in one hand, she held out the other hand to warm it.

"As soon as it's light enough, I want to check the camp and see if we can salvage anything," Bill said.

Dawn quickly developed into day, and Bill went back to the campsite. The wikiup had been knocked over, but, unexpectedly, nothing was really damaged. Inside the downed structure, he found the bison blankets intact, a light dusting of snow covering them. He gathered the blankets, shook the snow off, and went back to the canoe.

"Here," he said, handing one to Meri. Karen was now awake and sitting up in the canoe.

"Got a fire going, if you're interested," he said to her, gesturing toward the campfire.

The recovering woman slowly exited the canoe and approached the fire.

"How you feeling?" Bill asked her, handing her one of the bison blankets, which she draped around her.

"Like crap. Whaddaya think?" Her voice was hoarse.

"Well, it could've been worse," he said. "Wikiup was knocked over, but it seems to be in pretty good shape, overall. Added bonus: lots of fresh meat."

Winter Camp

After resetting the wikiup, Bill and Meri helped Karen get settled back inside. Bill got the fire going again, and the small dwelling warmed up rapidly.

As they were enjoying the warmth, the topic turned to the future.

"Way I see it," Bill said, "we've got two choices. Continue upriver or stay here for the winter. Thoughts?"

"I don't really care," Karen muttered from under her blanket.

Bill and Meri exchanged looks.

"Well," Meri finally said, "if we continue upriver, we'll get closer to the IP, but further away from wood — less fuel for fires. Considering winters here are hell, that might not be such a good idea."

"I'm thinking the same thing," Bill said. "If we dig in here for the winter, we should have time to gather enough wood and food. We can salvage that baby mastodon, and probably get some more big critters, like bison, and smoke enough to last us through the winter. Meri, do you think you'll be able to gather enough edible plants to prevent scurvy?"

She nodded. "Yeah. With a little help, I should be able to. Storage might be a problem."

From under the blanket came a low voice: "I took underwater

basket weaving in college."

"That's a real course?" Meri asked.

"No," Karen said. "It's not, but I did take an actual basket weaving course, so if you can gather the right material, I can make a bunch, even from here."

"What do you need?" Bill asked.

Karen told him.

"We should be able to find that near the river. Meri, you mind finding that stuff while I take care of the mastodon? After I get that done, I'll help out."

"Yeah, just as long as somebody with a rifle is nearby, it shouldn't be a problem."

"Great. Okay. Next topic, shelter," Bill said. "Ain't no way, no how, we're all three gonna want to stay cramped up in this wikiup all winter, so we're gonna have to do something different."

"What are you thinking?" Meri asked.

"A sort of dugout. We can dig into the side of the hill, which will get us out of the wind, and the mass of the earth will provide some thermal protection. Build a small fireplace, and it'll stay pretty warm, as long as we don't have a bunch of gaps letting in the wind."

"That's going to take a bunch of digging and log cutting," Meri said.

"Yep. Either that or the wikiup. Any other suggestions?"

Meri and Karen thought about it, then shook their heads.

"Looks like we'll be entering the shire," Karen said.

Once again, Meri looked at her strangely.

"Hobbit shire," Bill interpreted.

It took most of the day for Bill to erect smoking racks and clean the mastodon and Smilodons. Meri helped out in the afternoon to cut the meat into thin strips that were hung over the racks suspended above several small fires, serving to dry and smoke the meat, not cook it. By the time he was finished, the snow had mostly melted away, leaving the ground bare, but wet.

Bill realized that somebody would have to stay awake all night watching the fires, and preventing any wild animals from taking their food. He wasn't up to the task, not after having already spent one night on guard. He mentioned this to Meri, who told him she could handle a bunch of it. Giving him some stew, she sent him to bed in the wikiup.

Karen had managed to make it out to the main fire. She sat on a log watching the interaction between the married couple, not saying anything, nor offering to help.

Bill awoke after midnight. Karen was asleep, buried under a bison blanket. The glow of the fires showed Meri still awake, sitting watch. It was still cold, but not as cold as the night before, so Bill crawled out from under his bison blanket, put his boots on, grabbed his rifle, and joined Meri at the fire.

Giving her a quick kiss, he asked how the night was.

"Quiet, so far. A few coyotes and wolves howling in the distance, but no sign of any big cats."

The cats were Bill's biggest worry. He considered them far more dangerous than the wolves or bears. And it wasn't just the Smilodons they had to worry about, but also lions and cheetahs. Of course, they were also deep in the territory of the short-faced bear, one of the largest, most aggressive bears that ever existed. On top of that, it was a carnivore. Not just a part-time carnivore like the grizzly and black bears of Earth, but total full-on meat-eating carnivore — it ate vegans, not vegetables. It was also huge, taller than a human and weighing in at roughly a thousand kilos (or, a kilo kilo as Bill thought of it), several hundred kilos heavier than the largest grizzly. Not an animal

Bill ever hoped to meet.

"I'm up for taking over if you want to get some sleep," Bill said.

Stifling a yawn, Meri said, "Sounds good to me. Wake me at daylight, then you catch a couple of more hours of sleep. We're gonna be busy building tomorrow, and I don't think Karen's going to be too useful."

Sadly, Bill had to agree.

"What do you think we should do?" Meri continued.

"Keep on keeping on. It's all we can do. I figure either she'll come out of this, or she won't. Either way, we can't all give up."

Meri nodded. She then got up, gave Bill a goodnight kiss, entered the small wikiup, and crawled under the blanket that Bill had just vacated, not even taking off her boots.

Construction on the winter dwelling began the next day. Both Bill and Meri dug into the slope of the bluff they had taken refuge on during the night of the mastodon stampede. As with any physical venture involving tools in this brave, new world, the work soon resulted in numerous blisters, which Bill found amazing considering how callused his hands had become. It wasn't their first time down this road, so they just worked over the pain.

By the end of the day, an area roughly five by five meters had been hacked out of the bluff. Meri suggested using the mastodon's hide as the back wall, covering the dirt and reducing the amount of water that would seep into the dwelling.

It took several more days, most of which were spent cutting and dragging logs before they had an actual structure in place. Karen was able to help a little, mostly by keeping watch. At Meri's suggestion, the couple began moving the dirt from the original excavation over the exterior walls of the building, adding more insulation and reducing the number of gaps.

A small fireplace was constructed in a corner against the bluff. Meri had found some clay near the river's edge, so they used that as mortar for the stones, and eventually, for a pipe that served as a chimney.

By the time December rolled around, the hobbit-hole, as they were now calling it, was completed, and attention turned back to securing their food supply. Bill dug another hole in the bluff near the hobbit-hole to store the dried meat in. With the temperatures hovering around freezing, Bill wasn't too worried about the food spoiling. What he was worried about, though, was wild animals. He suggested they keep the edible plants that Meri and Karen had gathered in the hobbit-hole. "At least that way we can discourage some of the little critters, like mice, from eating too much," he said.

Karen had healed completely from her surgery within two weeks, but it was another couple of weeks before she was in full physical form. Her mental form, though, was a different matter. Bill had discussed this with Meri when the two of them were alone, usually when hunting. Bill was worried that Karen might do something stupid, like commit suicide. Meri didn't think so but agreed that they should keep a close eye on her. Karen's depression wasn't bad enough to make her completely incapable of doing anything, but it was certainly strong enough to affect her decision making and level of effort she applied to anything.

Another couple of weeks into winter, Karen finally started pulling out of her depression, but declined to take back the role of expedition leader.

"I'm not really up to decision making," she said to Bill when he broached the subject. "If you don't mind, I'd rather continue as we're doing. At least you're managing to keep us alive."

Bill couldn't argue with that logic.

As he retrieved wood for that evening's fire, a cold wind blew hard from the north, burning their exposed flesh like a frozen fire. Had it not been for the warm bison coats they were all wearing, Bill was certain he would have become a human popsicle in just a few minutes.

Meri's pregnancy had advanced to the point that she no longer walked in a lithe manner; rather she tended to "waddle like a duck," as she put it. Bill didn't think so, but he wasn't about to argue with a hormone-laden pregnant lady armed with a rifle in the middle of a wilderness. She no longer accompanied Bill on hunts, instead keeping the hobbit-hole clean and cooking dinner on the days he hunted. She also still spent a fair amount of her time gathering whatever edible plants she could find not covered with snow. Bill was constantly amazed at the variety of foods she would find them. *If it weren't for her*, he thought, *I'd probably be subsisting on bison and acorn, and getting scurvy in the process.*

Several months were spent in the hobbit-hole. Oftentimes Bill would go hunting solo, while Meri and Karen spent most of their time inside. One one such trip, he got caught in a blizzard. Luckily, he was near the river, so he was able to construct a mini-wikiup and had access to fuel from driftwood. That hunting trip, like many others, was successful.

Hard not to kill something on this planet, what with all the wildlife here, Bill thought, as he dragged home more meat on a travois. He still hadn't gotten over all the tick bites from earlier trips hauling fresh kills on his back.

As spring approached, the three of them were beginning to get a bit tired of each other. Even love can have a stretching point, Bill learned. It helped that he was able to get out and hunt often, or he was sure he'd turn bat-shit crazy.

Bill's thoughts turned to Meri's pregnancy. He didn't know much about pregnancies, other than how they started and how they were supposed to end, but he had learned a lot over the past several months. The biggest and hardest lesson learned was "never joke with a pregnant lady who is suffering morning illness." He wasn't sure which hurt worse, the silent treatment for two whole days or the slap across the face.

Karen was finally pulling her weight, but she wasn't the same Karen who started out leading their little expedition. Just being around her sometimes brought Bill down.

Yeah, she's missing her kid, he thought. *But, damnit, she's alive, and it looks like pretty good odds that we'll make it. So why doesn't she pull out of it and act that way?* Of course, Bill was pretty clueless when it came to the physiological components of depression, but that didn't stop him from mentally screaming when he was alone.

The grass he walked over was starting to turn green, and the trees along the river were budding. Looking down at the river from his position high on a bluff, more than a mile from the hobbit-hole, he thought, *Another month or so and we can start heading back upriver. Don't want to take a chance being on it if it's flooding. The ice breakup was a sight in itself. Glad we weren't on the river when that happened.*

As his gaze scanned the lowlands, he picked up signs of movement at the point where the flat lands of the river's edge met the bluff he was standing on. He pulled a small monocular from his shirt pocket and sighted in on the movement. It was a short-faced bear.

Crap, Bill thought. *That ain't good. Hope he's not heading downriver.*

Bill watched the bear for over an hour, confirming with relief that it was heading upriver. Away from his wife and future child. He breathed a little easier seeing that.

After the bear had moved on, Bill continued his hunt, his head on a swivel, watching for any threats. The action had become so automatic that he didn't even recognize he was doing it. He was soon rewarded with the sight of a small herd of flat-head peccaries, a distant relative of the common pig. They were larger than the peccaries on Earth and had longer tusks, something Bill had to worry about.

Last thing I need is to be gored by one of those. Hell, it's bad enough being thousands of klicks from civilized help. Just think how much worse it would be to be stranded, injured, alone, and nobody knowing where you were. Hello? Death, anyone?

Dropping to a crouch, Bill began to stalk the animals. Fortunately, the wind was in his face, so they wouldn't be able to smell him. Peccaries were notorious for having bad eyesight, so if he moved slow enough, they probably wouldn't even notice him. Every few steps he would stop and turn around, making sure he hadn't become prey for any other predators.

He had soon worked up to a distance of only 200 meters from the herd, most of whom were rooting around in the ground. Once again, he glanced around to ensure his safety. Satisfied, he extended the bipod of his rifle and got into the prone position. As he lined up his sights on the closest peccary, he once again wished for a rifle scope. While he was a good shot with the iron sights, he missed his rifle scope, which let him shoot groupings of less than a centimeter at a hundred meters. With the iron sights, he was happy to get a grouping the size of his palm at that distance.

Bill didn't bother aiming for a head shot. Without the scope, he wasn't confident he could make it. Rather, he aimed for just behind the shoulder, a spot that anywhere nearby would hit something vital.

The wind outside the hobbit-hole was howling, but thanks to

the small fire in the stone fireplace and the bison blankets on the floor, it was warm inside the small dwelling. This was a good thing. Meri lay on the blankets, gripping Bill's hand. Bill was amazed at the strength of the grip, which clamped down even more as Meri had another contraction.

Meri was in a basic birthing position, flat on her back, legs spread, knees up, and feet on the ground. Karen, sitting back on her heels at Meri's feet, had one hand under the bison blanket that served as Meri's skirt, which was hiked up on the knees.

"Just about there," Karen said. "I can feel the head crowning. Another couple of pushes and we'll have this little sucker outta there."

Meri screamed again. As she did, she clamped down on Bill's hand again, squeezing so hard his fingertips went white. *Jesus*, Bill thought, *how long is this gonna last?* He had been good standing by and doing all the other man stuff, but this whole birthing thing was freaking him out a bit. First off, he hated seeing Meri in pain, regardless of whether or not she was giving birth to their first child.

"One more push," Karen said.

Meri stopped screaming. The crush on Bill's hand let up. Meri lay there, sweat soaking her hair and brow, beads of moisture on her upper lip. She put her head back and panted. Bill didn't know what to do or say, so he just shut up.

It was only a couple of seconds before another contraction began. Meri's head came up, her hand clamped down on Bill's in her vise-like grip, and she screamed again.

"Push!" Karen practically yelled.

Meri went silent, holding her breath. Her face became beet red, and she exhaled with a quiet scream.

"It's coming," Karen said.

Then Meri flopped back, loosing her grip on Bill again.

"I've got it," Karen said, pulling a small, wet bundle from

under Meri's blanket. As she did, Bill could see the form of a human, umbilical cord still attached.

The feeling that came over Bill was one he had never experienced before. He wasn't sure he would even be able to describe it, but it was a combination of amazement, love, fierce protectiveness — a multitude of feelings that no one would recognize until their time came as a father.

As Karen cut and tied off the umbilical, Bill stared in amazement.

That's my son. I'm a dad. That's our son. I'm a dad, was pretty much all he thought.

Bill was awakened from his reverie when Meri asked, in a whispered voice, "How's our baby?"

It was hard for him to answer with the lump in his throat; fortunately, he didn't have to. Karen, who had wrapped their son in a small bison blanket, placed the small bundle on Meri's chest and said, "Healthy, and probably hungry."

Bill stared in awe at the little bundle on his wife's chest, and didn't even notice that Karen was cleaning up the remains of the birth, removing the placenta and replacing soaked bison rugs with a dry one. All he could do was stare at the future that lay on his wife.

Finally, he found his voice. "Hey, you're a mom."

Meri looked up at him, sweat-dampened hair plastered to her forehead, smiled, and said softly, "Hey. You're a dad."

The first night as new parents went relatively smoothly, considering that Bill had absolutely zero experience with babies, and no formal education in childbirth and dealing with newborns. Luckily, Meri had some babysitting experience with infants, and Karen had relatively recent memories of newborn childcare, since her son had been only two when they began the primary survey.

Without modern medicine and ultrasounds to tell them the sex of their child, they hadn't spent too much effort figuring out a name. Now, they agreed to name the boy after both their dads. After arguing their points on which name should be first, Karen settled it for them by having them do rock-paper-scissors. Meri won, so their son was given the moniker of Jonathan David Clark. Jonathan, better known as Jack Lewis, was Meri's father, the head of the *Corps of Discovery*. David Clark was Bill's dad, whom he always thought of a "The Colonel" (quote marks, capitalization, and all), a Lieutenant Colonel in the U.S. Air Force at the time Bill joined the *Corps*.

"Can we call him Jack?" Meri asked.

"Sure. Why not? Of course, that might make it a bit confusing when we get back to Hayek."

"Naw," Meri said. "Different last names. Besides, little Jack is a lot cuter than my dad."

Bill couldn't argue with that.

A week of being a father had started to wear on Bill, mainly on the lack-of-sleep department. *You'd think all the experience I've had not sleeping would pay off,* he thought, yawning. *Then again, I should feel lucky. Not like I have to be the one to wake up every other hour and feed the little guy.* Bill had plenty of sympathy for Meri but was secretly glad he didn't have to get sucked into that situation. *Heck, by the time we get back to Hayek, I bet he'll be sleeping through the night.*

Karen had taken over cooking while Meri took care of Jack and Bill continued his duties as hunter. Right now, though, it was a bit too dark for hunting, and a part of the antelope he had shot the day before was being cooked in a stew with some wild onions and cat-tail root flour.

Bill had just returned from gathering wood for the fire and sat down next to Meri and Jack on the bison rug that served as both floor and bed. Leaving his bison coat on, he leaned his rifle against the wall and gave Meri a quick kiss.

"How's he doing?"

Meri looked down at Jack, who was, once again, latched onto a boob, chowing down. "He's doing great, but you better bring me a lot of protein. This kid eats a lot, sorta like his dad."

"Who, me?" Bill asked.

Their repartee was suddenly halted when they heard a snuffling noise outside the closed door.

"What the hell?" Bill muttered, reaching for his rifle. Meri pulled a squalling Jack off her breast and wrapped him in a small bison blanket they had made for him.

The door was smashed in with a loud crash. Bill aimed and fired. The noise was deafening inside the contained environment; Jack screamed as the concussion from the shot assaulted his little ears. Meri placed her hands over his ears as Bill fired again.

Karen had grabbed her rifle and fired, too.

The creature roared: the largest bear Bill had ever seen. Its mouth was agape and its large teeth exposed. In the back of his mind, he recognized it as a short-faced bear. He fired again, and again, forcefully ejecting and loading each round after pulling the trigger. Each time he fired, the bear roared, but it continued its advance into the cabin.

As Bill chambered another round, he looked down to ensure the round was feeding — but there was no other round. His rifle was empty. There was nothing he could do to stop the bear from hurting his family.

Desperate, Bill threw himself onto his wife and child, covering them with his body. As he did, the bear reached out with its paw and swiped at him. Bill could feel the claws tear through his bison coat, shirt, and into his back.

He felt Meri moving under him, then heard and felt a PDW

fire. Meri kept firing until she, too, ran out of ammunition. The room was filled with cordite, the sound of crying baby, and the screaming of Karen. Bill didn't hear the bear anymore.

Tentatively, he stood up and turned around. The bear lay on the hobbit-hole's floor, only inches away, the top of its head blown away. He looked back at Meri, who was holding a PDW in her right hand while protectively holding Jack in her left arm.

"I think you killed it," he said.

Meri dropped the PDW, grabbed ahold of Jack with both hands, and began crying, while simultaneously trying to comfort the crying baby.

Karen was still holding her rifle, smoke rising from the barrel. All of them were stunned, Bill and Karen frozen into inaction.

"We need to get this outta here," Bill finally said. Only then did he realized his back hurt. *I wonder how bad it is?* he thought.

Despite the cold air blowing in from the broken entryway, Bill stripped off his coat and shirt.

"Here. Take a look at this," he said, turning his wounded back to Karen.

Karen set her rifle down. "You've got some pretty deep scratches here. Let's clean 'em up and bandage them. I think you'll be okay, but you're gonna have to take it easy for a week or so. Give those wounds time to heal."

Karen cleaned and dressed Bill's wounds, then suggested to Meri that the two of them dispose of the bear's carcass and let Bill rest with Jack.

It took the women more than an hour to finally get the giant bear out of the hobbit-hole. The most difficult part was trying to keep the blood out of their quarters as they cut the dead animal up. There was no way that the two women, with or without Bill's help, were going to be able to move an animal that weighed over a thousand kilos without cutting it up into parts. To their credit, when all was said and done, there was very little blood spilled on the floor that night, other than that from the multiple gunshot wounds that the bear had suffered before Meri literally blew its brains out.

Departure

Bill was first up in the morning. He stepped out of the hobbit-hole to gather more dead wood to add to the fire. *Man, what I wouldn't do for a cup of coffee,* he thought, not for the first time since crossing the Atlantic. It had been more than a week since the bear attack, and his back was finally on the mend. As the fire grew in the hearth, there was movement around him, and soon the crying of a baby, announcing to the world that he was not only awake but hungry.

The others soon joined him, Meri with a small bundle latched onto her breast.

"Maybe we oughta change his name to Limpet," Bill said. Meri answered him by sticking out her tongue.

Bill prepared breakfast, this time bear stew. *Big surprise,* he thought as he dropped the meat cubes into the pot suspended over the fire.

It had become warm during the night, and Meri suggested they eat outside. Bill agreed but suggested they get a fire going outside as well. "After all, it may be warmer, but it's still a bit chilly."

Once the stew was ready, Bill served everyone and they stepped outside to take breakfast on the veranda. At least, that's what Bill called the collection of logs in front of the hobbit-hole that they sat on sometimes. They enjoyed the warmth of Meri's fire, the sunshine, and the meal.

Bill heard it first. A buzzing that soon turned into a drone. *I know that sound,* he thought. Looking wildly around, he spotted a dot in the air, halfway between the northern horizon and the apogee of the sky. It took a few seconds for what he was seeing to register on his brain.

"A plane! A fucking plane," he practically shouted, pointing upward. Meri and Karen turned and looked where he was pointing. Little Jack was completely oblivious, sound asleep in the baby carrier strapped across Meri's chest.

It soon became apparent that the plane was on an approach that would take it over the small group.

"Quick, we gotta get something out to attract them," Bill said, looking around for anything that would serve as a beacon.

"Clothing. Spread out clothes in the universal sign of distress. I'll get another fire going while you two set out it out."

"Make three," Meri said, unstrapping Jack from her chest and laying him down on the grass. "That's the international signal for distress — three of anything." Shucking out of her pack, she asked Bill, "Do you think they'll see a flare?"

"Don't know. Don't worry about it now. Get the clothes laid out and I'll start the fires. I'll dig out a flare if they get interested," he replied, grabbing several small pieces of wood.

Meri and Karen soon had clothing spread out on the slope, laid out on the grass in the shape of the letters SOS.

Bill got a small fire going, using some of the burning wood from the original fire. Once that was blazing, he and the women gathered enough material for the third fire, set to resemble the three points of a triangle.

The fires burning well enough and the plane almost upon them. "Keep throwing green wood them," he told Meri and Karen.

He ran into the hobbit-hole and dug one of their few flares out of his battered pack, then returned outside. Bill now recognized the plane as one of the DeHavilland DHC-4 Caribou's that the *Corps* used for aerial surveys in the secondary survey stage. It was just like the plane Meri had served on during her first survey on Zion, over a year ago.

The smoke turned a heavy white. It was obviously clearly visible to the plane's occupants, as the craft began to alter course slightly to pass directly over them.

Bill pulled the flare out of the pack and pulled the pin, holding the flare in one hand, and the striker cord in the other. As it became apparent that the plane was definitely seeking them out, he raised the flare above his head and pulled the cord. The flare shot up into the sky.

In less than a minute, the plane flew directly over them, at least a thousand meters up. They watched as it droned on, then slowly banked and made its way back.

Bill wasn't sure if it was the smoke from the hobbit-hole's chimney or the sheer excitement of being rescued, but his eyes were watering. He shouted, inarticulately, and he wasn't the only one. Meri and Karen were also screaming, yelling, and crying.

The plane flew over them again. This time, the wings waggled in recognition.

Big sobs broke from Bill. Finally, the nightmare was almost over. Meri rushed over to him, hugging him and crying. Karen just stood there, racking big sobs coming from deep within her.

As the plane banked again, they could see it climbing. Rather than cruise over them a third time, the Caribou circled above them, gradually gaining altitude. The rear cargo door opened, and soon a large object fell out of it.

As the object fell, four appendages spread from its sides,

resolving themselves into shrouded propellers. Bill recognized the object as a rescue flitter, a single-seat flying car with a litter under it, usually used to rescue injured ground survey Explorers.

The three watched, mouths agape, as the flitter descended.

With a cloud of dust bursting out from under it as it approached the ground, the flitter landed, not more than 20 meters from their location, facing up the slope.

Not moving, the three watched as the top of the flitter opened, and a light-skinned brown man exited it, PDW in his hand.

"Bill?" he asked. "Meri?"

It took Bill a moment, but then he was rushing forward. "Jordan!" He embraced him as if his life depended on it. In a way, it did.

Releasing him, Bill stepped back while Meri also hugged the young man. "Thank God you're here," she said, tears streaming down her face.

Karen had just collapsed to sit on the ground, sobbing uncontrollably.

"Christ almighty," Jordan said, as Meri released her hold on him. Holding her at arm's length and looking among the three Explorers, and then at Jack, still in his swaddling, he said, "We wrote you off months ago."

"Yeah, well, we don't kill easy," Bill said.

"Hold on a sec. I gotta let the crew know what's up."

Pulling a radio from his belt, Jordan called up to the craft above, "Romeo Zero One, Rescue Zero One, over."

"Romeo Zero One. Go ahead, Rescue Zero One, over."

"Romeo Zero One, be advised, I've got three crew members of Forty-Two Two down here." Looking down at Jack, he continued, "Along with a fourth survivor, an infant. Over."

"Copy that, Rescue Zero One — four survivors, one's an infant. Got names? Over."

"Bill Clark, Meri Lewis, and," looking over at Karen, Jordan raised his eyebrows in question.

"Karen Wilson," Bill answered.

"Karen Wilson, over," Jordan said into the radio.

"Confirming Clark, Lewis, and Wilson. What about Weaver, over?"

Bill shook his head.

"Negative on Weaver, over."

"Roger, negative on Weaver. Stand by."

"Damn, man. What the hell happened?" Jordan finally asked, looking at his former roommate. "We thought you were dead."

"Damned near," Bill replied. "Somebody snuck an EMP bomb on our flight, causing us to go down in the Eurasian Alps. Meri, here," he gestured to his wife, "and Ben Weaver managed to safely land us in a lake. We've been making our way home ever since."

"Fuckin' GLF," Jordan said, shaking his head. "Fuckers did a lot of damage. What happened to Ben?" he asked.

"Shark attack in the Caribbean," Bill said, his mind flashing back to that horrible scene.

"What happened?" Meri asked, picking up Jack and holding him.

By this time, Karen had gotten control of herself and joined the group, snot still running down her nose and tear tracks streaking through the dust of her face.

"The Gaia Liberation Front decided to simultaneously attack the gates and every single survey we had running. They basically attacked us in force, killing a lot of good people, and shutting down gate operations for several months. We're still trying to figure out everything they did. Luckily, most of them were killed, but we've still got a number in custody. Remember

Brenda Lightfoot?" he asked Bill.

Bill had to dig back into his memory, and then remembered the woman from Colville, a small town in central Washington State. He had met her his first week on Hayek, even before Explorer training began. A Native American who was a graduate of Washington State University.

"Yeah, what about her?"

"She's one of them. Did a shitload of sabotage, including that Caribou incident of yours."

The incident took place during Bill's Caribou transition flight, where somebody had sabotaged the plane causing a propeller blade to shear off and cut through the flight deck, decapitating the Instructor Pilot. Bill had to make an emergency landing, alone, supported only by another pilot on the radio. He still had nightmares about it, despite the counseling he went through after the incident. Like most Explorers, Bill had his own amount of post-traumatic syndrome disorder to deal with, and that was only the first instance.

"What happened to her?" Meri asked. It was clear to Bill, from her tone, that his wife was royally pissed.

"She's in custody," Jordan answered. Under his breath, Bill heard him mutter, "I hope that bitch hangs."

At that moment, Jordan's radio sounded again.

"Rescue Zero One, Romeo Zero One, over."

Jordan replied, "Go ahead Romeo Zero One, over."

"Rescue Zero One, we're gonna RTB and see about getting a proper retrieval. We'll drop some more supplies. Advise all to stay put. We'll be back in less than forty-eight hours, over."

"Roger that, Romeo Zero One. Copy, supply drop and return in forty-eight." Jordan looked up at the twin-engine plane as it approached at a lower altitude. Turning to the others, he said, "Right. Like I'm gonna trek several hundred miles when I could wait for a ride."

"Is that Brad on the other end?" Meri asked.

"Yeah," Jordan said. "He's the one that actually identified you, using binoculars."

"Who's Brad?" Bill asked.

"Old friend," Meri said with a smile. "We've known each other practically our whole lives, growing up on base. I helped him out once, years ago," she said, cryptically.

Clearly there was more to the story.

Once more, the plane flew over them. This time, though, the object dropped was attached to a parachute that deployed soon after it left the aircraft.

The plane waggled its wings once again, then turned west and headed toward the horizon.

The parachuted bundle landed on the ground several hundred meters away. Jordan said, "Let me."

Climbing back in the flitter, Jordan took off and flew to the grounded bundle. In a couple of minutes, he had it secured in the litter and was back at the small makeshift encampment.

He hopped out of the flitter. "Well, let's see what they dropped off."

Lowering the litter to the ground, he extracted the bundle, which was over a meter and a half long and about half a meter in diameter. It was a container designed to carry supplies to be air-dropped.

It opened up lengthwise; Bill saw a number of food packets. The ones on the top were the *Corps*-issued field rations. Field rations were similar to the U.S. Army's HDRs, Humanitarian Daily Rations, with the meals and some sundries in vacuum-packed retort pouches rather than cans. One of Bill's favorite sundries was a chocolate-covered coconut bar. Each field rat also came with a small chocolate bar, specifically designed for the tropics so it wouldn't melt in the tropical heat (or even in one's mouth), crackers, and peanut butter. An accessory packet was included, with the most popular item in it being a packet of field toilet paper. Looking at the manna from heaven, Bill couldn't remember the last time he'd had toilet paper. *Geez, how many months has it been*, he thought. While grass and leaves did the job, they certainly weren't squeezably soft!

"So, who's this little guy?" Jordan asked, looking at Jack with a raised eyebrow.

Standing up straighter, Bill said, formally, "Jack, meet Jordan Washington. Jordan, meet Jonathan David Clark, our son."

That caused both of Jordan's eyebrows to rise, almost to his hairline.

"Son, as in, you two?" he asked, gesturing to Bill and Meri.

"Um, yeah," Meri said. "What, you think we adopted him?"

Everyone laughed, but the comment also reminded Bill of something. "Crap, I almost forgot. We've gotta quarantine this planet, it's a Class II planet."

"What do you mean?" Jordan asked.

"Class II, as in 'already occupied by humans' is what I mean," Bill said.

"You sure?"

"Damned right he's sure," Karen said, speaking up for the first time since Jordan landed. "We've got physical evidence in the form of a spear point, and we saw a bunch as we left Gibraltar."

"Well, not a lot we can do until we're back in touch with civilization," Jordan said.

"Guess you're right about that. Hey," Bill said, turning to the women, "how about we gather up our clothes so they don't blow away?"

Jordan helped collect the worn and ragged clothing.

After extinguishing the now-unnecessary fires, the four sat

down to enjoy lunch, the first in almost a year that didn't require any of the three survivors to kill and clean it. Of course, Jack wasn't interested in the food provided by the *Corps*.

As they ate, Jordan caught them up on the news back on Hayek and in the *Corps*.

"Matt finally proposed to Nicole," he told them, referring to Matt Green, Bill and Jordan's roommate from training. Matt was a Southern good ole boy from Memphis, Tennessee, and Nicole Andrews was a Kiwi from New Zealand. It was a wonder that the two could even communicate with their rather distinctive, and sometimes impossible to understand, accents.

"About time," Bill said. "I thought he did that the first week they met. Remember him serenading her in the Cave Bear Cave?" This was one of the outdoor beer gardens on Sacajawea Base that the roommates used to hang out at.

The two men smiled with the fond memory of that evening. The strains of John Denver's *Follow Me* passed through Bill's mind, recalling that event.

Jordan told them about the impact that the GLF had had on the *Corps*, base operations, and on Hayek in general. Along with the gates at Bowman Field, they had also managed to sabotage many gates operating between Hayek and Earth. Luckily, those were rapidly re-opened, and only had a minimal impact on Hayek's economy. It was the gates between Hayek and the newer opened parallel planets that took a while. All surveys and explorations were halted until gate operations were back to normal.

"Your dad ordered it that way," Jordan said to Meri. It was clear he was a bit uncomfortable about it.

"Dad always did put duty and the *Corps* before family," Meri said, looking down at Jack, now feeding on her breast.

"How's Thep doing?" Bill asked, referring to their fourth roommate, Thepakorn Daeng, a tropical botanist, originally from northern Thailand.

Jordan looked down. Finally, he looked up at Bill with a lost look and, almost in a whisper, said, "Dead."

Bill felt the shock run through him. "What happened?"

"He was at one of the gates, actually going through it, about to go on a survey, when it fucking exploded." Jordan looked away. Bill could see the anguish on his face. Jordan and Thep were close, much like Bill and Matt were, so he understood what the young Californian was feeling.

"Geez. Sorry, dude."

"Yeah, well, that was, like, last year. Know what I mean?" Jordan replied, shrugging it off.

Bill could see it still hurt Jordan. He glanced over at Meri; she saw too.

"Anyhow, things are pretty much back to normal. The Commandant decided to re-open the gate to Planet 42, so here we are. They finished the Initial Survey months ago," he said sheepishly, clearly expecting an outburst of anger from the three. "They found your plane, but without contact, decided not to do anything."

That got Bill thinking. "What were you doing in the plane? You're a biologist, not an aerial surveyor."

"Yeah, well, when things went to shit, they did whatever they could to get things back together. We were a bit short on the whole manpower thing, thanks to the fuckin' GLF. Lots of people killed and hurt in their attacks. Turns out that the one GIS class I took was enough for the *Corps* to consider me for aerial survey, so there I am, operating a geographic information system at a thousand meters, rather than collecting flora and fauna at ground level. Go figure."

Placing her hand on his knee, Karen said, "Well, I, for one, am happy as hell that you were in that plane. Thanks."

Bill didn't think he'd ever see a black man blush, but he was proven wrong at that moment.

Jordan, as a trained biologist, was an experienced ground survey crew Explorer, so sleeping in the wild on an unexplored planet was nothing new for him. What was new was seeing the survivors' hobbit-hole set up, with spread-out bison hides serving as floor and blankets, and a fire going in the home-made fireplace.

After lunch, Bill took Jordan around, showing him the canoe that had carried the crew over several river systems.

"Hard to believe it's still functional, after all the abuse we've put it through," Bill said, as the men looked upon the beached canoe, its sail hanging limply down the mast.

"Damn, man. How far you come in that thing?"

"Beat me. At least several thousand klicks. Down the Ohio, up the Mississippi, and up the Missouri to here. And, I gotta say, I got no problem not going another klick in the damned thing."

"With any luck, you won't have to," Jordan said, rubbing his mustache. Bill remembered the last time Jordan did that, days before he was required to shave it off prior to beginning Explorer training.

Bill realized just how much they had changed. Despite being in his early twenties, Jordan was looking older, with faint lines creasing his face, cutting down in vertical stripes on either side of his mouth. His hair was cut to regulation shortness, but the mustache, which had been rather faint when they first met, was fuller now, and clearly not regulation. Bill was also different. When he first met Jordan, he had the typical complexion of a western Washington resident, or, as he called it, the aqua tan. He was also clean-shaven and had short hair. Now, he was sunblasted and tan, with hair that hadn't seen a barber in almost a year, hanging to his shoulders. He sported a full beard, albeit a bit scraggly, and a full mustache. Meri had recently told him that he had fine crease lines radiated from his eyes, a combination of squint and laugh lines. Had Bill thought about it, he doubted his own father, "The Colonel," would have recognized him. Had he been able to look in a mirror, he probably wouldn't be able to, either.

As Jordan looked at the canoe, becoming somewhat introspective. "Whattaya think about bringing it back?".

"Bringing what back?" Bill asked.

"The canoe. To put it in the museum."

"Hey, you want to carry it back, that's fine by me, but don't expect me to help. I'll be damned glad to finally be rid of it."

Bill thought a moment longer. "Actually, if you really want a great museum piece, I think you oughta try and get the outrigger we used to sail across the ocean. We stashed it on the banks of the New River near Pamlico Sound."

Jordan turned to Bill. "Y'know, that would be freakin' amazing. Ain't nobody else in *Corps* history done anything that epic. Not even Janice Goodland. When we get back, be sure to give me the coordinates, and I'll see what I can do. Class II planet or not, that's something to consider."

"Deal," Bill said.

Two days later, another twin-engine aircraft came into sight, from the direction the Caribou had departed. It was one of the heavy-lifter cargo planes in the *Corps'* inventory, a C-123 Provider. The fire was going, and since it was no longer an emergency, Bill didn't order two more fires established. The four adults watched as the plane came close, eventually passing over them, wings waggling in recognition.

Circling back, it came closer to the ground, eventually running parallel to the river at the top of the bluff, a bare ten meters above the ground, the cargo ramp in the back down. It was operating barely above stall speed. As it roared near them, Bill saw a parachute emerge from the back, pulling an object out of the plane.

The parachute yanked it out of the plane, and the short drop to the ground meant it didn't spend too much time in the air. Bill recognized the method as a low-altitude parachute extraction. He suspected there would be more.

The object landed in a puff of dust, even on the grassy prairie, the special pallet collapsing under the impact. Bill knew from experience that the pallet was mostly heavy-duty cardboard, designed to take the force of the impact and collapse, preserving the integrity of whatever it carried. That object turned out to be a rubber bladder, large enough for several hundred gallons of water or fuel. Being yellow, Bill suspected it was for diesel.

A second parachute emerged, this one with a small bulldozer, configured on the same type of pallet.

"They're gonna build an airfield," Meri said, upon seeing the second extraction.

Bill put two and two together. One bulldozer plus fuel, plus whatever other equipment the plane would drop, meant one airfield suitable for a STOL — a Short Take-Off and Landing plane. This meant they intended to bring in one of the STOL planes, like the DHC-4 Caribou that found them, to extract them.

A third parachute dropped from the rapidly departing plane several hundred meters away. Bill couldn't see what the object was, but he suspected it was a road roller.

A fourth object was extracted before the C-123 raised its nose and increased speed. The aircraft circled around, gaining altitude, and eventually, regurgitating another pallet of equipment and number of parachutes attached to people.

"Engineers," Jordan said.

Within minutes, the pallet and three engineers were on the ground. After unstrapping themselves from their parachutes, they approached the four Explorers.

The spokesman was a grizzled veteran in his late twenties.

"Who's in charge?" he asked.

All eyes turned toward Bill.

"Guess I am," he said.

The engineer approached Bill, hand outstretched.

"Ken Schmitt."

"Bill Clark," Bill said, grasping the hand.

"Well, Bill. Let's get you guys outa here and home."

Bill couldn't say anything for a moment due to the lump that had suddenly appeared in his throat. Finally, he was able to say, "That'd be mighty fine."

Looking at the two women, Ken nodded. "Ma'ams. We'll have you back on Hayek shortly." Then he turned to the engineers and practically shouted, "What are you guys doing standing here? We got a runway to build!"

Minutes later, both the bulldozer and steamroller were in operation.

The Caribou had left the area, returning to wherever it had come from.

"Wow," Meri said. "To think, they're doing this for us."

Jordan gave her a long look. "The *Corps* doesn't leave anyone behind if they can help it."

Ken explained that a rough airfield would be ready to accept a Caribou the next day and that the priority was to evacuate them as soon as possible.

The engineers had jumped with their primary gear, along with extra food rations.

"May not be good, but it'll keep you alive," Ken said as they ate around the fire in the evening. Bill was kind enough to offer the engineers some bison, which they gratefully accepted. In kind, he gratefully accepted their field rats.

In less than twenty-four hours, the engineers had an operational airfield in place. Of course, the concept of "operational" probably wasn't one that would suffice on Earth, unless one was operating in Laos during the Vietnam War. The dirt runway had been scraped from the prairie, and flattened as much as possible with the road roller. It was barely over 200 meters long.

Another twenty-four hours later, the first Caribou landed on the makeshift airfield. It braked, turned, and circled back to the waiting people at the other end of the field, blowing dust into their faces and grit into their teeth. As it came to a halt, the rear ramp lowered. An older man stepped down the ramp onto the beaten ground.

As he walked toward the small gathered group, Meri clearly recognized him. Handing Jack to Bill, she took off running toward him, her rifle banging against her back. She practically jumped into his open arms, hugging him and burying her face into his shoulder. He hugged her back. Even from the distance of almost a hundred meters, Bill could see the man's shoulders shaking from sobs. Slinging his rifle over his shoulder and cradling Jack, he, Karen, and Jordan, followed in Meri's steps.

The man Meri was embracing was the Commandant of the *Corps of Discovery*, Jack Lewis. Also known as Meri's father, and now Bill's father-in-law, and the grandfather of little Jack.

As the group approached him, Jack let go of Meri and held out his hand to Bill, wiping tears from his face with his other hand. "Bill, damned glad to see you."

"You too, sir," Bill said, taking the outstretched hand in his now-callused palm.

Releasing his hand, the Commandant reached out to Karen. "Karen," he said as she took his hand.

"Commandant," Karen replied.

Still holding her hand, he covered it with his other one. "You'll be glad to know that we notified Tran as soon as we heard. He and your son are being brought over so they can meet you when we land at the IP."

Big tears began to flow from Karen's eyes, and she grasped the Commandant in a fierce hug. Bill's eyes watered and a lump formed in his throat as he watched Karen sob once more.

Letting go of her after what seemed an eternity, Lewis looked around the small encampment. "Well, let's get that bird loaded and get you guys home." It was then he noticed the bundle in Bill's left arm.

"Say, who's this guy?" he asked.

Meri took Jack from Bill's arm, and said, with a great deal of pride, "Dad, meet your grandson, Jack. Jack, this is your grandfather."

Lewis's eyebrows went up. He looked from Jack to Meri, and then to Bill. "I thought maybe Karen was the mom," he said, more in the way of a question than a statement.

"Bill and I decided to get married when we thought we might not make it back," Meri explained. "And, well, let's just say that the birth control implants clearly aren't one hundred percent effective," she finished with a rueful smile.

"Wow. Just wow," said Lewis. "Well, hello there, young man," he said to little Jack. Jack yawned in return.

"Well, let's not tarry any longer, Lewis said. "Lots of people waiting to see you three — excuse me, you four," the last directed at little Jack. "So, let's not hold them up any longer."

Turning to Schmitt, he said, "Ken, leave the construction equipment here for now. We'll bring it back later. Your guys can either stay with it or come back now, though. Your choice." Turning to the flight crew chief and his assistant, both of whom had joined the group while the Commandant was greeting the found survivors, he said, "Help gather up anything the Trekkers want taken back to Hayek."

Jack turned to Bill and asked, "What do you want brought back?"

"We'll carry our survival equipment, but it'd be great if they brought the bison blankets, and the canoe," Bill said. "We had a wikiup, but we used the wood for firewood. We've also got a bigger catamaran stashed away on the east coast, that the *Corps* might be interested in. Got us from the Med to Ti'icham."

"Make it happen," Lewis said to the air crew, who promptly went to where the canoe was beached on the riverbank. Lewis's comment made Bill smile, thinking about how Karen used to imitate that guy from that old spaceship television show.

"Let's break down the hobbit-hole," Bill said to Meri and Karen, the latter of whom had finally composed herself and was no longer crying. "It'll be faster since we know what we're doing, and I'd like to get out of here asap."

"Dad, could you hold Jack while we get our stuff?" Meri asked her father.

Holding out his arms, he said, "I'd be honored."

As he took Jack in his arms, Lewis softly spoke to him. "Hey there, little guy, I wish your grandmother was alive to meet you. You'd have loved her."

That statement brought a wistful look to Meri's face. Her mother had died while she was a toddler; she had no real recollections of her. Bill's mom had died when he was six. He still remembered how much he had cried at her funeral, so he empathized with Meri.

It didn't take more than a few minutes to pack everything and get it loaded into the Caribou. Prior to loading the canoe, the crew removed the emergency flitter, putting it adjacent to the one Jordan had landed. The crew chief explained that they would retrieve it when they came back for the runway building equipment.

The pilot and co-pilot exited the craft at that point, and Bill was introduced to them by the Commandant.

"This young man is a great pilot and explorer, despite being a pain in my ass for too many years to count," Lewis said as he introduced the pilot, Brad Maeda.

"Are you still pissed about that?" Brad asked Jack, smiling. "Hell, you woulda done the same thing."

"Yeah, maybe. But you got Meri involved. I wouldn't have done that."

Brad shrugged, and Bill raised his eyebrows, questioningly.

"Meri helped me go through a gate and run my own private rescue mission back when we were in high school," Brad told him.

"Hmph," Lewis grunted. "Used her as a spy, you mean."

"Intel, sir. Aren't you the one who keeps harping on about gaining all the intel you can?"

Lewis didn't say anything.

The canoe took a bit longer, as the mast and sail had to be removed. Bill first thought they'd have to remove the outrigger, but the Caribou's interior space proved big enough that they were able to load it without doing so. They put it in on a diagonal, so the outrigger, which was against the bulkhead, was a meter or so above the canoe, which rested on the Caribou's deck. The crew made sure it was safely secured.

"Last thing we need is a loose canoe in here," the crew chief said as he tightened the straps.

After everything was loaded in the front of the cargo section of the plane, the human cargo boarded. Web seats had been set up against the bulkheads so that passengers could sit, albeit not very comfortably. That was the problem with being considered supernumerary cargo.

Unlike commercial flights, the Caribou had both seat belts and shoulder harnesses. The only one to not buckle in was little Jack, who was held by his mother. The crew chief visited each passenger, ensuring they were properly buckled in, then worked his way through the spaces left by the canoe, poked his head into the cockpit, and announced that all were secured and they could take off.

The engines were started, and soon they were roaring, a great thundering noise that the three Trekkers hadn't experienced for almost a year.

Conversation in the noisy Caribou wasn't easy. You had to shout to be heard, so there was very little talking during the flight. Despite the noise, Bill took the time and effort to describe to Lewis the situation on Planet 42 regarding sentient life.

The *Corps* recognizes three types of planets. A Class I planet is one that is similar to Earth or Hayek in terms of development by a sentient species, usually a human one. There were sub-classifications ranging from just entering the agriculture revolution to those civilizations whose technology surpassed Earth's. A Class II planet has humans or hominids but hadn't reached beyond the nomadic, tribal, hunter-gatherer stage. Both classes were off limits to exploitation, and settlement. Only Class III planets, those without any sentient beings, were open for discovery.

This edict dated back to the time of the gate's inventor, Dr. Tim Bowman. Bowman didn't want a repeat of 1492 Earth, where European explorers "found" America, leading to the death of approximately ninety percent of its population from imported diseases. He said, "I couldn't live with that on my soul."

When Bill was going through the *Corps'* orientation after finishing Basic Militia Training, he remembered Commandant Lewis saying, "Our primary objective is to survey new parallel planets to ensure that no other humans or hominids exist there before opening them to settlement. That is our number one priority! Anything beyond that is just pure gravy."

Upon hearing Bill's report, Lewis said, "Well, crap. There goes a shitload of money. But if what you say is true, we're gonna have to shut this operation down asap."

"It's true." He pulled a stone point from a pocket and handed it to the Commandant. "We found this near our crash site. We also saw a bunch of hominids, we think they were Neanderthals, at Gibraltar."

Lewis turned the stone point in his hand, clearly recognizing it as a Paleolithic tool.

"Pretty strong evidence," he finally said, closing his hand around the point and leaning back in his seat, as if both relieved of a burden and hit by disappointment.

Return

Had the Trekkers tried to continue their journey up the Missouri, then up the Clark Fork, and finally down the Snake and Columbia Rivers (Bill still thought of them in Earth terms), it would have taken three or more months. And that was if the snow was cleared from the passes in the numerous mountain ranges they would have had to cross. Bill had experienced a small avalanche while skiing at Washington State's Crystal Mountain Resort once while going to school at the University of Washington. It wasn't something he wanted to ever repeat, so he was glad to be flying over the snow-capped mountains, rather than trying to wend his way through them on foot.

As it was, the Caribou got them to the IP in less than two days. Total flying time was six hours, but the late start from their encampment meant they had to stop for the night en route. One simply does not try to land a plane in the dark on a supposedly uninhabited planet with little to no rescue services. They spent one night at a forward base in what Bill knew as Montana.

It was strange being hailed as heroes, despite the fact that all they had done was survive. Even stranger was the hot shower with unlimited water. Bill and the others had been using their portable hand-held showers that fit on their canteens for so long, they had almost forgotten what it was like to have more than a liter for a shower. Bill spent an eternity under the solar-heated water, rubbing off several months' worth of grime. Of course, the dirt ground into his fingertip whorls wouldn't come out for months, so he didn't even bother to try and remove it. Nor the dirt under his fingernails.

Finally, Bill stopped the flow of water, grabbed the towel, and wiped himself dry. It was a far cry from what they had been doing while trekking. The feeling of actually being clean, not just not stinky, was wondrous. Then he got dressed in newer clothes. They weren't exactly new; they belonged to one of the base occupants who gave them up so that Bill wouldn't have to stay in the ragged, remnants of his uniform. It was strange putting on new clothes. They felt stiff, and the scent of the laundry detergent tickled his nose.

Dried and dressed, Bill went to the rec room, where his newly cleaned bride and son waited for him. Bill had taken over parental duties so Meri could wash up first. He wasn't totally clueless.

The airfield was set up in the usual *Corps* fashion. There was a small control tower, an operations building with a combination mess hall and recreation room, a shower, and crew quarters. In the rec room, Meri, Jack, and Jack Lewis were sitting in a corner. Little Jack was in Big Jack's lap, held in a protective grandparent bear hug.

Meri, red hair still wet from her shower, was sipping on a drink, clearly one of the daily tots the *Corps* provided to Explorers in the field. Along with coffee, that was one of the things about civilization that Bill had missed. *Well, that and showers. And cooked meals. And clean sheets.* He stopped that train of thought.

As Bill joined them, Lewis asked, "What's your poison?"

He thought for a second. "I'm not sure. I'd like a beer, but I also wouldn't turn down a whiskey." Even though he was still in his early twenties, Bill had developed a taste for whiskey on his first survey. The *Corps* only issued a single tot to each Explorer for each evening, so he had to make up his mind between the two. Beer or whiskey?

Handing little Jack back to Meri, Lewis got up and said, "Allow me," gesturing for Bill to take the seat near his.

"But I haven't decided," Bill said.

"That's okay. Sit," the commandant commanded.

Bill sat.

Within minutes, Lewis was back with a canteen cup and a small shot glass, handing both to Bill. "Here, you deserve it."

The cup contained beer, one made by mixing local water with a beer concentrate. The shot glass contained whiskey.

"Thanks!" Bill took a sip of the beer first. The first sip led to a second, and the second led to a deep draught. Bill let out a sigh. "Man, that tastes good."

Meri giggled, holding up her cup to toast with him. Bill then noticed that an empty shot glass was on the table next to her.

Lewis sat down, once again taking Jack from Meri. Jack, sound asleep, didn't even acknowledge the hand-off.

The small group was shortly joined by the area commander, Dave Cheng. Bill and Meri had worked under him on Zion when he was the area commander for the Caribbean surveys. The native Californian of Hmong descent raised his glass to the couple. Briefly overcome with emotion, it took him a minute to say, "Damn glad you're here."

"Us, too," Meri said.

"Well, supper's almost ready. You guys hungry?"

"Starved," said Bill.

"Just as long as it's not bear or bison stew, I am," Meri added.

After drinks and a supper that consisted of a lot of potatoes and vegetables with spices that made them drool as the scent filled their nostrils, and what seemed like several hours telling the tale of their trek, the Trekkers were shown to their sleeping quarters. These were typical *Corps* field operations: four walls, a roof, and posts to string hammocks from. On the posts were adjustable LED lights so one could read while lying down, and a single outlet for charging electrical devices. There was also a small table with four folding chairs. A light was above the table. All the electricity came from solar panels on the roof, or if there was a creek or river nearby, a small water-powered turbine. Bill and Meri had stayed in similar quarters on their first parallel planet survey on Zion.

Their packs had been brought into the cabin, but they were still wearing the required survival equipment, and each had their personal rifle.

Bill and Meri looked around the spartan quarters, then at each other.

"You want to sleep in a hammock tonight?" Bill asked her.

She shook her head.

Turning back to Jordan, he asked, "Any way we can get some things off the 'bou?"

"Sure," Jordan said. "What you need?"

"A bunch of bison skins. We got kinda used to sleeping on them, and I somehow don't think Jack would be too interested in trying out a hammock yet."

"Let's go," Jordan replied.

It was dark outside, a bad time to be out on a strange planet, especially since some of the larger predators were nocturnal, so the two men took some time standing outside the door, letting their eyes adjust.

The trip out to the Caribou and back took only a few minutes, and nothing appeared out of the darkness to bother them. That didn't mean nothing was out there. In the distance, Bill could hear wolves howling on one side of camp, and coyotes on the other.

Bill and Meri spread out blankets for themselves and Jack while Karen spread out some for herself. Meanwhile, Jordan held on to Jack. It was obvious from the way he held the infant that he was more scared of dropping him than he had been of going out into a predator infested wilderness in the dark. He was clearly relieved when Meri took Jack back.

"See you guys in the morning," Jordan said.

It wasn't as hard to fall asleep as Bill had thought it would be. Despite the sheer excitement of being rescued, it had still been a long day. Combined with the great meal, and then more alcohol in one sitting than he'd had in a year, that was a recipe for lethargy. Realizing that nobody needed to stand watch and that when it came to midnight feedings, there wasn't much he could do to help, he said goodnight to his family, kissing each in turn, then collapsed between two bison blankets.

Bill awoke just before dawn. Through one of the cabin's windows, he could see the sky turning a lighter shade, the bottoms of the clouds turning pink with dawn's early light. *Evidence of Rayleigh scattering*, he thought, as the sun's rays penetrated more of the atmosphere than they would when directly overhead. The shorter wavelength of the blue light scattered, leaving the longer wavelength of red to strike the clouds.

Bill rolled out of their makeshift bed, then got up and noticed that the cabin was considerably cooler than it had been the night before. He then saw what he had missed the night before: a small woodburning stove in one of the corners. He quietly made his way over to it and re-stoked the almost dead fire.

Soon, the fire was warming up the cabin. Bill decided to take the opportunity to get some coffee, so he got dressed and grabbed his rifle. The others were still asleep, so Bill made his way back to the operations building, which also served as the mess hall.

He wasn't surprised to see people already there, enjoying coffee, tea, breakfast, or all three. The cooks noticed him enter and one yelled across the room, "Take a seat anywhere. I'll bring it to you!"

Bill nodded his thanks and joined Jordan and Ken Schmitt. Both had cups of coffee and plates of food before them. Bill could only stare. He hadn't seen eggs or bacon for as long as he could remember. And maple syrup-covered flapjacks? Fuggedaboudit!

In just a few seconds, a similar platter, along with a steaming hot cup of coffee, was placed before him. Bill thanked the cook, then automatically went for the spork stashed in his shirt pocket. He didn't even notice what he was doing until Jordan said, "What, you don't like our knives and forks?"

Bill blushed while laughter erupted around him. One of the older Explorers joined them at the table, telling Bill, "Don't sweat it. Happens to every Trekker. Give it a couple more days and you'll remember what civilization's like."

Rather than spending a lot of time talking, Bill ate quickly. He told the others he wanted to bring Meri some coffee, juice, and food because he was sure a certain son of his would be taking up a chunk of her time in the morning. Those Explorers who were parents nodded in understanding.

He cleared his empty plate and utensils and got a tray to carry food and coffee back to the cabin, making sure he had a second cup for himself on the tray.

Needless to say, Meri was not only awake but quite pleased to see the tray of food Bill brought her. And as Bill had suspected, a certain young infant-turned-limpet was latched onto mom, have breakfast first. Karen was already gone, probably in the latrine.

Bill set the tray down beside Meri, and handed her a fork, saying, "They have this weird utensil here. Sorta like a spork, but with longer tines."

Meri laughed. Growing up in the *Corps*, she immediately understood. "Yeah, it's going to take a bit before we become civilized again." She forked some of the scrambled eggs into her mouth.

Bill sat quietly, sipping his coffee, as his wife and son continued with their breakfast. Meri seemed to take exquisite joy in drinking her orange juice. And like Bill, she appeared to find the bacon to be like ambrosia.

After breakfast, Bill offered to take the tray back to the rec room/mess hall, mainly because he detected a certain odor emanating from a certain infant.

"You're just trying to get out of diaper duty," Meri said.

"Won't deny it. When we get back to civilization where there're real diapers and diaper wipes, then I'll be glad to help out. Well, not really glad, but more likely? But skins and moss or grass? Yuck!"

"Get out of here and let a real woman show you what it takes," Meri said, laughing. "We'll join you in the rec room shortly."

Bill returned to the rec room and found almost the entire base assembled. Some were still eating, but most had finished and were sitting or standing around. It was a mixed group of men and women, and even more ethnically mixed, running the gamut across the human spectrum. Bill recognized a few Explorers from his survey time on Zion and nodded to them, getting nods of greeting back in return. He also saw Karen sitting at one of the tables enjoying her first civilized breakfast. Seeing him, she smiled and gave a thumbs-up, then held up her spork.

"Commandant said he wanted an all-hands meeting," Jordan said when Bill joined him after depositing his tray.

Bill suspected he knew what the Commandant was going to say, but he kept his mouth shut. *I could be wrong, so why say anything?*

When Meri entered with Jack, a murmur went up around the room. Meri just smiled and waved, making her way over to Bill. One of the sitting Explorers got up, offering the new mom a place to sit. Meri thanked him and sat down.

"What's happening?" she asked.

"Appears your dad called an all-hands meeting." Turning to Jordan, he asked, "Any idea when this meeting starts?"

Before Jordan could answer, the door opened, and in walked Lewis and the area commander. Cheng's look was anything but inscrutable. Bill could tell he was definitely not a happy camper.

"Listen up," Lewis said, looking around at the quickly quieting crowd. "Effective immediately, we're shutting this planet down."

As the room erupted in shouts of dismay and murmurs from the veteran Explorers, Lewis raised his hands. "What's the primary objective of the *Corps of Discovery*?" he asked.

"Exploration!" said one man.

The rest became thoughtful, and it didn't take long before somebody ventured the answer, sounding as if she was quoting from a text, which she was. "The *Corps of Discovery's* primary purpose is to survey new parallel planets to ensure that no other humans or hominids exist there before opening them to settlement."

Lewis nodded. "Exactly! And that's why we're shutting this planet down. We've upgraded it from Class III to Class II, thanks to information and evidence provided by Bill Clark, Meri Lewis — I mean, Meri Clark — and Karen Wilson. They not only found Neolithic tools in Eurasia but actually saw tool-bearing, cloth-wearing hominids that resembled Neanderthals before sailing through the Strait of Gibraltar. It doesn't look like humans have made it to this side of the ocean, but we're not taking any chances.

"Luckily, this survey was just getting started, so we don't have too much to clean out. But, I want everyone chipping in to remove all manufactured artifacts and get things back to the IP, and then to Hayek. Once all artifacts are gone, those of you who are pyromaniacs get your chance. I want every base burned to the ground. Not much we can do about the runways other than spread some grass seed on them. Nature will take its course and wipe them out in a few years. And, I'm betting that's probably decades or centuries before those Eurasian hominids make their way to this continent."

Looking around the now-quiet room, Lewis asked, "Any questions?"

"When do we start?" Cheng asked.

"Immediately. As soon as that plane out there deposits our Trekkers at the IP, the pilot will be notifying the IP commander to start the evac process. I expect we'll have some birds landing by mid-afternoon, so be ready by then.

"I know it's going to take some time to pull out all the infrastructure, like the solar panels, wiring, et cetera, but the sooner you can load up your personal gear, the sooner you can help strip this place."

"All right people, let's get cracking," Chen announced in his booming Marine Corps voice. Bill remembered first meeting Cheng, and hearing the phrase, "once a Marine, always a Marine." Cheng was proud of his service in the U.S. Marine Corps but was also proud of his service in the *Corps of Discovery*.

As the room emptied, Bill heard Cheng mutter, "Good thing we didn't have to deal with any boats."

Lewis gestured the three Trekkers over.

"I don't want you guys doing anything except getting your gear together. We need that plane back here immediately, so once you're packed and ready, we're out of here."

Bill and Karen nodded, while Meri held out Jack and said, "It'll go a lot faster if somebody'll watch this little guy."

Lewis took little Jack, saying to him, "Your mom fights dirty."

"Gee, I wonder where I got it from," Meri said as she headed out the door.

In less than fifteen minutes, the three Trekkers, along with Jack and Commandant Lewis, were at the rear of the Caribou, watching as Brad Maeda and his co-pilot did a pre-flight inspection. The crew chief was present, but his assistant wasn't.

Watching the two of them brought back memories of Bill and "The Colonel" doing the same thing. Fourteen-year-old Bill learned to fly on an old single-engine Cessna. Every flight started with a checklist that Bill had to follow religiously. "If you don't have the checklist, you might forget something. And if you forget something, you might die. Never pre-flight without a checklist," "The Colonel" would tell him.

Soon the pre-flight was completed, and everyone boarded through the passenger door at the rear on the pilot's side. Once the door was shut, the engines started, and the crew chief made sure everyone was properly strapped in.

"Where's the assistant crew chief?" Bill asked, over the roar of the engines.

"Helping break down the base. Don't really need him on this flight, so why waste the gas carrying his lazy ass home?" the crew chief said with a grin.

Only minutes after they boarded, they were given permission to take off. Brad turned the plane into the wind, gunned the engines, and soon the plane was rumbling down the steel-planked runway. Within fifteen minutes the plane reached its cruising altitude. The passengers were told they could unbuckle, and if necessary, use the small toilet. That would require them making their way over, under, and around the canoe, though. The crew chief warned them that they might experience turbulence, so staying buckled in was the best course of action.

As the plane roared along, conversation wasn't too practical, but it turned out that drinking coffee was. The crew chief brewed up a pot in the small galley (really, just a one-burner electric hotpad and an electric drip coffee machine) and passed around the brew. Bill took his black with sugar. He still couldn't get over how sweet sugar was. The only sugar he'd had for the past nine months was mainly from fruits and berries they harvested along the way. Even the pemmican they made, which contained fruits and berries, wasn't as sweet as the single spoonful of sugar he dumped in his coffee.

The flight lasted almost two hours. Meri, Bill, and Lewis spent the time passing Jack around until he fell asleep from the airplane's drone. Bill was ever grateful that the infant hadn't had ear problems on take-off. He remembered some of the flights he had been on where a child screamed practically the whole way. At the time he had thought, *Why don't those stupid parents shut that stupid kid up?* Thinking about that made him uncomfortable, especially now, realizing that how kids react isn't always in control of the parents.

Soon after Jack fell asleep, the crew chief came around and told them that they were approaching the IP, and checked to make sure everyone was properly strapped in. Then he said a few words over the small microphone attached to his earphone headset, reporting to the pilot.

Bill could feel the plane's angle change as it descended toward the ground. Turning around in his seat, he looked out the small portal at the imposing figure of Mt. Rainier. *Mt. Tahoma, damnit. I'm on Hayek, not Earth. Well, almost on Hayek.* He glanced over at Meri and Karen, who were also staring out the windows. Meri's eyes were clearly wet, but Bill could see tears streaming down Karen's face. *I'm glad she made it,* he thought. *Damn close, though.*

As the plane landed with a bounce and a chirping of wheels on the pierced steel planking runway, Jack woke up. Still too small to do anything physical, he seemed to look around and then yawn.

"Almost home, little guy," Bill said, even though he knew the infant couldn't hear him over the roar of the reversing engines.

Soon the plane pulled up to the operations building, the propellers wound down, and everyone unstrapped from their seats. Brad came out of the cockpit. "Quite the crowd out there."

He turned to Karen. "Ms. Wilson, would you mind departing first? There's a couple of young men out there waiting for you."

For a second, Karen had a deer in the headlights look. Then, turning to Meri, she asked, "How do I look?" while simultaneously trying to straighten her uniform and brush her hair from her face.

"You look fine. Now get out there."

The crew chief opened the door, dropped the small steps, then stepped aside, gesturing for Karen to exit first.

Slinging her pack on her back, and grabbing her rifle, which she slung over her shoulder, she tentatively made her way to the door. She stood there for a second, then stepped out and down into the bright sunshine.

Bill could see her descend the few steps to the ground, then heard her squeal with pleasure. He finally got his first glimps of Tran, Karen's husband, and their son, Jeff, through the open door as the two rushed toward Karen. Tran, a man of Vietnamese descent, embraced her in a hug, literally lifting her off the ground as she wrapped her arms around his neck. Bill thought that quite a feat, as Tran was several inches shorter than Karen.

As Bill and Meri collected their equipment and rifles and made their way to the door with Jack, Bill saw Karen crouching down in a squat and looking at Jeff. When they had last seen each other, Jeff was two. Now he was three and had lived a third of his life without his mother. Bill wondered if he remembered.

Karen must have said something that tickled his memory, for the young toddler suddenly reached out and wrapped his little arms around his mother's neck. Karen mirrored him, hugging the young boy. Bill could see tears streaming down Tran's face.

Meri exited the Caribou next, holding Jack. Bill could hear people cheering, but didn't see them until he finally stepped through the small door.

All personnel from the base were present, and a sign had been erected that read, "Welcome Home Trekkers." For a man used to being around only three other people, it was quite overwhelming. He started to step back into the plane, but felt the pressure of Lewis's hand on his shoulder.

"You'll be fine," Lewis said. It was clear to Bill he understood.

Bill finally made his way down the small steps. Looking over at Karen, he was glad to see her finally smiling. *About time*, he thought. She had been through a lot, and Bill was glad to see it was finally over for her. He doubted she would be applying for field duty any time soon.

The Field Manager, the young Asian admin type who had

welcomed Bill to Zion on his first survey, approached Lewis. "We're scheduled to open the gate in an hour. I presume you'll want to get the Trekkers through immediately."

Lewis nodded at her. "Yeah, the rest of it can wait. How's the evac going?"

She glanced down at her tablet for a second. "Pretty good. We only had a handful of bases operational, and they've all been notified. Each has their own 'bou, so it shouldn't take more than twenty-four hours to evac and get everyone here."

As she was saying that, Bill could hear the hydraulics of the cargo doors of the Caribou whining. Turning around, he saw the rear ramp drop, then several men entered the rear of the plane.

Then, a deep southern drawl said, "Well, look at what the cat dragged in." Actually, that was Bill's interpretation; what he heard was "Wail, looky what the cat dun drug in."

Turning to the voice, he saw his former roommate, Matt Green, with a wide grin on his face. Meri gave him a one-armed hug, then Matt approached Bill, who reached out his hand. Matt bypassed the hand and gave Bill a bro hug. "Welcome home, dude."

Bill couldn't say anything. Once more, his throat had constricted and the lump wouldn't let him talk.

Eventually, the two friends let go of each other, and Bill found he could speak again. "Hey, I hear you're engaged.

"Damn skippy. Been waiting for my best man to show up so I can make it official," Matt said, grinning.

"Well, I'm here. So, when's the date?"

"Good question, we'll have to ask Nicole when we cross over."

"She's not here?" Meri asked, surprised.

"She was, but she managed to break a tooth last week. Slipped coming out of the cockpit and smashed her mouth against a bulkhead. Broke the tooth and needed stitches for her upper lip."

"Ouch," Bill said as Meri visibly winced.

"She going to be all right?" Meri asked.

"Yeah, but they couldn't save the tooth, it was so damaged, so the oral surgeon's gonna do an implant."

Bill wasn't familiar with the process so decided to keep his mouth shut until he learned more.

By this time, the three Clarks were surrounded by well-wishers, patting them on the back and saying "Welcome home," or words to that effect. It was a bit overwhelming for them, and seeing their increased agitation, Commandant Lewis yelled to the crowd, "Hey. Little room here. Give the Trekkers some space. Ain't you got any manners?"

The crowd laughed but parted. Some understood what the Trekkers were going through, having been there, done that. Others, out of just plain respect.

Soon the attention of the crowed turned to the rear of the Caribou where the canoe was emerging from. Once it was fully out of the plane, one of the men went back into the aircraft and retrieved the mast and sail. Bringing it out, he attached it to the canoe, showing the Trekker's small water vessel in its full glory.

As promised, within the hour the gate opened, and the Trekkers, along with their canoe (carried by other Explorers) and the Commandant, crossed back into Hayek. Immediately after they crossed over, a caravan of trucks crossed into Planet 42.

"Going to help evacuate," Lewis explained, as the gate shut down, leaving them on the tarmac of Bowman Field on Hayek.

Trekker

PART FOUR

HAYEK

Trekker

Homecoming

After passing through the gate, the Trekkers were once again subjected to a large crowd, with banners saying "Welcome Home Trekkers" and "Welcome back Meri," among others. It seemed as if the entire population of Sacagawea Base was present. It wasn't just the Explorers, but their families, too. Thousands packed the small airfield.

Probably most important to the families was to see Explorers making it home after being lost off-world for so long. Their husbands and wives were doing the same thing; seeing proof that one could survive such a trek brought them hope for their own loved ones.

There was a small stand set up near the gate, clearly for a bout of public speaking. Bill knew he wasn't up to the task. *Hell, I almost failed Public Speaking in high school I was so afraid to talk.* Fortunately, it appeared he didn't have to.

Commandant Lewis climbed the few steps up to the platform and approached the microphone. The cheering crowd finally started to quiet.

"I want to thank all of you who showed up today. It means a lot to our three Trekkers right now," he paused for a second, "I mean, our four Trekkers. Can't forget my grandson," he added with a smile.

"Anyhow, I'm sure most of you are aware of just how difficult it is for someone who's been on a trek to re-assimilate back into society. And, I've got to say, I don't recall any other time when the time or distance on a trek was as long as these three Explorers experienced. Keeping that in mind, I'm sure they'd appreciate it if you gave them a little space for the next couple of days.

"Once they're civilized, we'll bring them back for a proper introduction," he said with a chuckle. The crowd reciprocated with their own chuckles and soft laughter.

Turning a little somber, he then said, "And we'll also be having a memorial service for the Explorer who didn't return, Ben Weaver. The time and place will be announced in *The Explorer* and via the various news outlets and user lists."

Looking over at Bill, Lewis asked, "Anything you want to add?"

Bill started to shake his head but then felt a nudge in his ribs. Meri nodded and gestured to the podium. Bill's eyes went wide with fright. His wife nodded again, saying, "They deserve to hear from us."

Bill reluctantly climbed the podium.

"And don't show any fear," he heard Meri say on his way up the steps.

Yeah, right, he thought as he stepped onto the podium platform.

As he approached the microphone, he didn't quite know what to say.

"Hi," he started off, too a ripple of laughter.

"I'm not really good at public speaking," he began, "but I just wanted to say thanks to all those who stood by, waiting for us, and especially those who rescued us."

He paused for a moment to collect his thoughts, then resumed. "I'm glad we're here. But one of us is missing. If you don't mind, I'd appreciate it if you took a moment to honor our friend and fellow Explorer, Ben. Ben, along with my wife, Meri, saved our lives. Our plane was sabotaged, and if it hadn't been for his flying skills, we would have crashed and died. Instead, he put us down in one piece. We lost Ben shortly after crossing the Atlantic. Please, let's give Ben a moment of silence."

Bill bowed his head. He wasn't particularly religious, but he did believe in honoring those who deserved it.

After about thirty seconds, Bill spoke once more. "Thank you. Ben would have appreciated this."

Bill could feel his eyes smarting, and wiped them with his hand.

"Thank you," he said again, leaving the podium and descending to the safety of his wife.

After the little ceremony, Bill joined the others at a couple of jeeps waiting to transport the Trekkers home. Karen came over to Bill and Meri, gave each of them a hug, and said, "Thanks. I owe you two, big time."

"Yeah, well, I think it's mutual," Bill replied.

Meri nodded in agreement. "Forget about us. Go spend time with the fam. You've spent enough time with us." Karen smiled, turned, and headed off to rejoin her husband and son.

Lewis ushered them over to one of the jeeps and into the back of while he climbed into the passenger seat. Bill and Meri tossed their packs on the floorboards. He and Meri still held onto their rifles, as befitted Explorers, and were still wearing their survival vests and belts. As the driver started the vehicle, Lewis informed the young couple that they would be staying with him until things straightened out.

"Your apartment was given to another couple a month or so

after you were reported missing," he said. "The *Corps* actually brought all your personal stuff over to me." He turned back toward the front of the jeep, obviously lost in thought. Bill could only imagine what was going through his mind, thinking about his only child lost on an unexplored planet, thousands of miles away, and nothing he could do to facilitate a rescue.

Turning back to the couple, he said, "It's all still boxed up. I wasn't sure what to do with it." It was obvious he struggled with that memory.

Meri smiled, leaned forward, and gave her dad a peck on the cheek. "We'll figure it out. Besides, it shouldn't take more than a day for us to get another apartment."

"Nonsense," Lewis said. "Just stay with me for a bit. There's no rush, and the Commandant's quarters are big enough for all of us, as you well know."

Bill wasn't sure how that would work out, but if it was something Meri wanted, he wasn't about to argue.

They pulled up in front of the Commandant's quarters. The building was similar to the board and batten cabin that Bill had lived in while going through training. Of course, befitting his position as Commandant of the *Corps*, this building was bigger than the cabin on Jaskey Lane, about twice as big.

Lewis hopped out of the front seat. "Here. Hand me a pack or two."

Bill grabbed the pack in front of him and handed it over to Lewis. It wasn't as heavy as it had been. There was no food and a lot less ammunition than when they started.

Meri climbed out of the other side of the jeep holding on to Jack and her rifle. Bill grabbed her pack and got out.

The driver offered to carry equipment up to the house, but Lewis told him not to bother. "Not a whole lot to carry."

The driver nodded, then shook Bill and Meri's hands. "A real honor. Welcome home." Then he hopped back into his jeep and sped away.

Bill still wasn't used to the whole hero-worship thing. As far as he was concerned, they were just lucky. *Hell, if it hadn't been for Ben and Meri getting us down, Karen leading us across most of the planet, and Meri's survival skills, we wouldn't be alive. What the fuck did I contribute?*

Meri opened the front door and stepped in like she owned the place. In a way, she did. She had spent a number of years living there when Lewis first became Commandant, not moving out until she joined the *Corps* and started training. She even lived there while attending Hayek University in nearby Milton, the capital of Hayek.

Lewis followed her, then Bill closed the door and set Meri's pack down next to his, which Lewis had deposited on the foyer floor.

Meri had stopped and was slowly turning in a circle, looking around at the familiar settings. Bill had been to the Commandant's Quarters on several occasions.

"So, I'm thinking the guest room might be better for you three," Lewis said.

"Yeah, I don't think my old bedroom would really work," Meri said with a grin. "Kinda small." Bouncing Jack in her arms, she said to him, "So, wanna check out the new digs? You know, you're lucky. Grandpa wouldn't let me go in there when I was a kid, but here you are, about to stay there." Jack just drooled.

"I'm not saying you were a holy terror," Lewis said, "but, you were. Couldn't let you go in anywhere civilized."

Meri stuck her tongue out at him.

"C'mon," she said to Bill.

Bill grabbed both packs and followed Meri down the hall, past a set of stairs, and turned right into a room big enough to be called a suite. They entered a sitting room first, where Bill plopped the packs down on the floor.

Off to one side was a bedroom, and he could see a bathroom attached to it. Large windows allowed Hayek's sunshine to enter, creating a warm environment.

Meri went into the bedroom, then came back, handed Jack to Bill, and gave her dad a hug.

"Where did you get the crib?" she asked.

"The attic," was his response.

"Is that my old crib?"

"Yep. Once I found out that the sole infant on the trek was yours, I radioed ahead and had Janice Goodland dig it out for you. That okay?"

"Yes. Most definitely, yes."

Bill went in and saw the crib. Next to it was a changing table, and under it was a stack of cloth diapers. "Hey, real diapers."

Meri came back in with a great big smile plastered across her face. "Great. That means I'm no longer the lone diaper changer." Turning to Bill, she said, "Guess what?"

"Don't need to guess. Already know what you're gonna say. Okay, show me what I need to know before he has another blowout."

Before Meri could do so, the doorbell rang. Lewis said, "Excuse me," and left the two alone in the small quarters with Jack.

Bill found a small bar and had decided to fix a drink. He opened the cabinet. "Hey," he called, "there's some Irish Mist here. Want a glass?"

"You sure you're willing to share?" Meri asked, laughing. Ever since their first survey, where the traditional bottle was opened upon returning to base, Bill had become hooked on the whiskey and honey mead liqueur.

"Why not? I'm not paying for it."

He filled two glasses. Before he could hand one to Meri, her father appeared at the door to their quarters. "Bill, there's a visitor for you."

Lewis stepped aside and in strode an older version of Bill, one with salt and pepper hair and a practically white goatee.

It took a second for Bill to realize he was looking at his father, "The Colonel."

"Dad?" he asked, handing both glasses of Irish Mist to Meri without conscious thought.

"Bill." His father came over and shook Bill's hand. Bill stared at him, stunned.

Letting go, his father stepped back. "Damn, it's good to see you, son. Look at you! You look like a man, now!"

Bill felt uncomfortable. Perhaps it was because he *was* a man, proven in the wilds of Zion and Planet 42; perhaps it was because his father was saying that in front of his wife; or maybe it was because, in all his life, his father had never praised him nor shown him any affection, especially after his mother had died when Bill was six. Bill was still in shock just seeing his father, whom he had last seen on Earth just before joining the *Corps*.

Confused, he asked, "Dad, what are you doing here? I didn't think the Hayek government let military officers come to Hayek."

"They don't," "The Colonel" said. "But, they don't stop civilians from crossing over. I retired shortly after Jack," he gestured to Jack Lewis, "told me that you were MIA and presumed dead. On top of losing your mom, that pretty much took the wind out of my sails, so I retired and decided to migrate. I would've been here earlier, but I wasn't near a phone or the internet for the past couple of days."

"Sorry I didn't tell you beforehand, Bill," Lewis said. "I wasn't sure where your dad was and wanted to surprise you."

"Well, that you did," Bill said.

"Crap, where are my manners? Dad, I'd like you to meet my wife, Meri. Meri, my dad, David."

Meri went up to Bill's dad, placed her hands on his shoulders, leaned in and gave him a peck on the cheek. "Glad to finally meet you, sir. You raised one hell of a son."

"Yep, I think so, too," "The Colonel" agreed.

"Oh, yeah, and this is our son, your grandson," Bill continued, turning just enough that Dave could see Jack's face. "Jack, meet your grandfather. Dad, meet your grandson, Jonathan David Clark."

The next couple of days were mainly spent relaxing in the Commandant's quarters, with occasional forays into the wilds of civilization. It didn't take too long to get used to people and modern amenities again. To Bill's surprise, he found the hardest thing about adjusting to being back on Hayek was not having to carry his rifle all the time. That and not having to be on full alert with full situational awareness.

Both grandfathers spent as much time with them, and Jack, as possible. Bill's dad had more free time, so he was around more than Meri's dad, who still had to run the *Corps*.

On the third day back, Bill, Meri, and Karen began the process of debriefing. The three presented themselves at a small room in the terminal at Bowman Field, wearing their uniforms. Above the left chest pocket were ribbons indicating the medals they had been awarded before their final survey. Bill and Meri each had a single ribbon representing a Survey Medal, indicating that they had completed a survey. Karen had the same, but hers also had three small metal pine cones on it, indicating that she had been on fifteen surveys. Each pine cone meant that the Explorer had been on five surveys. An acorn would have indicated a single survey. Karen also wore a Purple Heart ribbon, meaning that she had been injured in the line of duty during a past survey.

For what seemed like days on end, the three would meet with a panel of veteran Explorers, one of whom was Janice Goodland, the lead instructor of the *Corps'* Survival Training Program. Goodland was quite the character, a survivor of a trek when she was doing surveys. Missing her left arm from just above the elbow, she also had a hideous scar that ran down the left side of her face from the edge of her eye to her jawline. This was partially covered by long, silver-streaked black hair.

The three learned that none of the three Monarchs assigned to survey Planet 42 returned. Their plane, 42/2, was discovered intact; 42/1 wasn't. It was presumed that the crash killed all aboard, though it was possible that the crew parachuted to safety and were currently trekking to the Initial Point. Since the plane had gone down in the Sudanian Savannah, just north of the Guinean forest belt south of the Sahara Desert, the *Corps* still held out hope. The trio was told that with their rescue, the *Corps* was going to do a more thorough search using a Monarch, but if nothing was found in the next couple of weeks they would call it off. "If they're out there," Janice said, "we suspect they're doing the same thing you did, trekking across Ti'icham. In the meantime, we're sending a crew out to recover the plane."

There was no sign of 42/3. The *Corps* had determined that it had possibly gone down somewhere over the South Atlantic. The *Corps* considered the possibility of survivors low to nonexistent.

Sometimes all three would be in interviewed in the same room with the same panel, and sometimes they would individually meet with different panels. The whole purpose was to extract as much information from the three survivors to help future Explorers.

The first topic of discussion was the final flight. The panel focused on two issues. First, why the plane went down; and second, how they managed to safely land, particularly in an area surrounded by mountains.

Meri explained about the EMP bomb, and how it destroyed all their electronics.

"How did you know it was an EMP bomb?" asked a panelist.

"That's all it could've been," Meri said. "What other kind of device could possibly have fried every unprotected electronic device in the plane? All our tablets were fried, too. The only devices not destroyed were the two protected tablets in the Faraday cage."

"Could the electrical damage have come from a natural event, such as a solar flare, a coronal mass ejection, or possibly a sprite?" another panelist asked.

It took Bill a second to remember what a sprite was — an electrically induced luminous plasma that developed above cumulonimbus clouds in the upper atmosphere. If it struck a plane, it could do electrical damage similar to what the Monarch experienced.

"Definitely not," Meri said with authority. "First, any solar flare or CME would have caused some pretty major auroras, and we never saw any during our time in Eurasia, and somebody was on watch at night at all times. As to the sprite, we were above clouds, but nobody reported anything. And besides, a sprite would've only damaged the Monarch's electronics, not our personal tablets."

Bill spoke up. "I have to agree. My tablet was in my cargo pocket, and it got fried."

"So, assuming this EMP bomb exists and did the actual damage, where is it?"

"It should be still at the crash site," Meri answered. "If I recall correctly, once I pulled it out of the plane and showed the others, we just tossed it aside. It's most likely at the spot where we camped."

Pulling up an aerial image of the lake that 42/2 was still floating on, they were asked to identify their campsite.

Bill pointed. "Right here. If anything's left, it's gonna be there."

"Isn't this where you found the artifacts?"

"No, that was on the other side of the lake," Meri said, indicating where she and Ben had found the point.

The discussion then turned back to the "supposed" EMP bomb. Meri was asked why it wasn't found during a pre-flight inspection. She explained that the bomb was actually hidden aboard the plane in an area not likely to have been included in any inspection.

"Do you look in every hanging locker when conducting a pre-flight inspection?" she asked the panelists. They had to agree they didn't, but it looked like that was about to change, much like how the inspection procedure changed after Bill's sabotage experience during flight transition training.

After a lengthy discussion about the EMP bomb, the topic turned to the last flight. Every aspect of it was covered, to the best of the survivors' memories. At one point, Karen pointed out, "Hey, this was almost a year ago. Do you remember everything that happened nine months ago?" Bill was glad to see some of the former spunk emerging from her. *Damn, Karen's back*, he thought.

The takeaway on that part of the discussion was that it appeared Ben had done the best possible job, considering the circumstances.

Attention then turned to the sabotaged parachutes. Bill told the panel that every parachute aboard the plane had been deliberately cut.

"Are you absolutely certain all the parachutes had been

deliberately cut?" a panel member asked. "Even the crash seat 'chutes?"

The three survivors looked at each other, eyebrows raised.

"We don't know. We only salvaged the regular parachutes," Bill answered.

The three panelists looked at each other, obviously thinking the same thing.

As the panel was disbanding for the day, the lead panelist said, "It looks like Ben was the main one responsible for saving all of your lives during that flight. I'll be recommending him for the Honor Medal with Crossed Tusks." This was the highest lifesaving medal, indicating that one risked one's life to save another. The crossed tusks were miniature replicas of mammoth tusks, something that most Explorers got to see firsthand during their many surveys.

He turned to Meri. "I think you deserve it, too, so I'll be recommending one for you. You may not get it, but it's still an honor to be nominated."

Meri blushed, the red of her face almost matching her hair. "I'm honored, but Ben did most of the work."

Bill couldn't contain himself. "As I recall, there were two people who worked together to get us safely on the ground. If he doesn't nominate you, I'm sure Karen will. And I know I will!"

The panelist laughed. "And, there you go."

After days of interviewing (*more like interrogation*, Bill thought), the panels made their recommendations to the Commandant of the *Corps*. Even though the Clarks continued to live under the same roof as the Commandant, he never let on what the panels were saying or thinking.

Bill and Meri decided to take a break and visit the Cave Bear Cave, a beer garden on base that they used to frequent when they were Probies, or Probationary Explorers. Despite the fact that it was early spring, the outdoor patio was open, with propane heaters warming the patrons. Well, warming them enough. Spring east of the Cascades is anything but warm.

Bill had contacted Matt Green before heading over, requesting that he gather up as many of the old crew as possible and meet them there. When the couple arrived, with Jack firmly ensconced in a new front baby carrier, and joined by David Clark, Matt was waiting for them, along with his fiancée, Nicole. Jordan was there as well, along with Kim Brown, one of Bill's original co-aerial surveyors. Both women gave Bill a hug, but it was apparent their attention was focused more on Meri and Jack.

Bill noticed the new scar slicing down Nicole's lower mouth and commented on it.

"Yeah, not fun," she said. "Dr. Benson said it'll be another three months until they'll do the implant, but after that, you won't even be able to tell I lost the tooth."

The evening passed pleasurably, aided by several pitchers of the local home brew. It almost seemed like back when they were all Probies, full of hope and excitement. Now they were veterans. Still full of hope and excitement, but tempered by the reality of the job. All had lost a friend. Some had seen death up close. Most had faced death.

As the evening began to wind down, first Jordan, and then Kim left. "Gotta be up early," Kim said, giving both Meri and Bill a hug goodnight. "I'm really glad you made it. The *Corps* wouldn't be the same without this geographic genius," she said, nodding in Bill's direction.

At one point the group was approached by a man in his mid-twenties in the uniform of the Hayek Defense Force. "Bill?"

Bill looked up and immediately recognized him. "Sergeant

Renard," he said, standing to greet his former militia training sergeant.

"Just plain Pierre, tonight," he said, grasping Bill's hand. "Glad to see you made it back."

"Me, too," Bill laughed.

Bill introduced everyone. "Join us?"

"No, thanks. I just wanted to stop by and say welcome home. Glad you all made it back, especially this little guy," he said, gesturing to Jack.

Giving Bill another handshake, he bid the others goodnight.

Soon, the table was occupied only by the Clarks, Matt, and Nicole.

"So, when's the big date?" Bill asked. As soon as the words were out of his mouth, he felt a sharp rap on his shins. Startled, he looked at his wife. "What?" he asked, confused as to why he warranted a physical assault.

Nicole picked up on the byplay and laughed. "No need to be so cautious. We had planned on getting married once this survey was up, but between losing a tooth and you two showing up, things are a bit discombobulated right now." She turned to Matt. "What do you think?"

"Hell, I'd be happy tying the knot tonight," he responded.

Bill smiled at that. *Classic Matt. Direct, to the point, and completely lacking in tact.*

"Well, mate, let me tell you. No wedding is happening until I replace this tooth," she said.

Bill didn't even notice the missing tooth. But, then again, he wasn't a woman. What the hell did he know?"

"On the bright side," Matt said, "at least I've got my best man back."

Bill awoke early the next morning, feeling slightly hungover. Not the raging headache, dry-mouth, dry heaves, dizzy, blurred vision type, rather the not-feeling-on-top-of-his-game hung over. *Coffee, water, and aspirin. That oughta do it*, he thought, making his way into the living area. There was a carafe of coffee on the table, and Bill helped himself to a cup.

Damn, that tastes good, he thought as he took his first sip. It wasn't until he had quaffed down half the cup before he realized he was alone. *That's weird. I wonder where Meri and Jack are? Man, was I that drunk I didn't hear them leave? Come to think of it, did they get home last night?*

Racking his befuddled brain, Bill concluded that, yes, all three of them had made it back to the Commandant's quarters the night before.

As he sipped on the coffee, Meri came back into the suite from the main house, Jack on her hip.

"It's alive," she said.

"Yeah, barely. Where were you?"

"Talking with Dad. Seems they're planning a ceremony for this afternoon. Part memorial service, part 'honor the survivors' thing. You up to it?"

"I will be. Get enough coffee into me."

"Great. In the meantime, I'm going to take a bath. Can you watch Jack?"

"Yeah, but give me a minute to finish this cup and start another."

Smiling at Bill, she came over and gave him a kiss on the lips. "Doofus."

"Yeah, well, I'm your doofus," he replied.

The afternoon's ceremony was held in the base auditorium. Bill had first been in the building when he was going through Basic Militia Training. This time it was different. Rather than being one of about 250 people in the seats, he was one of a handful on stage.

The auditorium was filled beyond capacity. Had this been Earth, Bill was sure the fire marshal would have shut it down due to overcrowding and the lack of a quick exit. But Earth's rules didn't apply on Hayek. There were even videographers; Lewis had told Meri and Bill that the event was being broadcast live.

A podium with a microphone was center stage.

Christ, I hope they don't expect me to talk again. I'd rather face another Smilodon than that crowd, he thought, looking out over the assembled people.

Soon, Commandant Lewis was standing behind the podium with the Assistant Commandant, Lisa Ragnar, behind him.

"Ladies and gentlemen, thank you for joining us this afternoon. As most of you are aware, we're here to honor four Explorers, one of whom is no longer present.

"Almost a year ago, Hayek and the *Corps of Discovery* was attacked by the Gaia Liberation Force, with the purpose of shutting down the gates. This terrorist action not only killed many of our members but also left some stranded on surveys. Those on secondary surveys were the luckiest. We were able to rapidly reopen the gates and give them the needed support. Unfortunately, we also had a primary survey taking place at the time, with three survey crews out, along with their Initial Point support crew.

"While we were able to connect with the IP support crew fairly rapidly, we weren't so lucky with the survey crews. The sabotage by the GLF also took place on the individual survey crafts, as we have now learned. All three planes went down. Originally, we had presumed that the crews, twelve experienced Explorers, were lost to us.

"Less than a week ago, we were proven wrong, when most of the crew of 42/2 was discovered on the plains of Ti'icham on Planet 42. Unfortunately, one did not survive.

"Today, we honor that lost crew member, Benjamin Weaver. For those who haven't heard, Ben did an amazing bit of piloting, dead-sticking a Monarch safely into an alpine lake on the western edge of the Eurasian Alps. Ben's actions saved the lives of his fellow crew."

Looking down into the front row of the audience, he gestured. "Today we have Ben's parents here. They made the trip from Earth specifically for this ceremony," Lewis said as the older couple made their way up the side steps to the stage.

Spontaneous applause erupted.

Once the couple was next to Lewis, he held up several medals and certificates.

"Mr. and Mrs. Weaver, I'd like to present you with the Honor Medal with Crossed Tusks. This is the highest award the *Corps of Discovery* presents for those who risk their lives to save the life of another.

"You'll see your son's medal comes with three small metal acorns on it. That signifies that he saved the lives of three people at great risk to his own life."

At this point, Lewis bowed his head briefly, and then, looking back up at Mrs. Weaver, said, "One of those lives was that of my own daughter. Words cannot express how much I owe your son. He was a great man."

At that point, Ben's mom broke down and started crying. Bill could tell that Ben's dad was barely holding it in. The auditorium was so quiet Bill could swear he heard the ticking of the digital clock on the wall.

Lewis handed the first medal and certificate to Mr. Weaver.

"It's tradition that anyone who winds up on their own in the wild and has to make their way back to the *Corps* also receives the Survival Journey Medal. We colloquially call it the Trekker Medal. He certainly earned this one."

Again, another medal and certificate were handed to Mr.

Weaver. By this time, Mrs. Weaver had composed herself, but that wasn't to last long.

"Mrs. Weaver, Mr. Weaver. This is the hardest award for me to hand out. The Purple Heart. I wish it wasn't one I needed to give."

As he handed Mr. Weaver the third certificate and medal, a bagpiper at the opposite end of the stage began playing.

It took a couple of seconds before Bill recognized the song, *"Amazing Grace." Fitting,* he thought. Listening to the mournful wailing of the pipes, Bill felt a lump form in his throat. Meri reached over and grasped his hand, holding on tight. Karen, on his other side, did the same. The three suffered silently, along with their partner's parents. Bill's eyes grew wet, but he didn't release his grip on the hands of his companions to wipe away the tears.

Then, as the Weavers were about to return to their seats, Bill did release the hands of the two women. He stood and called to the couple. They stopped and looked at him.

Bill walked to them across the stage. "We've got some of Ben's personal items that we brought home with us with the intent of getting them to you." He reached into his pocket and pulled out a small packet. Handing it over to Ben's mother, he watched as she unwrapped it. Inside was Ben's St. Christopher medal, his *Corps* ID card, the photo of Ben and his parents, and the small gold coin.

She smiled sadly. Looking up at Bill, she said, "Thank you," in a soft voice, almost a whisper, then hugged him. It was obvious that Ben's father wasn't able to speak at that moment. He just nodded his thanks.

Bill then made his way back to his chair and Ben's parents returned to their seats.

Once Bill was seated, Lewis spoke again.

"Ben wasn't the only one on that trek." Turning toward the three seated Trekkers, he gestured to them to stand.

"Allow me to introduce the three Explorers who have made, what is undoubtedly the longest trek in *Corps* history. Ladies and gentlemen, I present to you Survey Commander Karen Wilson, Co-Pilot Meriwether Lewis Clark, and Aerial Survey Specialist William J. Clark."

The auditorium erupted in thunderous applause. It took almost a full minute before Lewis was able to speak again.

Lewis gestured for the three Explorers to join him at the podium.

"As you can imagine, each one has earned the Survival Journey medal, but, upon the recommendation of the review panels, each has also been awarded separate awards.

"Due to their continuous actions against threatening wildlife, each is awarded the Honor Medal. We present this medal to those who save another's life with potential risk to themselves. They each did this on numerous occasions."

In turn, Lewis pinned the medals on each Explorer.

"Karen Wilson is also awarded a second Honor Medal for her actions when a cougar attacked Meri Clark, assisting in killing the cougar. She is also awarded a third Honor Medal for her actions when a short-faced bear broke into their winter cabin and threatened all the occupants. Wilson, along with the Clarks, engaged the threatening bear at close quarters and helped stop its assault."

Lewis pinned the two medals on her chest. Turning to the audience, he said, "It's tradition for Explorers to wear ribbons on their uniforms, indicating the medals they have earned. A second medal is indicated by a small metal acorn that is pinned to the ribbon."

Turning back to the trio, Lewis continued. "Meriwether Lewis Clark is further awarded a second Honor Medal. During the trek, Wilson suffered from appendicitis. Meri, with Bill's assistance, operated on Wilson, performing a successful field appendectomy. Had she not done so, it is doubtful that Wilson would have survived.

"William J. Clark is further awarded a second Honor Medal for his actions in shooting a cougar that had attacked Meri. Without his quick actions, Meri would have undoubtedly been killed."

Turning back to Ragnar, Lewis picked up several more medals.

"While crossing the ocean, the three encountered a hurricane. Meriwether Lewis Clark risked her life to cut a broken mast loose from their outrigger canoe, preventing the canoe from being swamped. During this action, Lewis was twice tossed into the ocean. The quick thinking and actions of both Karen Wilson and William J. Clark, who risked their lives to pull her out of the water, undoubtedly saved her life. For this action, each is awarded the Honor Medal with Crossed Tusks."

For the third time in as many minutes, Lewis pinned medals to the three.

"Meriwether Lewis Clark is awarded a second Honor Medal with Crossed Tusks. At one point, Bill fell into a river and was knocked unconscious. While unconscious, he went over a waterfall. Without hesitation, Meriwether Lewis Clark jumped over the waterfall, putting herself at great risk, and rescued him. Without Meriwether Lewis Clark's quick reaction, it is doubtful he would have survived. William J. Clark is awarded a Purple Heart for injuries sustained in the fall over the waterfall.

"William J. Clark is also awarded a second Honor Medal with Crossed Tusks for his actions in saving Wilson, who was still incapacitated from her appendix surgery, from being trampled by a herd of stampeding mastodons. At great risk to himself, he assisted Wilson in climbing a bluff, practically carrying her.

Without his actions, it is likely Wilson would have been killed.

"William J. Clark is also awarded a third Honor Medal with Crossed Tusks. Near the end of the trek, when the short-faced bear broke into the cabin they had wintered in. Clark, after emptying his rifle into the bear, realized he had no other means of protecting his wife and son, so he threw his body over them, protecting them from the bear. Clark suffered wounds to his back from that attack, and is also awarded a second Purple Heart."

With that, Lewis pinned the final medal onto Bill's uniform.

Glancing down at his chest, Bill thought, *I'm gonna look like a fucking Christmas tree if they keep this up*. He also felt he didn't deserve the medals. *I'll have to take that up with Jack later.*

The ceremony soon wrapped up, and the award recipients were free to continue with their lives. Upon retrieving little Jack from "Aunt" Nicole, Bill and Meri sought out the Weavers. When they found them, Bill was surprised to find Lewis and Janice Goodland talking with them.

Commandant Lewis formally introduced the Clarks to the Weavers. The two couples spent the rest of the afternoon and evening together, with Bill and Meri telling the Weavers about their experiences with Ben.

Bill summed it up at the end of the evening, telling the Weavers, "You did a great job. Ben was a helluva guy, and I'm proud to have known him. If it weren't for him, we wouldn't be alive and our son wouldn't exist. We owe him."

He thought the Weavers left in better shape than they had arrived. When they had come to Hayek, all they knew was that their son was dead. They left knowing he had saved others. Not only that, but another whole generation existed because of his actions. While that would never replace their loss, it at least helped assuage their grief.

Trekker

Return to Planet 42

The day after the combination memorial service and award ceremony, Lewis came into the Clarks' living quarters and asked to speak with Bill. "You can join us," he added to Meri.

As soon as the three were seated, coffee in hand, the Commandant came directly to the point.

"We normally give Trekkers a bit of time off before sending them out again or putting them to work on base, but we need to get those downed birds off that planet immediately. To do that means going to the crash locations and crossing over." He looked at Bill. "You up to the task?"

Bill didn't respond, looking at Meri. She gave a brief, almost imperceptible nod.

"Okay, but why me?"

"Simple. You've been there. You know where things are, at least at your crash site. Plus, you're more experienced than most."

Bill couldn't argue with that. "So, does that mean going through the Bowman Field gate and flying all the way over?" he asked.

Lewis gave an actual belly laugh. "Good God! No! What do you think we are, crazy?"

"Well, the thought did cross my mind," Bill answered.

Lewis shook his head, still chuckling. "No. What we do is go to the nearest location on Hayek and open a portable gate. Saves time and money."

"Portable gate?" Bill asked, confused. "I thought those things ate energy like nobody's business. You know, the whole 'hurry up, we're burning neutrons' thing. How do you get enough energy to open a portable gate?"

Lewis laughed again. "Well, let's just say there's a bit of propaganda going on there. Gates don't take much energy. As a matter of fact, they require less than ten amps of 110 volts. Pretty much like a regular electrical outlet in a standard home. We can open a portable gate using a small gas-powered generator. We do it all the time."

Bill felt even more confused. "Then, why tell people to hurry up and act like it's costing a boatload of energy?"

"Simple. We don't want others knowing our secrets. Can you imagine what would happen if China, Russia, or the U.S. got its hand on the gate's secrets?"

Bill nodded. "I see."

Before heading back to Planet 42, Bill demanded and received a new scope for his old rifle. After mounting it, he spent a day on the rifle range making sure everything operated the way he wanted it to.

Jordan and Matt had also been tasked to help retrieve the downed planes, so Bill made sure the two of them spent as much time on the range as he did. While Jordan had plenty of experience operating in the wilderness amongst the various hungry creatures, Matt spent more time flying over the wilderness. He still had good situational awareness, but the situations one faced at an airfield were substantially less threatening than a biologist would face on a ground survey. The trio spent their time in the live action range, which consisted of moving targets, usually facsimiles of large felines, like Smilodons and lions, coming at them.

Just two days after being told of their task, the three Explorers were prepped and ready. Bill had spent most of a morning replacing his worn-out survival gear. The only things he decided to take with him from his original equipment were his rifle, the PDW, his sheath knife, and his canteens and cups. Everything else was brand new, even the ammunition. When asked about the replacement cost, he was told by the logistics staff that since he was replacing equipment that had been either lost, damaged, or worn out due to a trek, he wasn't financially responsible for it.

"We make people pay for doing stupid stuff, like losing it while drunk, or tossing it away 'cause they think it's too heavy to carry. If anything, you guys tried to bring back everything you could, so good on you."

After reporting to the Commandant's office the morning of departure, the three Explorers were given an itinerary and written orders, which had also been e-mailed to all those who were to provide them assistance with their task.

"Bill, I know you're fairly young, but I'm putting you in charge of this as survey leader," Lewis said.
"What you say goes. Listen to others, but the final decision is up to you."

The trio would make their way to the east coast of Ti'icham in one of the supersonic trains that operated in evacuated tubes, known as E-tubes. From there, they would catch a flight to Eurasia, landing at the port city of Jongen, at the mouth of the Rhine River, then a magnetic levitation train to Guerin, a small city, at the confluence of the Isère and the Rhône Rivers.

"Your old stomping grounds," Lewis said. "From there, you'll take a 415 to the lake with everything you need to recover the Monarch." The CL-415, was a seaplane used by the *Corps* for secondary surveys, and one that Bill was intimately familiar with, having served on one on his first survey. "In case you're wondering why we're not picking you up in Jongen, it's because it costs less to use mass transit, and is probably faster.

"Your job, once the operators open the gate, is to get that bird out fast, with as little impact as possible. We need that EMP bomb and the crash seat parachutes for evidence, so try to recover them, if you can. If you do find the bomb, be sure to put gloves on before handling it. There might not be any fingerprints left after being exposed to the elements for so long, but you never know.

"As to the extraction, you'll probably have to clear some land on this side of the gate to get both birds through. That area isn't heavily settled, and we don't operate gates in water. The operators tell me it's something about water and electricity not being a good combo. Who knew?" Lewis joked.

"Anyhow, once you've recovered the Monarch, you'll continue on with the 415, gate, and crew, and get the second bird. We've already dispatched an engineering unit to build a small field for you, so that should be a much easier retrieval. After you've recovered what's left of the plane, I want you to take some time and scout the area for any evidence of survivors. I don't want to shut a gate if there are. If not, we'll see about recovering the bodies.

"Once you've finished there, I want you to come back to Milton. I'll send another team out to recover the catamaran you used to cross the ocean. Along with our need to sanitize the planet, I think that'll make a great addition to the museum.

"Any questions?"

"Yeah," Bill said. "What do we do with 42/2 once we recover it?"

"Leave it there. We'll send out a crew to see what can be done to make it airworthy again." Lewis glanced around the group. "Everyone packed and ready?"

The three young men nodded.

"Good. Your E-tube leaves at noon. Make sure you're on it."

Lewis stood up, extended his hand to each of them. "Stay safe out there," he said, the standard *Corps* way of saying farewell to another Explorer.

As the three left the Commandant's office, they walked past his personal assistant/receptionist, an older woman, disabled from an injury she sustained on a survey years ago. She hadn't been there when they arrived.

"Hi Glenda," Bill said, stopping briefly.

"Bill, so good to see you," she said, coming around the desk, limping, and gave him a quick hug. "I'm so glad you and Meri made it back safely. The Commandant had been sick with worry ever since you went down."

Bill had suspected as such, as evidenced by all the new gray hair Lewis sported, but hadn't mentioned it. "Thanks, but it looks like I'm going right back out again."

Glenda shook her head. "I heard. I don't think it's right, but I'm not the Commandant."

"Nor are we," Bill joked. "Anyhow, I hope you don't mind, but we leave pretty soon and I'd like to spend as much time with Meri and Jack before I have to go."

"Oh, my. Yes, don't let me hold you up. You guys stay safe out there."

Meri and Jack accompanied Bill down to the skytrain station at the entrance to Sacajawea Base. Nicole was with Matt, looking suitably sad. Jordan stood off by himself, waiting for the other two. *Man, that sucks*, Bill thought.

Giving his wife and son a hug and kiss, he said, "Well, time to go."

"Stay safe out there," Meri said, looking like she was about to cry.

"Hey, don't worry about me. This'll be a walk in the park after everything we've been through," he said with a grin, trying to lighten the mood.

"Yeah, right," she responded. "Just remember, Tarzan, there are real people out there, and you don't know how they'll react. For all you know, they found the Monarch and consider it a deity, and you trying to take their god might not be a good idea."

"Hey, they might think I'm the god," he joked.

"Don't even," Meri said. "Just make sure you come back to us in one piece."

"I will," he said. He gave her another kiss, then kissed Jack on his forehead. "See you soon, little guy. Love you." Looking Meri in the eyes, he said, "I love you. Take care of him."

"I will. You take care of you," then she glanced over to Jordan and Matt, "and look out for those two. God knows, Matt's not as good in the wild as he thinks he is, and Nicole's definitely worried."

"Will do," Bill said.

A train pulled into the station.

"Love you," Meri said.

With a brief smile toward her, Bill turned and called the other two Explorers to him. "Let's go, guys. Long ride ahead, and this train won't wait for us."

The three boarded, being careful not to bump other passengers with their backpacks and rifles.

As the door closed, Bill could see Meri and Nicole standing next to each other, watching them. He waved; Meri waved back, their son held in her arms.

The train pulled out. Bill kept an eye on Meri until she faded from sight. He turned to the other Explorers. "Well, this is it, guys."

The ride to the E-tube station only took about fifteen minutes, whereupon they had to find the right track. Bill had ridden on the magnetic levitation trains, but not on the E-tube. They were completely different. The maglev trains were mainly regional transportation systems, designed for rapid movement with minimal environmental impact on Hayek. The E-tubes were designed for trans-continental travel. There were only a few lines running, mainly from coast to coast on Ti'icham. Unlike the maglevs, there were no windows to look out at the passing scenery, as the trains operated in enclosed evacuated tubes. Of course, the high speeds the trains traveled at made up for any lack of scenic viewing.

Hell, even flying in a jet 10,000 meters in the air, there's not much of a view, so what does it matter if we don't see the landscape flashing past at 1,200 kilometers per hour? Bill thought as he boarded. *Let's see. A jet normally travels around 950 klicks an hour, and we've got about 4,800 klicks to go, that's...about five hours. At 1,200 klicks, that's about four hours. Yeah, think I'll take the faster time. And no fucking Air Nazis, security lines, or other bullshit to put up with.*

The three found their platform. Soon, the train pulled into the station and disgorged hundreds of passengers. Watching them all reminded Bill of old movies he watched as a teen, that took place during World War II when most of the country traveled by train. Here on Hayek, that was still the case. Planes were really only used for intercontinental travel, and even then, usually for high-priority stuff, such as sanitizing a possible Class II planet. Most intercontinental travel was still by ship.

The three boarded, found their assigned compartment, then divested themselves of their packs and other equipment.

"Ain't gonna wear it if I don't have to," Bill said, dropping his vest and survival belt on one of the empty seats. The others followed suit. Three hats contributed to the pile.

Soon, an announcement came over the cabin's speaker, advising the occupants to buckle up and prepare for rapid acceleration. Minutes later, the train began moving. Bill didn't particularly notice the build-up of speed. In just a few minutes, the train's conductor came back on the speaker announcing they had reached their cruising speed of 1,200 kilometers per hour. The train was scheduled for four stops between Milton and Neponsit, in the Massachusetts Canton.

When they arrived in Neponsit, almost five hours later (due to stops along the way), an Explorer was waiting for them.

"Bill Clark?" the Explorer asked as they exited the train.

"Yeah," Bill said.

"Hi, I'm Patrick Spanner. *Corps* said to get you on a flight to Jongen asap, so I'll be taking you out to the airfield."

"Great," Matt said in his Memphis drawl. "Finally make it to damnyankee country, and they kick me out before I even get a chance to see it."

Jordan punched Matt in the shoulder. "Sure you ain't some un-reconstructed rebel?" he joked. The two had been friends and roommates for well over a year.

Rubbing his shoulder, Matt replied, "Only when it comes to sweet tea, barbeque, and grits."

"I've got a Kenji waiting outside. Airfield's about ten minutes away. You guys need to use the restroom before we go?"

"It can wait," Bill said, after looking at the other two, both of whom shook their heads.

A couple of minutes later the four were climbing in the back of the Kenji, a pickup truck that was converted to carry passengers. Benches ran along the sides of the bed, under a small roof, tall enough for somebody to squat under.

The ride to the airfield in the early evening darkness was short, but somewhat cold due to the open sides of the Kenji.

They went inside the small terminal and checked in at the ticket counter. Once the ticketing agent confirmed their flight information, she issued them boarding passes, with a warning, "Don't forget to make sure all firearms are unloaded before boarding." Bill had totally forgotten about that, being used to having a loaded rifle with him at all times.

Spanner walked with the three men out the terminal and onto the tarmac. "The Commandant wants me to report when you've taken off. The airline's actually been holding the flight until you got here."

Before climbing the boarding steps into the small passenger jet, the three pointed their rifles at the ground and ejected the magazines, putting them in ammo pouches on their belts. They then each extracted the remaining round from their rifle. Letting the rifles hang from their slings, they retrieved the magazine, put the extra cartridge in it, and replaced the magazine into the pouch. After slinging his rifle, Bill repeated his actions with his PDW, first by removing the magazine from the pistol grip, which he placed in a cargo pocket, and then pulling the charging handle back and catching the ejected cartridge as it left the small carbine. Holding the carbine against his ribs with his arm, he retrieved the magazine from his pocket, fed the round into it, then put the magazine back into his pocket.

They then climbed the stairs and entered the plane. A flight attendant offered to show the Explorers where the in-flight rifle rack was. Bill was surprised at this; other than the airplanes flown by the *Corps*, he had not been on any civilian aircraft since migrating to Hayek almost two years ago. He knew people could fly with firearms, considered a total no-no on Earth, but he didn't even think about how to store them in-flight.

Once the rifles were racked and survival equipment and hats stashed in the overhead bins, and the three men settled into their seats, the flight attendant came by and gave each of them a small zippered bag. "Airline amenity kit, courtesy of Freedom Air," she told them. Bill opened his and found a pre-pasted toothbrush, eye shades, earplugs, and a pack of tissues.

The pilot gave the usual "Welcome aboard" speech he had heard a number of times before. As Bill had expected, an eight-hour flight was in store for them, with an arrival in Jongen at around eleven o'clock in the morning local time. Bill's chronograph was still set for Alpha Time, how all Hayek and *Corps* time was kept, much like Zulu Time on Earth. The prime meridian for Alpha Time was in the center of Milton. *Let's see, six o'clock now, and we're three hours ahead of Milton, add in another six hours, so that'll put us nine hours ahead, so that means we'll be landing around two A.M., our time. Oh, joy. Just what I wanted to do, hit the ground running when I should be pushing some serious REM cycles.*

Jordan had the window seat and Matt was crammed in the center. Bill turned to them and said, "Looks like we'll be landing around two in the morning our time, so you guys might want to catch up on your beauty sleep."

"I'm thinking they might serve something to help with that," Matt said, as the plane began taxiing toward the runway.

Bill was still wide awake, sipping on a whiskey, when the rising sun began streaming through the open windows. He glanced down at his chrono, still set on Alpha time. It was barely past ten PM. *Great*, he thought. *Now I'll never get any sleep.*

When he looked again, it was because Matt was shaking his shoulder.

"Hey, I gotta use the latrine, so wake up and move over."

Bill shook his head groggily and moved his legs so Matt could squeeze past him.

Jordan was sound asleep, head resting against the bulkhead, and a small line of drool running from the corner of his mouth down his chin.

Bill looked at his chrono. *One o'clock. AM or PM?*

It took his fuzzy brain a second to figure out that it was one in the morning Alpha Time.

Might as well use the restroom, too, he thought, taking the amenity kit from the seat pocket and getting up.

There was a small line to use the lavatory, but it moved fairly fast. Soon, Bill was done with his toilet, and with fresher teeth and a cleaner mouth, headed back to his seat.

Just as he sat down, Jordan woke, so both Matt and Bill had to move legs to let him get by. By the time he returned, the flight attendants were serving breakfast.

Bill asked for two coffees with his breakfast, joking with the flight attendant, "No sense making two trips."

A half hour later the plane landed in Jongen.

Bill easily spotted the Explorer on the tarmac as they exited the plane. She was the only one wearing the distinctive brown utilitarian *Corps* field uniform, same as them. Seeing them, she waved.

On the tarmac, they separated from the rest of the passengers, most of whom had luggage to collect in the terminal. The three Explorers had all their luggage with them, strapped on their bodies in one manner or another.

"Which one of you's Bill Clark?" the Explorer asked.

"That would be me," Bill said.

She reached a hand out to shake. "Hannah Botha," she said, then looked at Jordan. Answering his unspoken question, "Yeah, my dad was a racist Afrikaner who fled South Africa. I'm a Hayeker, born and raised."

Jordan shrugged. "Hey, we all come from somewhere."

Bill didn't quite understand the byplay and decided to let it slip.

"I take it you're here to get us to the maglev?"

"Yeah, the station's right on the other side of the terminal, but Commandant Lewis wanted eyes on the ground, so to speak."

"I'm beginning to think the old man doesn't trust us," Matt said.

"Well, not like any of us know how to read a map or anything," Bill agreed.

Hannah chuckled, and said, "Follow me."

"Give us a sec," Bill said, extracting a magazine from his ammo pouch, then loading his rifle. The other two did the same. Then Bill loaded his PDW and strapped it back in place. "Now I'm ready."

They soon arrived at the maglev train station. It was almost two hours until their train departed, so Hannah offered to give them a quick tour of Jongen. They left their survival equipment at the courtesy counter, and carrying only their rifles, hopped in a jeep she had parked in the terminal lot.

As far as cities went, it was quite small, about half the size of Milton. Not many cities were that big on Hayek, a planet with a population of barely over forty million, most of whom had crossed over from Earth less than twenty years ago. Everything still looked new. Bill was surprised that there was even a maglev in Eurasia.

"It was one of the first things put in after the initial seaports were developed," Hannah told them. "Nuclear's far less polluting than airplanes, so I guess Parallel wanted to make sure enough infrastructure was developed fast to avoid having a bunch of planes polluting the air.

"We've only got lines on the mainland right now, and mostly just here in the Canton of Constant. This line runs down to Buffett, a port on the coast of Marseilles at the mouth of the Rhône River, with stops along the way, including your stop at Guerin. They're putting another line to the English Channel, which should be done in another year or so."

"That fast?" Bill asked, surprised.

"Oh, yeah. Lots of indentured servants paying off their passage to Hayek are employed by Parallel to build the maglev infrastructure. That's what my dad did. Average time to pay off is four years, but some bust their butt and get out in three. All depends on how bad you want it, I guess."

It was Bill's first real experience hearing about the indentured servants. He knew passage to Hayek from the U.S. was pricey, about $100,000 per person, and he had wondered how people were able to afford it. He found out after he made the crossover that some worked for the company that actually controlled the gates, Parallel, Inc., parent company of the *Corps of Discovery*. He had always wondered what those people did to pay their passage and now knew.

The time had come to return to the station and complete the next leg of their journey.

Thanking Hannah, the three boarded the train and were soon watching forested country with small farms flash by at 600 kilometers per hour. Bill felt a sense of disconnect, having traveled through this part of France on Earth. Seeing smaller farms, few towns and mostly forest reinforced just how different Hayek and Earth were.

In a bit over an hour, with just enough time to have lunch in the dining car, the train arrived in Guerin.

As with every other stop along the two-day journey, the trio was met by an Explorer at the terminal. This time, though, Bill knew her.

"Mindy!" he practically yelled. The two embraced. Mindy had been the pilot and crew commander of Bill's first survey on Zion. A dark-haired woman in her mid-thirties, she was an excellent pilot.

"So, you flying the 415?" he asked.

"Yep. But, being short of pilots, I'm dragooning yours." She turned to the other two. "Jordan, good to see you again." After giving him a brief hug, she turned to Matt. "You must be Matt Green."

"Guilty as charged."

"Good. You're gonna be my co-pilot, along with whatever scut-puppy stuff Bill has you doing. I'm Mindy Hubert, and I'll be doing the main flying." She looked at Bill and added, "and working under you. How'd that happen?

Bill shrugged. "Karma?"

Mindy laughed, then led them out of the station. "I've got a Kenji waiting; the airfield isn't all that close."

Once they were on the road in the truck-turned-jitney, she said, "Had there been any type of road out there, even a dirt path, I'm sure we'd be hauling this stuff in a truck. As it is, no road, so we fly. Besides, that'll just give us a head start on getting to the second crash site."

Five minutes later they were at the airfield and boarding the CL-415. As Bill climbed in, he stopped and looked around. He knew that the planes were practically identical, but he could have sworn it was the same seaplane he had run remote sensing platforms on in the Carib on Zion.

"Is this Zebra 21?" he asked, calling the plane by its former call sign.

"Yep, same plane, different designation though. It's Romeo 21 now."

There were a couple of other Explorers in the cabin. "Boys, this is Bill Clark," Mindy said to them. "He'll be leading this little foray. The other two are Jordan Washington and Matt Green."

The two Explorers introduced themselves as gate operators. The tall East Asian guy was Ken Tanaka, and the shorter Hispanic-looking gal was Estela Cruz.

Everyone got settled in, Bill at his former workstation. Within minutes Mindy had clearance from the field and they were airborne.

With less than twenty kilometers to go, the flight to Grand Lac de Laffrey was so short that Mindy never took the plane above the tops of the surrounding mountains. The seaplane soon settled on the calm waters of the small lake. From take-off to landing took less than five minutes.

To think, that trip took us four days, Bill thought, remembering the time spent walking through a forest, making rafts, and floating downriver. *Was that really less than a year ago?*

As Mindy slowed the plane, she called back to Bill, "Where'd you say the Monarch was?" Her voice was somewhat tinny over the intercom system.

"On the long beach on the east side of the lake."

Mindy maneuvered the plane toward the beach Bill had indicated. Soon, they were stopped. "Okay, let's get it tied down to a tree and get the gate equipment out," she said, after shutting down the engines.

Bill remembered his last walk into the frigid waters of the lake, so he was glad they had a small inflatable boat. Bill and Jordan got the boat inflated and out the door. With Jordan holding the rope that held the boat steady, Bill climbed aboard the small craft, then helped the gate operators load equipment into it.

It took several trips before they had all the equipment necessary to create a gate big enough to bring the survey plane through, and to clear enough space to park the plane once it was on Hayek. The forest, as on Planet 42, extended practically to the lake's shore. And since it was nearly as wild, being on Hayek's frontier, somebody had to keep watch. That meant fewer hands to do the work.

Several hours were spent clearing space for the Monarch's fuselage. The goal was to separate the wings from it, which allowed for a much smaller gate. Bill, having no experience with chainsaws, took over the watch, the snarling of the saws assaulting his ears. He still wasn't used to the cacophony of civilization.

It was dusk when they finished.

"No sense going over in the dark," Bill said. "Let's call it a day." He turned to Mindy. "How's the bird set up for overnighting?"

"All prepped. We've got enough for two weeks operation."

"What about sleeping spaces? We've got six people, but only four racks."

"Rotate every night, is what I'm thinking."

"That works. We'll go by teams. Pilots are one team, gate ops another, and the really cool guys the third," Bill said with a grin.

"Wait a minute," Matt argued, also grinning. "What about you and Jordan? You didn't identify your team."

"Shut up, Matt," Jordan said. "And what say we get aboard before the night hunters come out."

The team climbed aboard the inflatable and went back to the seaplane.

Supper consisted of flight rats and the daily tot. Flight rats contained a pre-made entree and a dessert. These differed from field rations in their variety, contents, and weight. Flight rations were for use in airplanes with amenities such as microwaves. While edible cold, they were better warmed, and the packaging was designed to allow for microwaving. These came in sealed dishes and included an accessory packet with coffee or tea, sugar, and a non-dairy creamer. As flight crews could carry condiments and spices, none were provided, nor were any utensils. Flight rations were broken down into breakfast and lunch/supper meals. Most were vegetarian, but some had fish or meat.

The daily tot was a holdover from the British and U.S. Navies. Rum in the British Navy and usually whiskey, which was cheaper than rum, in the U.S. Navy. The *Corps* had revived this practice.

Everyone was up early. Breakfast consisted of more flight rats, and as soon as everyone was done eating dawn had broken.

Stepping out of the 415, Bill wasn't surprised to feel the cold spring air. It stung his nostrils as he breathed in. This close to the mountains, all the cold, heavy air flowed down into the valley. *Not as cold as the Great Plains*, he thought, basking in the relative warmth of the rising sun.

Once ashore, the gate operators got the generator started and prepped the gate for opening.

Bill had tried to get some information out of them the night before on how the gate operated but was completely shut down. Apparently gate operators, all of whom held PhDs in physics, were heavily recruited and had better lives than what they could have found on Earth, both in terms of money, academic freedom, and actual freedom. Of course, one of the downsides was that they were never allowed to return to Earth, even for visits or family deaths.

Before the sun had gotten too high, Cruz announced that they were live. "Gate's open, and I can see your plane just a hundred meters down the beach."

"Okay folks, listen up," Bill announced. "Matt, Jordan, and I are going through to get the plane. First thing is to see if we can find the EMP bomb. If we find it, great. We'll pass it through to you, Mindy.

"Regarding getting the plane back, we'll dump the avgas in the lake first and then Matt and I'll tow it back." At the shocked looks, he said, "Yeah, I know. Pollution. But, don't worry. We'll light it up and burn it off before we leave.

"Jordan," he went on, "I want you providing watch. We were lucky last time I was here. No wild animals. But we've also got to watch out for the hominids. You see a predator, don't hesitate. Take it out. You see a hominid, you make the call. I'm not gonna hamstring you; I trust your judgment.

"When we get the plane back, pass the chainsaws through and we'll cut the wings off. Wings go through first, then the fuselage. Put the wings in the forest, and keep room for the fuselage. Any questions?"

There were none.

Bill didn't bother stripping off his boots, sock, or pants like the last time he was in the lake. Rather, he just stepped through the gate, immediately assessed for threats, then walked around the gate and out of sight.

Stepping up onto the beach, he waited for the other two who joined him almost immediately. The walk to the plane didn't take long. The area looked the same as it had before, only with less green vegetation.

Searching around where he thought Meri had tossed the bomb, he soon found it under a shrub.

Pulling a pair of surgical gloves on, he said, "I'm gonna take this back to Mindy. Matt, you get the plane untied from the tree. If you've gotta cut the rope to do so, fine. But be sure to get all the rope. I want this place sterile." With that, he made his way back to the gate.

An hour later, the wings and fuselage of 42/2 were back on Hayek. As the last order of business, Bill took a survival flare and shot it into the lake where the avgas was floating. As expected, it went up with a *whumph,* the concussion and heat wave washing over Bill as the gate closed.

Bill inspected the plane. The crash seat parachutes were still onboard. Rather than inspecting them himself, he removed them, wearing surgical gloves, and stored them in the same locker on Romeo 21 where Mindy had placed the bomb. He locked the locker and put the only key in his pocket. As far as he could tell, only three people had touched the bomb since it was planted: Meri, him, and Mindy, the latter two wearing gloves. *I doubt they'll find anything,* he thought, *but no sense taking chances.*

Looking at their handiwork lying on the beach in pieces, Bill said, "Good job. Now, let's get that second bird."

Airborne within minutes, Bill pulled his tablet out and tied in with the plane's WiFi, which hooked into the local internet system. He sent a message updating Commandant Lewis.

He then sent an e-mail to Meri letting her know they had made the first recovery and were back on Hayek, safe and sound.

The flight south took them to the port at the mouth of the Rhône River, Buffet. The CL-415 had been lightly loaded with fuel when it left Guerin; it wasn't safe to land on water, or even land, with full tanks. The next leg of the journey would take longer, so now the tanks were filled. The flight was over 3,500 kilometers and expected to take almost twelve hours. Thanks to modifications to the fuel capacity, the plane would be able to make it without having to stop for refueling enroute.

While eating lunch in the airfield's small cafe after the plane was fueled, Bill and Mindy talked about the next leg and pored over flight charts. Finding no airfields between them and their destination, they decided to Remain Over Night at the small airfield rather than attempt the long flight in the dark.

"No sense spending the rest of the day and all night flying after having gotten up early," he told the crew. "Dinner can be done on the local, but be back by 2000 hours. We stay on the plane tonight. I want to be wheels up before dawn, which is 0715. That means we're wheels up at 0645. So, plan on being up no later than 0600 hours."

Sunrise the next morning was seen through the plane's port windows at cruising altitude. As with all long flights, there was really nothing to do if you weren't flying the plane, so Bill read and watched movies. The lack of connection to the internet, being so far from civilization, left out the option of emailing his wife, or anyone else for that matter.

The day droned on. Finally, after a butt-numbing eleven-hour flight, they arrived over their destination. Below, Bill could see a rough field hacked into the mostly treeless savanna.

Mindy's voice came over the intercom, "Flight attendants prepare for landing. Ladies and gentlemen, please put your seat trays up, if you have any, your seats in the upright position, and fasten your seat belts, as you might need them." Bill chuckled at the dry humor. It seemed most *Corps* pilots had the same shtick in one form or another.

The approach was direct and soon they were on the ground and parked next to a Caribou on the dirt runway.

Stepping out of the craft, Bill was assaulted by the heat and humidity of the Sudanian Savanna. After spending a winter on the high plains and spring in northern latitudes, to be thrown into the African heat was a shock to his system. It was apparent the others felt it, too.

As he approached the small group of Explorers on the field, he could see that they were the same engineers that had built the field on Planet 42 for their rescue, along with Brad Maeda and his co-pilot.

"Bill, my boy. Glad to see you," Ken Schmitt said, taking Bill's hand. "Welcome to hell."

"Thanks, Ken. Hot enough for it. Thanks for prepping the field." This was directed to all the engineers.

"Hey, our pleasure. Boss wants it, we do it. Anytime, anywhere, anyhow, that's our motto."

"Great, so where's the crash site?"

Ken pointed to a spot with a flagged stake. "If I'm correct, right there. We'll know as soon as your crew gets the gate open."

"Gotcha. Well let's get them going. Do you have a flitter around?"

"Got one in the 'bou. What're you thinking about?"

"Once we go through, I want to fly around and see what we can find."

Jordan piped up. "Uh, hey Bill. Maybe you're not the best one to do that. How much time you got in a flitter?"

Bill had to admit, not much.

"Well, I've probably got the most time in one here, so if you don't mind, I'd prefer to be the one doing the survey."

"Got me there. We'll discuss it in the morning, and I'll tell you what I want."

Darkness was fast approaching, so Bill suggested they call it a night. They buckled down for more delicious flight rats and a tot in the planes.

After getting Tanaka and Cruz oriented the next morning, and watching them begin setting up the gate, Bill called Jordan over. As they walked toward the Caribou where the flitter was stored, Bill told Jordan what he was thinking.

"If they didn't go down with the Monarch, odds are they parachuted out. And if their chutes were sabotaged like ours, odds are they came down pretty damn fast. I'm betting nobody survived. You tracking?"

"Yeah," Jordan said. "Major suckage."

"Yep. Anyhow, once we determine if they were heading north or south, I'll want you to backtrack and see if you can spot anything. Run a standard search pattern. Look for parachutes. Even after this much time, I doubt they're completely buried in sand or covered with vegetation. You should be able to spot something. Just look for colors out of the ordinary."

Jordan nodded.

They extracted the flitter from the back of the Caribou and unfolded the propeller shrouds. Jordan climbed into the single-seat passenger compartment and started the flitter up, raising a cloud of dust. Bill could smell the African dust as the cloud rose.

Jordan maneuvered the flitter toward where the gate was.

Tanaka and Cruz had a smaller gate set up this time. Since the plane wasn't intact, there wasn't the need for a large gate.

In less time than it took to prep and open it at Grand Lac de Laffrey, the two had the gate open.

"Schmitt, you and your guys have any problem going over?" Bill asked the engineer.

"Hey, we're Explorers, too. Let's do it."

"Brad, you okay with sending John over?" Bill didn't ask

John; it was Brad's decision.

"Ase kaite inai," he responded.

"Huh?"

"It's Japanese for no sweat," the pilot said.

"Oh, okay. Well, here the plan. Ken, you and your guys and John will help Matt recover parts. I'm gonna stand watch; not because I'm lazy or because I'm in charge, but because I've probably got more ground time than anyone else here, including Jordan.

"Once we identify which direction this plane was heading, Jordan's gonna take a flitter and look for signs of survivors." Everyone there knew what he really meant, and survivors wasn't the correct word.

"Mindy and the gate operators stay on this side. Mindy, you maintain watch." She nodded.

"Two things I don't want anyone touching without gloves: the crash 'chutes and anything that looks like an EMP bomb." Bill held up his tablet and showed them an image. "This is what the one in my plane looked like. If you see it, don't touch it. Just call me over.

"When we go over, I'm gonna take some quick pics, and then just pick stuff up and bring it back. Any questions?"

There were none.

"Okay, Jordan, go for it. Rest of you, follow him."

In a blast of dust, Jordan lifted off and cruised through the gate, circling the crash site visible through the opening. He stayed in the air until the remaining Explorers had made it through. All looked warily around while Jordan set down.

"Matt, Ken, keep watch while I take photos," Bill ordered.

After several minutes of photography, Bill looked around the site in a holistic manner. Jordan joined him.

"I'm thinking they were southbound. That look like it to you?"

"Yep, tail's to the north, nose to the south. Unless they spun out and pancaked, that's the most reasonable deduction."

"Okay, go see what you can find. And, don't exceed, or come even close to exceeding, the range on that thing."

"Yessir," Jordan said, mockingly tossing Bill a salute.

As the others began gathering parts of the crashed plane, Jordan boarded the flitter, and with another cloud of dust, rose and headed north, gaining altitude until he was hovering about 100 meters above the ground. He then began flying in a pattern similar to an aerial survey, going west for a klick, then turning and going east two klicks.

An hour after departing, Jordan returned.

The others stopped working when he landed, congregating around the flitter to hear what he had found.

Getting out, he shook his head.

"Found 'em," was all he said.

Everyone nodded in understanding.

"All right, let's finish this task first. Everyone back to work."

As the others got back to grabbing plane parts and taking them through the gate, Bill asked, "Jordan, how easy will they be to recover?"

Jordan took a deep breath, dropped his head slightly, then breathed out. "Pretty easy. They're all desiccated. I'll probably be able to bring back two at a time."

"You good for that?" Bill asked.

"No, but it's gotta get done." Brightening slightly, he then said, "But, hey, I managed to pull your still-kicking ass out of the bush, so it ain't all bad."

"And don't you forget that, man. We're all glad you did. Just think, Jack doesn't have to deal with grass in his diapers anymore," Bill said, trying to lighten the mood.

The sands were practically empty of plane bits when Jordan

returned with the first load. Everyone stopped working to watch as he guided the flitter through the gate and landed it on Hayek. Everyone on Planet 42 followed him through.

As he exited the flitter, he said, "Little help here, please?"

Without a word, Brad and Mindy unhooked the litter slung under the flitter and dragged it out from under the craft. Inside were two desiccated beings, too dry and shrunken to identify their gender, let alone who they were. As the first body was gently lifted out of the litter, Bill raised his arm in a slow salute. It was something he had seen his father do many a time, but not a *Corps* tradition. The others followed suit, maintaining the pose until the second body had been placed on the ground next to the first.

Both bodies still had their parachutes attached to them. Bill didn't say anything about wearing gloves. It was too late for that.

Turning to Jordan, he asked, "How much juice you got left?"

"Pretty much maxed out," Jordan said.

"Okay. Brad?"

"Yeah?"

"Can you change the flitter batteries for fresh ones? I want to recover the other two bodies and get out of here as soon as possible."

"Sure, give me a couple." Brad headed off to the parked Caribou. Looking over his shoulder, he yelled to Jordan, "Bring the flitter on over."

Two hours later and the remaining bodies were back on Hayek, along with all the pieces of the Monarch. The second set of bodies had received the same honors as the first two. All four were encased in rubber body bags that the crew had brought with them. Bill had found the EMP bomb, and, following the same protocol as the first time, secured it in the locker.

Then he gathered the group. "Ken, you guys know what you need to get things back, so nothing new from me. We'll be taking the remains of the Explorers home tomorrow morning, along with the evidence. Mindy, you refuel yet?" Seeing her nod, he said, "Good.

"Ladies and gentlemen, it's been an honor serving with you. I wish our expedition hadn't finished this way, but we all knew it was probable. Let's get some rest. Romeo 21, we take off at first light."

The Final Return

The return flight was just as boring as the outbound leg. They finally made radio contact with civilization when they were halfway across the Mediterranean. Bill was able to talk with the Port of Buffett's control tower and requested they make immediate contact with *Corps* headquarters and relay that the site was cleaned and four bodies recovered. An hour later they were informed that the *Corps* had been notified and that the response from the Commandant was "Well done. Regrets on the findings."

As they approached the Port of Buffett, darkness was spreading over the land.

Upon getting landing instructions, Mindy informed the crew that an honor guard of the local militia would be meeting the plane. They had offered to stand guard over the remains of the dead Explorers while the crew spent some time ashore.

Exiting the plane, Bill was surprised to find more than a couple of militia members. Apparently, an entire company had come out. The captain approached Bill and saluted. "Captain Rogers, sir. We heard about the remains and wanted to offer our condolences and our services." Bill wasn't sure if saluting in return was proper, but he did it anyhow.

"Thank you, Captain. Your services are greatly appreciated.

As you can imagine, we're pretty tired, especially our pilot and co-pilot."

"Understood, sir. Once you're ready, we've got restaurant reservations set up for you and your crew. We suspect you'll prefer to stay in the plane overnight?"

Bill nodded.

After locking up the plane, the six crew members were given a ride to a nearby restaurant for dinner. *A step up from the airfield cafe*, Bill thought, as he dined on a plateful of fettuccine Alfredo.

Not having to fly to Grand Lac de Laffrey, the plan was to have Bill, Jordan, Matt, along with the remains and the evidence, take the maglev from Buffett to Jongen. The train was scheduled to depart at ten o'clock in the morning, so the crew had plenty of time to get ready.

When Bill awoke, shortly after dawn, he was surprised to see a militia truck pulled up outside the plane, about 100 meters away. Militia members still surrounded the plane, facing outward, maintaining their vigil.

Jordan had awoken shortly before him and started a pot of coffee, so Bill got a cup and took a few swigs, feeling the heat of the brew on his lips and tongue, while the scent of the coffee wafted upward. He then headed out the aircraft's door.

As he stepped outside, the same militia captain who had greeted them the night before approached him, and saluted again. Bill returned the salute, still feeling like a bit of a fraud, until he remembered, *Hey, I'm a militia member, too.*

"Good morning, sir," the captain said. It was obvious he was tired.

"Good morning, Captain. Were you out here, awake, all night?"

"Yes, sir. It's the least we can do." Gesturing toward the trucks, he said, "I hope you don't mind, but I took the liberty of having some coffins delivered. I didn't think it was right that the remains return home in body bags."

Bill was briefly overcome with emotion, amazed at the young captain's consideration.

"Thank you, Captain. Not only do I not mind, but I'm grateful."

"With your permission, then, I'll transfer the remains."

"Certainly. Let me let the crew know what's happening, first."

While the captain turned toward the truck to arrange matters, Bill returned to the plane. Everyone was awake by now, so he filled them in on the situation.

"Should we do a formal transfer?" Mindy asked.

"I think the captain's already got that in mind," Bill said. Looking out the window, he could see militia members lining up in two rows, each facing the other, between the plane and the truck. Four caskets had been placed on the ground near the truck.

The remains of the Explorers had been placed in the cargo hold before they left the Sudanian Savanna, so all six crew members exited the plane and approached the hold. Mindy opened it.

Jordan and Bill entered the hold and picked up the first body bag, carefully handing it to Matt and Ken. As the two walked the remains between the assembled militia, each militia member raised their hand in salute, holding it until the body passed.

As they passed the second body bag out, it was picked up by Mindy and Estela, who carried their human burden through the same honor guard.

When they passed out the third body bag, they were surprised to see the young militia captain and his senior NCO. The older sergeant briefly crossed himself before grasping the handles on his side of the bag.

Bill and Jordan carried the final bag through the honor guard, arriving at the only casket with an open top. Gently, they laid the body to rest in it. As the militia member closed the lid, everyone saluted.

A second militia member placed the flag of Hayek atop the casket. It was yellow with a stylized porcupine in the center and the words "Don't Tread On Me" underneath. All four caskets bore the same flag.

It took a moment before he was able to speak, and all he could say was, "Thank you," to the captain.

"Our honor, sir," he replied. He then directed several of the militia to load the coffins on the truck.

"As soon as you're ready, we'll get you over to the train station."

"Thanks, Captain."

Mindy gave Bill a hug before he left Romeo 21 for the final time.

"Glad we got to work together again," she said. "Just wish it had been under different circumstances."

"Me, too."

While Bill, Jordan, and Matt were returning to Milton in the same manner they arrived, Mindy would be flying back with the gate and the gate crew.

The rest of the trip back passed in a blur. At each transfer between transport modes, the remains were treated with respect, usually with a local militia component out to provide an escort and honor guard.

Finally, the crew arrived in Milton.

As the trio exited the E-tube, Bill wasn't surprised to find his wife and son waiting for him or to see Nicole waiting for Matt, or to see Commandant Lewis waiting for all three of them. He *was* surprised to find hundreds of Explorers.

Meri held back until Lewis had approached Bill and told him that there was a team of investigators from the Hayek Public Safety Force who would take control of the evidence, and that the Explorers were there to honor the fallen Explorers.

Bill, Matt, and Jordan were glad to finally hand over the evidence to the inspectors. Throughout the long journey from Buffett, the three had maintained physical control of it. Bill was tired of wearing surgical gloves.

The four caskets were brought out from the cargo section of the E-tube, flags still draped over them.

As they were carried through the terminal, every Explorer rendered a salute. Every civilian stopped, many of them placing their hands over their hearts. All knew of the attack by the GLF and the damage suffered by the *Corps of Discovery*, along with the physical and economic damage to Hayek.

Bill watched the coffins exit the building and then turned to his wife, who had made her way to him through the crowd. The two kissed each other and hugged, Meri holding Jack to the side so as not to crush him.

"And the hunter, home from the hills," she said, quoting Robert Lewis Stevenson.

Bill just nodded.

Lewis said, "Outstanding job, Bill. Go home, spend time with the family, and report to my office tomorrow morning. Bring your compadres with you," he added, referring to Matt and Jordan. "In the meantime, we'll be having a memorial service for the crew of 42/1 in two days. We're waiting for some of the crew's parents to come over from Earth."

Trekker

The Meeting

Bill was still groggy the next morning when he arrived at the Commandant's office. It wasn't because he was still tired from the trip, despite the jetlag. It also wasn't because he hadn't had a sufficient quantity of caffeine. He had. It was because he was the father of an infant. And that infant had decided that anyone sleeping was not a good idea. *Of course, Jack really didn't decide that, but it sure seemed like it*, Bill thought.

Glenda greeted him and, taking pity on him, brought him a fresh cup of coffee.

Thanking her, he took a big gulp. *Must...have...more...coffee....* he thought as he drank the bitter brew.

Bill was soon joined by Jordan and Matt, both of whom looked far fresher and more alert than Bill.

"Man, you look beat," Jordan said.

Just you wait, Bill thought. What he said was, "Yeah, Jack had a bad night."

"Ouch. Feel your pain, brother. I know what you mean. My younger sister was the same way. Drove me up a wall."

Glenda said, "The Commandant will see you now."

The three entered the Commandant's office. Lewis was standing in front of the desk and gestured the three of them to take seats.

Then Lewis said, "Once again, I want to state how proud I am of you three. You did a great job sterilizing the sites.

"Jordan, I especially want to thank you for the job you did in recovering the remains of the dead Explorers. It's not often the *Corps* is able to recover a body under such circumstances. It goes a long way to helping the families get closure. Don't be surprised if you're approached and thanked by any of them over the next several weeks. They've been waiting almost a year to find out what happened."

Jordan nodded.

"So, just to let you know what's happening. Shortly after you three handed over the evidence to the HPSF investigators, they called me and said they had both fingerprints and DNA on some of it. Not just yours, and not just Meri's. They're not saying much else, other than that the trial against the Gaia Liberation Front terrorists they caught should be starting in mid-June.

"As you know, that's pretty much the beginning of the training cycle for the new Explorers. Because of all the death and destruction caused by the GLF, we had to bring more Probies in from Earth than we were planning on.

"So, what I'm saying is that between the trial, where you, Bill, are a prime witness, and the need for some experienced hands to train a bunch of Earth Probies, you three won't be going out on any more surveys this year."

Bill was in shock. Yeah, he was just back from hell on Earth, *Well, hell on Planet 42*, but surveying was what he signed up for. He felt like he was being punished.

"Damnit, Jack," he said, feeling the heat rise to his face, "that's not fair. We're good. Damned good, and we should be out there doing the job we're trained for."

Out of the corner of his eye, he could see Jordan and Matt nodding in agreement.

Moving around his desk during this outburst, the Commandant sat down. Leaning back, he laced his hands in front of him, resting them on his practically nonexistent gut, and smiled.

"About that," he said. "Do you know the *Corps'* secondary objective?"

Bill and the others grew silent.

"Our secondary objective, which isn't really talked about much, is to explore parallel Earths that *are* developed, and identify technologies that might prove useful to the *Corps*, Parallel, and Hayek."

Sitting back, the Commandant's smile grew even bigger.

"Think about that for a second. New worlds, new civilizations, new cultures, to boldly go, and all that crap. Interested?"

"Oh, hell yeah!" Jordan said.

Bill was a bit suspicious. "I'm waiting."

"Well, here's the deal, men. It's a rather dangerous society we'd be sending you into, but it's got some really intriguing technology that just might make explorations even easier and safer, along with potentially reducing pollution. They speak English, so you'd mostly fit in. Mostly."

Looking directly at Jordan, he said, "You'd be in the most danger."

"Hell, I grew up in South-central LA and been on several ground surveys," Jordan said. "What could be more dangerous than that?"

"About that," the Commandant said.

For the next half-hour, he filled the three Explorers in, explaining exactly what the new civilization was like that they would be exploring.

It turned out that the *Corps* actually monitored a number of Class I planets, always seeking out useful technologies and knowledge. Just as with most human activity, it was a mix of good and bad, and pure evil. The *Corps* didn't discuss what they found outside of the higher command, but they were aware.

"So, after we get through the training session, can I count on you?" Lewis asked the trio, whom Bill was starting to think of as the Three Amigos.

Bill and Matt turned to Jordan. Nothing was happening unless he agreed.

After several seconds, Jordan finally said, "Yeah. What the fuck. I'm in."

The other two nodded, each saying "I'm in."

"Okay, then. We'll start prepping you. Lots of culture and history you'll need to know before you cross over. You can tell your wife," he said to Bill, "and if you marry that fine Kiwi, you can tell her," he said to Matt. "Otherwise, tell nobody. If this was the Hayek Defense Forces, we'd classify this as *Top Secret, Kill*. Got me?"

All three nodded.

"Outstanding." Turning to Bill, he said, "Until the new Probies show up, I want you and Meri to take some time off, and don't either of you report in for at least forty-five days. Got that?"

"Yes sir," Bill responded.

"Okay, then. Get outta here."

The three stood and left.

Several hours later, the Clark family was ensconced in Lewis Landing, a small homestead on the banks of the Nisqually River in Cascadia. It was originally founded by Meri's grandfather and was now a vacation retreat from the hectic *Corps* schedule that Commandant Lewis and the Clarks operated under.

Bill managed to get some spring Chinook salmon fishing in, so supper consisted of a baked salmon. Meri did an amazing job, which wasn't difficult, considering the quality of the fish. Regardless, her culinary skills pushed the supper into extravagant territory.

"So, how'd the meeting with Dad go?" Meri asked over the meal.

"Interesting," Bill said. "Did you know that, as prime witnesses to the Gaia Firsters' sabotage, we're gonna have to stay around for the trial?"

Meri nodded.

"Are you also aware that we'll be helping out with the new Probies?"

Again, she nodded. "What about after that, though?" she asked.

"Well, how well do you know Earth history, especially U.S. history?"

"A bit. It's part of our education, but not a major focus. Why?"

"What do you know of the Confederate States of America?"

THE END (for now)

Dear Reader,

Thanks for buying *Trekker*, the second in the *Corps of Discovery* series. I hope you enjoyed it.

As an independent author, I don't have a marketing department or the exposure of being on bookshelves. If you enjoyed Trekker and the *Corps of Discovery* series, please help spread the word and support the writing of the rest of the series by writing an Amazon review or telling a few friends about the book.

Thanks again,

James S. Peet

Trekker is my second novel, the sequel to *Surveyor*. Both are available on Amazon in paperback format, and on Amazon, Kobo, Barnes & Noble, and other online e-book sellers in e-book format. My third novel, *Explorer*, will be out soon, so if you'd like advance notice of it, please join my e-mail list at www.jamespeet.com.

James S. Peet is a modern-day Renaissance Man. He's lived on four continents, six countries, and visited countless more. He's been a National Park Service Ranger, a police officer, a tow-truck driver, a college instructor, a private investigator, a fraud examiner/forensic accountant, an inventor, and an entrepreneur. His other writing endeavors include *Surveyor: Book I in the Corps of Discovery Series*, several articles on modern sea piracy, economics, and the private investigation of fraud. He lives on the top of a small mountain in the foothills of Washington's Cascade Mountains with his wife, dogs, barn cats, and whatever adult daughter returns to the nest. He's attended 10 colleges and universities, two law enforcement academies, and has three degrees (all in geography) and multiple certificates (he really likes learning). *Trekker* is his second novel in the *Corps of Discovery* timeline. Be sure to watch for future releases.